Ray Bradbury
selects stories of soaring imagination and spine-tingling
suspense from his own works . . .

S Is for Space

"A collection of Ray Bradbury's finest stories!"

—Boston Pilot

"Beautifully written . . . The author's best science fiction
to curdle the blood and tingle the spine. Once begun, this
is not to be set aside!"

—Wyoming Tribune

"Bradbury wraps fantasy in miniscule details of reality,
so that the reader believes all and is ready for anything!"

—Horn Book Magazine

S
IS FOR SPACE

Ray Bradbury

RL 5, IL 6-up

S IS FOR SPACE

A Bantam Book / published by arrangement with
Doubleday & Company, Inc.

PRINTING HISTORY

Doubleday edition / August 1966
Bantam edition / November 1970

2nd printing . November 1970	8th printing . November 1974
3rd printing .... March 1971	9th printing .... April 1976
4th printing .... March 1972	10th printing .... April 1977
5th printing . November 1972	11th printing .... March 1978
6th printing .... August 1973	12th printing .... April 1978
7th printing .... July 1974	13th printing . September 1979

For Charles Beaumont
who lived in that little house
halfway up in the next block
most of my life.

And for Bill Nolan
and Bill Idelson, friend of Rush Gook,
and for Paul Condylis . . .

Because . . .

CONTENTS

	1
INTRODUCTION	
Chrysalis	3
Pillar of Fire	27
Zero Hour	69
The Man	81
Time in Thy Flight	95
The Pedestrian	101
Hail and Farewell	107
Invisible Boy	117
Come into My Cellar	127
The Million-Year Picnic	145
The Screaming Woman	157
The Smile	173
Dark They Were, and Golden Eyed	179
The Trolley	195
The Flying Machine	201
Icarus Montgolfier Wright	207

S IS FOR SPACE

INTRODUCTION

Jules Verne was my father.

H. G. Wells was my wise uncle.

Edgar Allen Poe was the batwinged cousin we kept high in the back attic room.

Flash Gordon and Buck Rogers were my brothers and friends.

There you have my ancestry.

Adding, of course, the fact that in all probability Mary Wollstonecraft Shelley, author of *Frankenstein,* was my mother.

With a family like that, how else could I have turned out than as I did: a writer of fantasy and most curious tales of science fiction.

I lived up in the trees with Tarzan a good part of my life with my hero Edgar Rice Burroughs. When I swung down out of the foliage I asked for a toy typewriter during my twelfth year, at Christmas. On this rattletrap machine I wrote my first *John Carter, Warlord of Mars* imitation sequels, and from memory tapped out whole episodes of *Chandu the Magician.*

I sent away boxtops and think I joined every secret radio society that existed. I saved comic strips, most of which I still have in great boxes down in my California basement. I went to movie matinees. I devoured the works of H. Rider Haggard and Robert Louis Stevenson. In the midst of my young summers I leapt high and dove deep down into the vast ocean of Space, long long before the Space Age itself was more than a fly speck on the two-hundred-inch Mount Palomar telescope.

In other words, I was in love with everything I did. My heart did not beat, it exploded. I did not warm toward a subject, I boiled over. I have always run fast and yelled loud about a list of great and magical things I knew I simply could not live without.

I was a beardless boy-magician who pulled irritable rabbits out of papier-mâché hats. I became a bearded man-magician who pulled rockets out of his typewriter and out of a Star Wilderness that stretched as far as eye and mind could see and imagine.

My enthusiasm stood me well over the years. I have never tired of the rockets and the stars. I never cease enjoying the good fun of scaring heck out of myself with some of my weirder, darker tales.

So here in this new collection of stories you will find not only *S is for Space*, but a series of subtitles that might well read: *D is for Dark*, or *T is for Terrifying*, or *D is for Delight*. Here you will find just about every side of my nature and my life that you might wish to discover. My ability to laugh out loud with the sheer discovery that I am alive in a strange, wild, and exhilarating world. My equally great ability to jump and raise up a crop of goosepimples when I smell strange mushrooms growing in my cellar at midnight, or hear a spider fiddling away at his tapestry-web in the closet just before sunrise.

You who read, and I who write, are very much the same. The young person locked away in me has dared to write these stories for your pleasure. We meet on the common ground of an uncommon Age, and share out our gifts of dark and light, good dream and bad, simple joy and not so simple sorrow.

The boy-magician speaks from another year. I stand aside and let him say what he most needs to say. I listen and enjoy.

I hope you will, too.

RAY BRADBURY
Los Angeles, California
December 1, 1965

CHRYSALIS

Rockwell didn't like the room's smell. Not so much McGuire's odor of beer, or Hartley's unwashed, tired smell—but the sharp insect tang rising from Smith's cold green-skinned body lying stiffly naked on the table. There was also a smell of oil and grease from the nameless machinery gleaming in one corner of the small room.

The man Smith was a corpse. Irritated, Rockwell rose from his chair and packed his stethoscope. "I must get back to the hospital. War rush. You understand, Hartley. Smith's been dead eight hours. If you want further information call a post-mortem—"

He stopped as Hartley raised a trembling, bony hand. Hartley gestured at the corpse—this corpse with brittle hard green shell grown solid over every inch of flesh. "Use your stethoscope again, Rockwell. Just once more. Please."

Rockwell wanted to complain, but instead he sighed, sat down, and used the stethoscope. You have to treat fellow doctors politely. You press your stethoscope into cold green flesh, pretending to listen—

The small, dimly lit room exploded around him. Exploded in one green cold pulsing. It hit Rockwell's ears like fists. It hit him. He saw his own fingers jerk over the recumbent corpse.

He heard a pulse.

Deep in the dark body the heart beat once. It sounded like an echo in fathoms of sea water.

Smith was dead, unbreathing, mummified. But at the

core of that deadness—his heart lived. Lived, stirring like a small unborn baby!

Rockwell's crisp surgeon's fingers darted rapidly. He bent his head. In the light it was dark-haired, with flecks of gray in it. He had an even, level, nice-looking face. About thirty-five. He listened again and again, with sweat coming cold on his smooth cheeks. The pulse was not to be believed.

One heartbeat every thirty-five seconds.

Smith's respiration—how could you believe that, too one breath of air every four minutes. Lungcase movement imperceptible. Body temperature?

Sixty degrees.

Hartley laughed. It was not a pleasant laugh. More like an echo that had gotten lost. "He's alive," he said tiredly. "Yes, he is. He almost fooled me many times. I injected adrenalin to speed that pulse, but it was no use. He's been this way for twelve weeks. And I couldn't stand keeping him a secret any longer. That's why I phoned you, Rockwell. He's—unnatural.

The impossibility of it overwhelmed Rockwell with an inexplicable excitement. He tried to lift Smiths' eyelids. He couldn't. They were webbed with epidermis. So were the lips. So were the nostrils. There was no way for Smith to breathe—

"Yet, he's breathing." Rockwell's voice was numb. He dropped his stethoscope blankly, picked it up, and saw his fingers shaking.

Hartley grew tall, emaciated, nervous over the table. "Smith didn't like my calling you. I called anyway. Smith warned me not to. Just an hour ago."

Rockell's eyes dilated into hot black circles. "How could he warn you? He can't move."

Hartley's face, all razor-sharp bone, hard jaw, tight squinting gray eyes, twitched nervously. Smith—*thinks*. I know his thoughts. He's afraid you'll expose him to the world. He hates me. Why? I want to kill him, that's why. Here." Hartley fumbled blindly for a blue-steel revolver in his rumpled, stained coat. "Murphy. Take this. Take it before I use it on Smith's foul body!"

Murphy pulled back, his thick red face afraid. "Don't like guns. You take it, Rockwell."

Like a scalpel, Rockwell made his voice slash. "Put the gun away, Hartley. After three months tending one patient you've got a psychological blemish. Sleep'll help that." He licked his lips. "What sort of disease has Smith got?"

Hartley swayed. His mouth moved words out slowly. Falling asleep on his feet, Rockwell realized. "Not diseased," Hartley managed to say. "Don't know what. But I resent him, like a kid resents the birth of a new brother or sister. He's wrong. Help me. Help me, will you?"

"Of course." Rockwell smiled. "My desert sanitarium's the place to check him over, good. Why—why Smith's the most incredible medical phenomenon in history. Bodies just don't act this way!"

He got no further. Hartley had his gun pointed right at Rockwell's stomach. "Wait. Wait. You—you're not going to *bury* Smith! I thought you'd help me. Smith's not healthy. I want him killed! He's dangerous! I know he is!"

Rockwell blinked. Hartley was obviously psychoneurotic. Didn't know what he was saying. Rockwell straightened his shoulders, feeling cool and calm inside. "Shoot Smith and I'll turn you in for murder. You're overworked mentally and physically. Put the gun away."

They stared at one another.

Rockwell walked forward quietly and took the gun, patted Hartley understandingly on the shoulder, and gave the weapon to Murphy, who looked at it as if it would bite him. "Call the hospital, Murphy. I'm taking a week off. Maybe longer. Tell them I'm doing research at the sanitarium."

A scowl formed in the red fat flesh of Murphy's face. "What do I do with this gun?"

Hartley shut his teeth together, hard. "Keep it. You'll want to use it—later."

Rockwell wanted to shout it to the world that he was sole possessor of the most incredible human in history. The sun was bright in the desert sanitarium room where

Smith lay, not saying a word, on his table; his handsome face frozen into a green, passionless expression.

Rockwell walked into the room quietly. He used the stethoscope on the green chest. It scraped, making the noise of metal tapping a beetle's carapace.

McGuire stood by, eyeing the body dubiously, smelling of several recently acquired beers.

Rockwell listened intently. "The ambulance ride may have jolted him. No use taking a chance—"

Rockwell cried out.

Heavily, McGuire lumbered to his side. "What's wrong?"

"Wrong?" Rockwell stared about in desperation. He made one hand into a fist. "Smith's dying!"

"How do you know? Hartley said Smith plays possum. He's fooled you again—"

"No!" Rockwell worked furiously over the body, injecting drugs. Any drugs. Swearing at the top of his voice. After all this trouble, he *couldn't* lose Smith. No, not now.

Shaking, jarring, twisting deep down inside, going completely liquidly mad, Smith's body sounded like dim volcanic tides bursting.

Rockwell fought to remain calm. Smith was a case unto himself. Normal treatment did nothing for him. What then? What?

Rockwell stared. Sunlight gleamed on Smith's hard flesh. Hot sunlight. It flashed, glinting off the stethoscope tip. The sun. As he watched, clouds shifted across the sky outside, taking the sun away. The room darkened. Smith's body shook into silence. The volcanic tides died.

"McGuire! Pull the blinds! Before the sun comes back!"

McGuire obeyed.

Smith's heart slowed down to its sluggish, infrequent breathing.

"Sunlight's bad for Smith. It counteracts something. I don't know what or why, but it's not good—" Rockwell relaxed. "Lord, I wouldn't want to lose Smith. Not for anything. He's different, making his own standards, doing things men have never done. Know something, Murphy?"

"What?"

"Smith's not in agony. He's not dying either. He wouldn't be better off dead, no matter what Hartley says. Last night as I arranged Smith on the stretcher, readying him for his trip to this sanitarium, I realized, suddenly, that Smith *likes* me."

"Gah. First Hartley. Now you. Did Smith *tell* you that?"

"He didn't tell me. But he's not unconscious under all that hard skin. He's aware. Yes, that's it. He's aware."

"Pure and simply—he's petrifying. He'll die. It's been weeks since he was fed. Hartley said so. Hartley fed him intravenously until the skin toughened so a needle couldn't poke through it."

Whining, the cubicle door swung slowly open. Rockwell started. Hartley, his sharp face relaxed after hours of sleep, his eyes still a bitter gray, hostile, stood tall in the door. "If you'll leave the room," he said, quietly, "I'll destroy Smith in a very few seconds. Well?"

"Don't come a step closer." Rockwell walked, feeling irritation, to Hartley's side. "Every time you visit, you'll have to be searched. Frankly, I don't trust you." There were no weapons. "Why didn't you tell me about the sunlight?"

"Eh?" Soft and slow Hartley said it. "Oh—yes. I forgot. I tried shifting Smith weeks ago. Sunlight struck him and he began *really* dying. Naturally, I stopped trying to move him. Smith seemed to know what was coming, vaguely. Perhaps he planned it; I'm not sure. While he was still able to talk and eat ravenously, before his body stiffened completely, he warned me not to move him for a twelve-week period. Said he didn't like the sun. Said it would spoil things. I thought he was joking. He wasn't. He ate like an animal, a hungry, wild animal, fell into a coma, and here he is—" Hartley swore under his breath. "I'd rather hoped you'd leave him in the sun long enough to kill him inadvertently."

McGuire shifted his two hundred fifty pounds. "Look here, now. What if we catch Smith's disease?"

Hartley looked at the body, his pupils shrinking. "Smith's not diseased. Don't you recognize degeneration when you see it? It's like cancer. You don't catch it, you inherit a tendency. I didn't begin to fear and hate Smith until a week ago when I discovered he was breathing and existing and thriving with his nostrils and mouth sealed. It can't happen. It mustn't happen."

McGuire's voice trembled. "What if you and I and Rockwell all turn green and a plague sweeps the country—what then?"

"Then," replied Rockwell, "if I'm wrong, perhaps I am, I'll die. But it doesn't worry me in the least."

He turned back to Smith and went on with his work.

A bell. A bell. Two bells, two bells. A dozen bells, a hundred bells. Ten thousand and a million clangorous, hammering metal dinning bells. All born at once in the silence, squalling, screaming, hurting echoes, bruising ears!

Ringing, chanting with loud and soft, tenor and bass, low and high voices. Great-armed clappers knocking the shells and ripping air with the thrusting din of sound!

With all those bells ringing, Smith could not immediately know where he was. He knew that he could not see, because his eyelids were sealed tight, knew he could not speak because his lips had grown together. His ears were clamped shut, but the bells hammered nevertheless.

He could not see. But yes, yes, he could, and it was like inside a small dark red cavern, as if his eyes were turned inward upon his skull. And Smith tried to twist his tongue, and suddenly, trying to scream, he knew his tongue was gone, that the place where it used to be was vacant, an itching spot that wanted a tongue but couldn't have it just *now*.

No tongue. Strange. Why? Smith tried to stop the bells. They ceased, blessing him with a silence that wrapped him up in a cold blanket. Things were happening. Happening.

Smith tried to twitch a finger, but he had no control. A foot, a leg, a toe, his head, everything. Nothing moved. Torso, limbs—immovable, frozen in a concrete coffin.

A moment later came the dread discovery that he was no longer breathing. Not with his lungs, anyway.

"BECAUSE I HAVE NO LUNGS!" he screamed. Inwardly he screamed and that mental scream was drowned, webbed, clotted, and journeyed drowsily down in a red, dark tide. A red drowsy tide that sleepily swathed the scream, garroted it, took it all away, making Smith rest easier.

I am not afraid, he thought. I understand that which I do not understand. I understand that I do not fear, yet know not the reason.

No tongue, no nose, no lungs.

But they would come later. Yes, they would. Things were—happening.

Through the pores of his shelled body air slid, like rain needling each portion of him, giving life. Breathing through a billion gills, breathing oxygen and nitrogen and hydrogen and carbon dioxide, and using it all. Wondering. Was his heart still beating?

But yes, it was beating. Slow, slow, slow. A red dim susurrance, a flood, a river surging around him, slow, slower, slower. So nice.

So restful.

The jigsaw pieces fitted together faster as the days drifted into weeks. McGuire helped. A retired surgeon-medico, he'd been Rockwell's secretary for a number of years. Not much help, but good company.

Rockwell noted that McGuire joked gruffly about Smith, nervously; and a lot. Trying to be calm. But one day McGuire stopped, thought it over, and drawled, "Hey, it just came to me! Smith's alive. He should be dead. But he's alive. Good God!"

Rockwell laughed. "What in blazes do you think I'm working on? I'm bringing an X-ray machine out next week so I can find out what's going on inside Smith's shell." Rockwell jabbed with a hypo needle. It broke on the hard shell.

Rockwell tried another needle, and another, until

finally he punctured, drew blood, and placed the slides under the microscope for study. Hours later he calmly shoved a serum test under McGuire's red nose, and spoke quickly.

"Lord, I can't believe it. His blood's germicidal. I dropped a streptococci colony into it and the strep was annihilated in eight seconds! You could inject every known disease into Smith and he'd destroy them all, thrive on them!"

It was only a matter of hours until other discoveries. It kept Rockwell sleepless, tossing at night, wondering, theorizing the titanic ideas over and over. For instance—

Hartley'd fed Smith so many cc's of blood-food every day of his illness until recently. NONE OF THAT FOOD HAD EVER BEEN ELIMINATED. All of it had been stored, not in bulk-fats, but in a perfectly abnormal solution, an x-liquid contained in high concentrate form in Smith's blood. An ounce of it would keep a man well fed for three days. This x-liquid circulated through the body until it was actually needed, when it was seized upon and used. More serviceable than fat. Much more!

Rockwell glowed with his discovery. Smith had enough x-liquid stored in him to last months and months more. Self-sustaining.

McGuire, when told, contemplated his paunch sadly.

"I wish I stored my food that way."

That wasn't all. Smith needed little air. What air he had he seemed to acquire by an osmotic process through his skin. And he used every molecule of it. No waste.

"And," finished Rockwell, "eventually Smith's heart might even take vacations from beating, entirely!"

"Then he'd be dead," said McGuire.

"To you and I, yes. To Smith—maybe. Just maybe. Think of it, McGuire. Collectively, in Smith, we have a self-purifying blood stream demanding no replenishment but an interior one for months, having little breakdown and no elimination of wastes whatsoever because every molecule is utilized, self-evolving, and fatal to any and all microbic life. All this, and Hartley speaks of degeneration!"

Hartley was irritated when he heard of the discoveries. But he still insisted that Smith was degenerating. Dangerous.

McGuire tossed his two cents in. "How do we know that this isn't some super microscopic disease that annihilates all other bacteria while it works on its victim. After all—malarial fever is sometimes used surgically to cure syphilis; why not a new bacillus that conquers all?"

"Good point," said Rockwell. "But we're not sick, are we?"

"It may have to incubate in our bodies."

"A typical old-fashioned doctor's response. No matter what happens to a man, he's 'sick'—if he varies from the norm. That's your idea, Hartley," declared Rockwell, "not mine. Doctors aren't satisfied unless they diagnose and label each case. Well, I think that Smith's healthy; so healthy you're afraid of him."

"You're crazy," said McGuire.

"Maybe. But I don't think Smith needs medical interference. He's working out his own salvation. You believe he's degenerating. I say he's growing."

"Look at Smith's skin," complained McGuire.

"Sheep in wolf's clothing. Outside, the hard, brittle epidermis. Inside, ordered regrowth, change. Why? I'm on the verge of knowing. These changes inside Smith are so violent that they need a shell to protect their action. And as for you, Hartley, answer me truthfully, when you were young, were you afraid of insects, spiders, things like that?"

"Yes."

"There you are. A phobia. A phobia you use against Smith. That explains your distaste for Smith's change."

In the following weeks, Rockwell went back over Smith's life carefully. He visited the electronics lab where Smith had been employed and fallen ill. He probed the room where Smith had spent the first weeks of his "illness" with Hartley in attendance. He examined the machinery there. Something about radiations

. . .

While he was away from the sanitarium, Rockwell locked Smith tightly, and had McGuire guard the door in case Hartley got any unusual ideas.

The details of Smith's twenty-three years were simple. He had worked for five years in the electronics lab, experimenting. He had never been seriously sick in his life.

And as the days went by Rockwell took long walks in the dry-wash near the sanitarium, alone. It gave him time to think and solidify the incredible theory that was becoming a unit in his brain.

And one afternoon he paused by a night-blooming jasmine outside the sanitarium, reached up, smiling, and plucked a dark shining object off of a high branch. He looked at the object and tucked it in his pocket. Then he walked into the sanitarium.

He summoned McGuire in off the veranda. McGuire came. Hartley trailed behind, threatening, complaining. The three of them sat in the living quarters of the building.

Rockwell told them.

"Smith's not diseased. Germs can't live in him. He's *not* inhabited by banshees or weird monsters who've 'taken over' his body. I mention this to show I've left no stone untouched. I reject all normal diagnoses of Smith. I offer the most important, the most easily accepted possibility of—delayed hereditary mutation."

"Mutation?" McGuire's voice was funny.

Rockwell held up the shiny dark object in the light.

"I found this on a bush in the garden. It'll illustrate my theory to perfection. After studying Smith's symptoms, examining his laboratory, and considering several of these"—he twirled the dark object in his fingers—"I'm certain. It's metamorphosis. It's regeneration, change, mutation *after* birth. Here. Catch. This is Smith."

He tossed the object to Hartley. Hartley caught it.

"This is the chrysalis of a caterpillar," said Hartley.

Rockwell nodded. "Yes, it is."

"You don't mean to infer that Smith's a—*chrysalis?*"

"I'm positive of it," replied Rockwell.

Rockwell stood over Smith's body in the darkness of evening. Hartley and McGuire sat across the patient's room, quiet, listening. Rockwell touched Smith softly. "Suppose that there's more to life than just being born, living seventy years, and dying. Suppose there's one more great step up in man's existence, and Smith has been the first of us to make that step.

"Looking at a caterpillar, we see what we consider a static object. But it changes to a butterfly. Why? There are no final theories explaining it. It's progress, mainly. The pertinent thing is that a supposedly unchangeable object weaves itself into an intermediary object, wholly unrecognizable, a chrysalis, and emerges a butterfly. Outwardly the chrysalis looks dead. This is misdirection. Smith has misdirected us, you see. Outwardly, dead. Inwardly, fluids whirlpool, reconstruct, rush about with wild purpose. From grub to mosquito, from caterpillar to butterfly, from Smith to—?"

"Smith a chrysalis?" McGuire laughed heavily.

"Yes."

"Humans don't work that way."

"Stop it, McGuire. This evolutionary step's too great for your comprehension. Examine this body and tell me anything else. Skin, eyes, breathing, blood flow. Weeks of assimilating food for his brittle hibernation. Why did he eat all that food, why did he need that x-liquid in his body except for his metamorphosis? And the cause of it all was—radiations. Hard radiations from Smith's laboratory equipment. Planned or accidental I don't know. It touched some part of his essential gene-structure, some part of the evolutionary structure of man that wasn't scheduled for working for thousands of years yet, perhaps."

"Do you think that some day all men—?"

"The maggot doesn't stay in the stagnant pond, the grub in the soil, or the caterpillar on a cabbage leaf. They change, spreading across space in waves.

"Smith's the answer to the problem 'What happens next for man, where do we go from here?' We're faced with the blank wall of the universe and the fatality of living in that universe, and man as he is today is not prepared to go against the universe. The least exertion

tires man, overwork kills his heart, disease his body.
Maybe Smith will be prepared to answer the philoso-
phers' problem of life's purpose. Maybe he can give it
new purpose.

"Why, we're just petty insects, all of us, fighting on a
pinhead planet. Man isn't meant to remain here and be
sick and small and weak, but he hasn't discovered the
secret of the greater knowledge yet.

"But—change man. Build your perfect man. Your—
your superman, if you like. Eliminate petty mentality,
give him complete physiological, neurological, psychological control of himself: give him clear, incisive channels of thought, give him an indefatigable blood stream,
a body that can go months without outside food, that
can adjust to any climate anywhere and kill any disease. Release man from the shackles of flesh and flesh
misery and then he's no longer a poor, petty little man
afraid to dream because he knows his frail body stands
between him and the fulfillment of dreams, then he's
ready to wage war, the only war worth waging—the
conflict of man reborn and the whole confounded universe!"

Breathless, voice hoarse, heart pounding, Rockwell
tensed over Smith, placed his hands admiringly, firmly
on the cold length of the chrysalis and shut his eyes.
The power and drive and belief in Smith surged
through him. He was right. He was right. He knew he
was right. He opened his eyes and looked at McGuire
and Hartley who were mere shadows in the dim shielded
light of the room.

After a silence of several seconds, Hartley snuffed out
his cigarette. "I don't believe that theory."

McGuire said, "How do you know Smith's not just a
mess of jelly inside? Did you X-ray him?"

"I couldn't risk it, it might interfere with his change,
like the sunlight did."

"So he's going to be a superman? What will he look
like?"

"We'll wait and see."

"Do you think he can hear us talking about him
now?"

"Whether or not he can, there's one thing certain—
we're sharing a secret we weren't intended to know.
Smith didn't plan on myself and McGuire entering the
case. He had to make the most of it. But a superman
doesn't like people to know about him. Humans have a
nasty way of being envious, jealous, and hateful. Smith
knew he wouldn't be safe if found out. Maybe that
explains your hatred, too, Hartley."

They all remained silent, listening. Nothing sounded.
Rockwell's blood whispered in his temples, that was all.
There was Smith, no longer Smith, a container labeled
SMITH, its contents unknown.

"If what you say *is* true," said Hartley, "then indeed
we should destroy him. Think of the power over the
world he would have. And if it affects his brain as I
think it will affect it—he'll try to kill us when he
escapes because we are the only ones who know about
him. He'll hate us for prying."

Rockwell said it easily. "I'm not afraid."

Hartley remained silent. His breathing was harsh and
loud in the room.

Rockwell came around the table, gesturing.

"I think we'd better say good-night now, don't you?"

The thin rain swallowed Hartley's car. Rockwell
closed the door, instructed McGuire to sleep downstairs
tonight on a cot fronting Smith's room, and then he
walked upstairs to bed.

Undressing, he had time to conjure over all the
unbelievable events of the passing weeks. A superman.
Why not? Efficiency, strength—

He slipped into bed.

When. When does Smith emerge from his chrysalis?
When?

The rain drizzled quietly on the roof of the sanitarium.

McGuire lay in the middle of the sound of rain and
the earthquaking of thunder, slumbering on the cot,
breathing heavy breaths. Somewhere, a door creaked,
but McGuire breathed on. Wind gusted down the hall.

McGuire grunted and rolled over. A door closed softly and the wind ceased.

Footsteps tread softly on the deep carpeting. Slow footsteps, aware and alert and ready. Footsteps. McGuire blinked his eyes and opened them.

In the dim light a figure stood over him.

Upstairs, a single light in the hall thrust down a yellow shaft near McGuire's cot.

An odor of crushed insect filled the air. A hand moved. A voice started to speak.

McGuire screamed.

Because the hand that moved into the light was green.

Green.

"Smith!"

McGuire flung himself ponderously down the hall, yelling.

"He's walking! He can't walk, but he's walking!"

The door rammed open under McGuire's bulk. Wind and rain shrieked in around him and he was gone into the storm, babbling.

In the hall, the figure was motionless. Upstairs a door opened swiftly and Rockwell ran down the steps. The green hand moved back out of the light behind the figure's back.

"Who is it?" Rockwell paused halfway.

The figure stepped into the light.

Rockwell's eyes narrowed.

"Hartley! What are you doing back here?"

"Something happened," said Hartley. "You'd better get McGuire. He ran out in the rain babbling like a fool."

Rockwell kept his thoughts to himself. He searched Hartley swiftly with one glance and then ran down the hall and out into the cold wind.

"McGuire! McGuire, come back you idiot!"

The rain fell on Rockwell's body as he ran. He found McGuire about a hundred yards from the sanitarium, blubbering,

"Smith—Smith's walking . . ."

"Nonsense. Hartley came back, that's all."

"I saw a green hand. It moved."

"You dreamed."

"No. No." McGuire's face was flabby pale, with water on it. "I saw a green hand, believe me. Why did Hartley come back? He—"

At the mention of Hartley's name, full comprehension came smashing to Rockwell. Fear leaped through his mind, a mad blur of warning, a jagged edge of silent screaming for help.

"Hartley!"

Shoving McGuire abruptly aside, Rockwell twisted and leaped back toward the sanitarium, shouting. Into the hall, down the hall—

Smith's door was broken open.

Gun in hand, Hartley was in the center of the room. He turned at the noise of Rockwell's running. They both moved simultaneously. Hartley fired his gun and Rockwell pulled the light switch.

Darkness. Flame blew across the room, profiling Smith's rigid body like a flash photo. Rockwell jumped at the flame. Even as he jumped, shocked deep, realizing why Hartley had returned. In that instant before the lights blinked out Rockwell had a glimpse of Hartley's fingers.

They were a brittle mottled green.

Fists then. And Hartley collapsing as the lights came on, and McGuire, dripping wet at the door, shook out the words, "Is—is Smith killed?"

Smith wasn't harmed. The shot had passed over him.

"This fool, this fool," cried Rockwell, standing over Hartley's numbed shape. "Greatest case in history and he tries to destroy it!"

Hartley came around, slowly. "I should've known. Smith warned you."

"Nonsense, he—" Rockwell stopped, amazed. Yes. That sudden premonition crashing into his mind. Yes. Then he glared at Hartley. "Upstairs with you. You're being locked in for the night. McGuire, you, too. So you can watch him."

McGuire croaked. "Hartley's hand. Look at it. It's green. It was Hartley in the hall—not Smith!"

Hartley stared at his fingers. "Pretty, isn't it?" he

said, bitterly. "I was in range of those radiations for a long time at the start of Smith's illness. I'm going to be a—creature—like Smith. It's been this way for several days. I kept it hidden. I tried not to say anything. Tonight, I couldn't stand it any longer, and I came back to destroy Smith for what he's done to me . . ."

A dry noise racked, dryly, splitting the air. The three of them froze.

Three tiny flakes of Smith's chrysalis flicked up and then spiraled down to the floor.

Instantly, Rockwell was to the table, and gaping.

"It's starting to crack. From the collar-bone V to the navel, a miscroscopic fissure! He'll be out of his chrysalis soon!"

McGuire's jowls trembled. "And then what?"

Hartley's words were bitter sharp. "We'll have a superman. Question: what does a superman look like? Answer: nobody knows."

Another crust of flakes crackled open.

McGuire shivered. "Will you try to talk to him?"

"Certainly."

"Since when do—butterflies—speak?"

"Oh, Good God, McGuire!"

With the two others securely imprisoned upstairs, Rockwell locked himself into Smith's room and bedded down on a cot, prepared to wait through the long wet night, watching, listening, thinking.

Watching the tiny flakes flicking off the crumbling skin of chrysalis as the Unknown within struggled quietly outward.

Just a few more hours to wait. The rain slid over the house, pattering. What *would* Smith look like? A change in the earcups perhaps for greater hearing; extra eyes, maybe; a change in the skull structure, the facial setup, the bones of the body, the placement of organs, the texture of skin, a million and one changes.

Rockwell grew tired and yet was afraid to sleep. Eyelids heavy, heavy. What if he was wrong? What if his theory was entirely disjointed? What if Smith was only so much moving jelly inside? What if Smith was mad, insane—so different that he'd be a world menace?

No. No. Rockwell shook his head groggily. Smith was perfect. Perfect. There'd be no room for evil thought in Smith. Perfect.

The sanitarium was death quiet. The only noise was the faint crackle of chrysalis flakes skimming to the hard floor . . .

Rockwell slept. Sinking into the darkness that blotted out the room as dreams moved in upon him. Dreams in which Smith arose, walked in stiff, parched gesticulations and Hartley, screaming, wielded an ax, shining, again and again into the green armor of the creature and hacked it into liquid horror. Dreams in which McGuire ran babbling through a rain of blood. Dreams in which—

Hot sunlight. Hot sunlight all over the room. It was morning. Rockwell rubbed his eyes, vaguely troubled by the fact that someone had raised the blinds. Someone had—he leaped! Sunlight! There was no way for the blinds to be up. They'd been down for weeks! He cried out.

The door was open. The sanitarium was silent. Hardly daring to turn his head, Rockwell glanced at the table. Smith should have been lying there.

He wasn't.

There was nothing but sunlight on the table. That—and a few remnants of shattered chrysalis. Remnants.

Brittle shards, a discarded profile cleft in two pieces, a shell segment that had been a thigh, a trace of arm, a splint of chest—these were the fractured remains of Smith!

Smith was gone. Rockwell staggered to the table, crushed. Scrabbling like a child among the rattling papyrus of skin. Then he swung about, as if drunk, and swayed out of the room and pounded up the stairs, shouting:

"Hartley! What did you do with him? Hartley! Did you think you could kill him, dispose of his body, and leave a few bits of shell behind to throw me off trail?"

The door to the room where McGuire and Hartley had slept was locked. Fumbling, Rockwell unlocked it. Both McGuire and Hartley were there.

"You're here," said Rockwell, dazed. "You weren't

downstairs, then. Or did you unlock the door, come down, break in, kill Smith and—no, no."

"What's wrong?"

"Smith's gone! McGuire, did Hartley move out of this room?"

"Not all night."

"Then—there's only one explanation—Smith emerged from his chrysalis and escaped during the night! I'll never see him, I'll never get to see him, damn it! What a fool I was to sleep!"

"That settles it!" declared Hartley. "The man's dangerous or he would have stayed and let us see him! God only knows what he is."

"We've got to search, then. He can't be far off. We've got to search then! Quick now, Hartley. McGuire!"

McGuire sat heavily down. "I won't budge. Let him find himself. I've had enough."

Rockwell didn't wait to hear more. He went downstairs with Hartley close after him. McGuire puffed down a few moments later.

Rockwell moved wildly down the hall, halted at the wide windows that overlooked the desert and the mountains with morning shining over them. He squinted out, and wondered if there was any chance at all of finding Smith. The first superbeing. The first perhaps in a new long line. Rockwell sweated. Smith wouldn't leave without revealing himself to at least Rockwell. He couldn't leave. Or could he?

The kitchen door swung open, slowly.

A foot stepped through the door, followed by another. A hand lifted against the wall. Cigarette smoke moved from pursed lips.

"Somebody looking for me?"

Stunned, Rockwell turned. He saw the expression on Hartley's face, heard McGuire choke with surprise. The three of them spoke one word together, as if given their cue:

"Smith."

Smith exhaled cigarette smoke. His face was red-pink as he had been sunburnt, his eyes were glittering blue.

He was barefoot and his nude body was attired in one of Rockwell's old robes.

"Would you mind telling me where I am? What have I been doing for the last three or four months? Is this a—hospital or isn't it?"

Dismay slammed Rockwell's mind, hard. He swallowed.

"Hello. I. That is— Don't you remember—anything?"

Smith displayed his fingertips. "I recall turning green, if that's what you mean. Beyond that—nothing." He raked his pink hand through his nut-brown hair with the vigor of a creature newborn and glad to breathe again.

Rockwell slumped back against the wall. He raised his hands, with shock, to his eyes, and shook his head. Not believing what he saw he said, "What time did you come out of the chrysalis?"

"What time did I come out of—what?"

Rockwell took him down the hall to the next room and pointed to the table.

"I don't see what you mean," said Smith, frankly sincere. "I found myself standing in this room half an hour ago, stark naked."

"That's all?" said McGuire, hopefully. He seemed relieved.

Rockwell explained the origin of the chrysalis on the table.

Smith frowned. "That's ridiculous. Who *are* you?"

Rockwell introduced the others.

Smith scowled at Hartley. "When I first was sick you came, didn't you. I remember. At the radiations plant. But this is silly. What disease was it?"

Hartley's cheek muscles were taut wire. "No disease. Don't *you* know anything about it?"

"I find myself with strange people in a strange sanitarium. I find myself naked in a room with a man sleeping on a cot. I walk around the sanitarium, hungry. I go to the kitchen, find food, eat, hear excited voices, and then am accused of emerging from a chrysalis. What am I supposed to think? Thanks, by the way, for this robe, for food, and the cigarette I bor-

rowed. I didn't want to wake you at first, Mr. Rockwell. I didn't know who you were and you looked dead
tired."

"Oh, that's all right." Rockwell wouldn't let himself
believe it. Everything was crumbling. With every word
Smith spoke, his hopes were pulled apart like the
crumpled chrysalis. "How do you feel?"

"Fine. Strong. Remarkable, when you consider how
long I was under."

"Very remarkable," said Hartley.

"You can imagine how I felt when I saw the calen-
dar. All those months—crack—gone. I wondered what
I'd been doing all that time."

"So have we."

McGuire laughed. "Oh, leave him alone, Hartley.
Just because you hated him—"

"Hated?" Smith's brows went up. "Me? Why?"

"Here. This is why!" Hartley thrust his fingers out.
"Your damned radiations. Night after night sitting by
you in your laboratory. What can I do about it?"

"Hartley," warned Rockwell. "Sit down. Be quiet."

"I won't sit down and I won't be quiet! Are you both
fooled by this imitation of a man, this pink fellow
who's carrying on the greatest hoax in history? If you
had any sense you'd destroy Smith before he escapes!"

Rockwell apologized for Hartley's outburst.

Smith shook his head. "No, let him talk. What's this
about?"

"You know already!" shouted Hartley, angrily.
"You've lain there for months, listening, planning. You
can't fool me. You've got Rockwell bluffed, disappointed. He expected you to be a superman. Maybe you are.
But whatever you are, you're not Smith any more. Not
any more. It's just another of your misdirections. We
weren't supposed to know all about you, and the world
shouldn't know about you. You could kill us, easily,
but you'd prefer to stay and convince us that you're
normal. That's the best way. You could have escaped a
few minutes ago, but that would have left the seeds of
suspicion behind. Instead, you waited, to convince us
that you're normal."

"He *is* normal," complained McGuire.

"No he's not. His mind's different. He's clever."

"Give him word association tests then," said McGuire.

"He's too clever for that, too."

"It's very simple, then. We take blood tests, listen to his heart, and inject serums into him."

Smith looked dubious. "I feel like an experiment, but if you really want to. This is silly."

That shocked Hartley. He looked at Rockwell. "Get the hypos," he said.

Rockwell got the hypos, thinking. Now, maybe after all, Smith was a superman. His blood. That super-blood. Its ability to kill germs. His heartbeat. His breathing. Maybe Smith was a superman and didn't know it. Yes. Yes, maybe—

Rockwell drew blood from Smith and slid it under a microscope. His shoulders sagged. It was normal blood. When you dropped germs into it the germs took a normal length of time to die. The blood was no longer super germicidal. The x-liquid, too, was gone. Rockwell sighed miserably. Smith's temperature was normal. So was his pulse. His sensory and nervous system respond-ed according to rule.

"Well, that takes care of that," said Rockwell, softly.

Hartley sank into a chair, eyes widened, holding his head between bony fingers. He exhaled. "I'm sorry. I guess my—mind—it just imagined things. The months were so long. Night after night. I got obsessed, and afraid. I've made a fool out of myself. I'm sorry. I'm sorry." He stared at his green fingers. "But what about myself?"

Smith said, "I recovered. You'll recover, too, I guess. I can sympathize with you. But it wasn't bad ... I don't really recall anything."

Hartley relaxed. "But—yes I guess you're right. I don't like the idea of my body getting hard, but it can't be helped. I'll be all right."

Rockwell was sick. The tremendous letdown was too much for him. The intense drive, the eagerness, the hunger and curiosity, the fire, had all sunk within him.

So *this* was the man from the chrysalis? The same man who had gone in. All this waiting and wondering for nothing.

He gulped a breath of air, tried to steady his innermost, racing thoughts. Turmoil. This pink-cheeked, fresh-voiced man who sat before him smoking calmly, was no more than a man who had suffered some partial skin petrification, and whose glands had gone wild from radiation, but, nevertheless, just a man now and nothing more. Rockwell's mind, his overimaginative, fantastic mind had seized upon each facet of the illness and built it into a perfect organism of wishful thinking. Rockwell was deeply shocked, deeply stirred and disappointed.

The question of Smith's living without food, his pure blood, low temperature, and the other evidences of superiority were now fragments of a strange illness. An illness and nothing more. Something that was over, down and gone and left nothing behind but brittle scraps on a sunlit tabletop. There'd be a chance to watch Hartley now, if his illness progressed, and report the new sickness to the medical world.

But Rockwell didn't care about illness. He cared about perfection. And that perfection had been split and ripped and torn and it was gone. His dream was gone. His supercreature was gone. He didn't care if the whole world went hard, green, brittle-mad now.

Smith was shaking hands all around. "I'd better get back to Los Angeles. Important work for me to do at the plant. I have my old job waiting for me. Sorry I can't stay on. You understand."

"You should stay on and rest a few days, at least," said Rockwell. He hated to see the last wisp of his dream vanish.

"No thanks. I'll drop by your office in a week or so for another checkup, though, Doctor, if you like? I'll drop in every few weeks for the next year or so so you can check me, yes?"

"Yes. Yes, Smith. Do that, will you please? I'd like to talk your illness over with you. You're lucky to be alive."

McGuire said, happily, "I'll drive you to L.A."

"Don't bother. I'll walk to Tujunga and get a cab. I want to walk. It's been so long, I want to see what it feels like."

Rockwell lent him an old pair of shoes and an old suit of clothes.

"Thanks, Doctor. I'll pay you what I owe you as soon as possible."

"You don't owe me a penny. It was interesting."

"Well, good-bye, Doctor. Mr. McGuire. Hartley."

"Good-bye, Smith."

"Good-bye."

Smith walked down the path to the dry wash, which was already baked dry by the late afternoon sun. He walked easily and happily and whistled. I wish I could whistle now, thought Rockwell tiredly.

Smith turned once, waved to them, and then he strode up the hillside and went on over it toward the distant city.

Rockwell watched him go as a small child watches his favorite sand castle eroded and annihilated by the waves of the sea. "I can't believe it," he said, over and over again. "I can't believe it. The whole thing's ending so soon, so abruptly for me. I'm dull and empty inside."

"Everything looks *rosy* to me!" chuckled McGuire happily.

Hartley stood in the sun. His green hands hung softly at his side and his white face was really relaxed for the first time in months, Rockwell realized. Hartley said, softly,

"I'll come out all right. I'll come out all right. Oh, thank God for that. Thank God for that. I won't be a monster. I won't be anything but myself." He turned to Rockwell. "Just remember, remember, don't let them bury me by mistake. Don't let them bury me by mistake, thinking I'm dead. Remember that."

Smith took the path across the dry wash and up the hill. It was late afternoon already and the sun had started to vanish behind blue hills. A few stars were visible. The odor of water, dust, and distant orange blossoms hung in the warm air.

Wind stirred. Smith took deep breaths of air. He walked.

Out of sight, away from the sanitarium, he paused and stood very still. He looked up at the sky.

Tossing away the cigarette he'd been smoking, he mashed it precisely under one heel. Then he straightened his well-shaped body, tossed his brown hair back, closed his eyes, swallowed, and relaxed his fingers at his sides.

With nothing of effort, just a little murmur of sound, Smith lifted his body gently from the ground into the warm air.

He soared up quickly, quietly—and very soon he was lost among the stars as Smith headed for outer space . . .

PILLAR OF FIRE

He came out of the earth, hating. Hate was his father; hate was his mother.

It was good to walk again. It was good to leap up out of the earth, off of your back, and stretch your cramped arms violently and try to take a deep breath!

He *tried*. He cried out.

He couldn't breathe. He flung his arms over his face and tried to breathe. It was impossible. He walked on the earth, he came out of the earth. But he was dead. He couldn't breathe. He could take air into his mouth and force it half down his throat, with withered moves of long-dormant muscles, wildly, wildly! And with this little air he could shout and cry! He wanted to have tears, but he couldn't make them come, either. All he knew was that he was standing upright, he was dead, he shouldn't be walking! He couldn't breathe and yet he stood.

The smells of the world were all about him. Frustratedly, he tried to smell the smells of autumn. Autumn was burning the land down into ruin. All across the country the ruins of summer lay; vast forests bloomed with flame, tumbled down timber on empty, unleafed timber. The smoke of the burning was rich, blue, and invisible.

He stood in the graveyard, hating. He walked through the world and yet could not taste nor smell of it. He heard, yes. The wind roared on his newly opened ears. But he was dead. Even though he walked he knew he was dead and should expect not too much of himself or this hateful living world.

27

He touched the tombstone over his own empty grave. He knew his own name again. It was a good job of carving.

WILLIAM LANTRY

That's what the gravestone said.
His fingers trembled on the cool stone surface.

BORN 1898—DIED 1933

Born *again* . . . ?

What year? He glared at the sky and the midnight autumnal stars moving in slow illuminations across the windy black. He read the tiltings of centuries in those stars. Orion thus and so, Aurega here! and where Taurus? *There!*

His eyes narrowed. His lips spelled out the year: "2349."

An odd number. Like a school sum. They used to say a man couldn't encompass any number over a hundred. After that it was all so damned abstract there was no use counting. This was the year 2349! A numeral, a sum. And here he was, a man who had lain in his hateful dark coffin, hating to be buried, hating the living people above who lived and lived and lived, hating them for all the centuries, until today, now, born out of hatred, he stood by his own freshly excavated grave, the smell of raw earth in the air, perhaps, but he could not smell it!

"I," he said, addressing a poplar tree that was shaken by the wind, "am an anachronism." He smiled faintly.

He looked at the graveyard. It was cold and empty. All of the stones had been ripped up and piled like so many flat bricks, one atop another, in the far corner by the wrought iron fence. This had been going on for two endless weeks. In his deep secret coffin he had heard the heartless, wild stirring as the men jabbed the earth with cold spades and tore out the coffins and carried away the withered ancient bodies to be burned. Twisting with fear in his coffin, he had waited for them to come to him.

Today they had arrived at his coffin. But—late. They had dug down to within an inch of the lid. Five o'clock bell, time for quitting. Home to supper. The workers had gone off. Tomorrow they would finish the job, they said, shrugging into their coats.

Silence had come to the emptied tombyard.

Carefully, quietly, with a soft rattling of sod, the coffin lid had lifted.

William Lantry stood trembling now, in the last cemetery on Earth.

"Remember?" he asked himself, looking at the raw earth. "Remember those stories of that last man on Earth? Those stories of men wandering in ruins, alone? Well, you, William Lantry, are a switch on the old story. Do you *know* that? You are the last *dead* man in the whole world!"

There were no more dead people. Nowhere in any land was there a dead person. Impossible! Lantry did not smile at this. No, not impossible at all in this foolish, sterile, unimaginative, antiseptic age of cleansings and scientific methods! People died, oh my God, yes. But—*dead* people? Corpses? They didn't exist!

What *happened* to dead people?

The graveyard was on a hill. William Lantry walked through the dark burning night until he reached the edge of the graveyard and looked down upon the new town of Salem. It was all illumination, all color. Rocket ships cut fire above it, crossing the sky to all the far ports of Earth.

In his grave the new violence of this future world had driven down and seeped into William Lantry. He had been bathed in it for years. He knew all about it, with a hating dead man's knowledge of such things.

Most important of all, he knew what these fools did with dead men.

He lifted his eyes. In the center of the town a massive stone finger pointed at the stars. It was three hundred feet high and fifty feet across. There was a wide entrance and a drive in front of it.

In the town, theoretically, thought William Lantry,

say you have a dying man. In a moment he will be dead. What happens? No sooner is his pulse cold when a certificate is flourished, made out, his relatives pack him into a car-beetle and drive him swiftly to—

The Incinerator!

That functional finger, that Pillar of Fire pointing at the stars. Incinerator. A functional, terrible name. But truth is truth in this future world.

Like a stick of kindling your Mr. Dead Man is shot into the furnace.

Flume!

William Lantry looked at the top of the gigantic pistol shoving at the stars. A small pennant of smoke issued from the top.

There's where your dead people go.

"Take care of yourself, William Lantry," he murmured. "You're the last one, the rare item, the last dead man. All the other graveyards of Earth have been blasted up. This is the last graveyard and you're the last dead man from the centuries. These people don't believe in having dead people about, much less walking dead people. Everything that can't be used goes up like a matchstick. Superstitions right along with it!"

He looked at the town. All right, he thought, quietly. I hate you. You hate me, or you *would* if you knew I existed. You don't believe in such things as vampires or ghosts. Labels without referents, you cry! You snort. All right, snort! Frankly, I don't believe in *you*, either! I don't *like* you! You and your Incinerators.

He trembled. How very close it had been. Day after day they had hauled out the other dead ones, burned them like so much kindling. An edict had been broadcast around the world. He had heard the digging men talk as they worked!

"I guess it's a good idea, this cleaning up the graveyards," said one of the men.

"Guess so," said another. "Grisly custom. Can you imagine? Being buried, I mean! Unhealthy! All them germs!"

"Sort of a shame. Romantic, kind of. I mean, leaving just this one graveyard untouched all these centuries.

The other graveyards were cleaned out, what year was it, Jim?"

"About 2260, I think. Yeah, that was it, 2260, almost a hundred years ago. But some Salem Committee, they got on their high horse and they said, 'Look here, let's have just *one* graveyard left, to remind us of the customs of the barbarians.' And the gover'ment scratched its head, thunk it over, and said, 'Okay. Salem it is. But all other graveyards go, you understand, all!' "

"And away they went," said Jim.

"Sure, they sucked out 'em with fire and steam shovels and rocket-cleaners. If they knew a man was buried in a cow pasture, they fixed him! Evacuated them, they did. Sort of cruel, I say."

"I hate to sound old-fashioned, but still there were a lot of tourists came here every year, just to see what a real graveyard was like."

"Right. We had nearly a million people in the last three years visiting. A good revenue. But—a government order is an order. The government says no more morbidity, so flush her out we do! Here we go. Hand me that spade, Bill."

William Lantry stood in the autumn wind, on the hill. It was good to walk again, to feel the wind and to hear the leaves scuttling like mice on the road ahead of him. It was good to see the bitter cold stars almost blown away by the wind.

It was even good to know fear again.

For fear rose in him now, and he could not put it away. The very fact that he was walking made him an enemy. And there was not another friend, another dead man, in all of the world, to whom one could turn for help or consolation. It was the whole melodramatic living world against one William Lantry. It was the whole vampire-disbelieving, body-burning, graveyard-annihilating world against a man in a dark suit on a dark autumn hill. He put out his pale cold hands into the city illumination. You have pulled the tombstones, like teeth, from the yard, he thought. Now I will find some way to push your Incinerators down into rubble. I will make dead people again, and I will make friends in so doing. I cannot be alone and lonely. I must start manufacturing friends very soon. Tonight.

"War is declared," he said, and laughed. It was pretty silly, one man declaring war on an entire world.

The world did not answer back. A rocket crossed the sky on a rush of flame, like an Incinerator taking wing.

Footsteps. Lantry hastened to the edge of the cemetery. The diggers, coming back to finish up their work? No. Just someone, a man, walking by.

As the man came abreast the cemetery gate, Lantry stepped swiftly out. "Good evening," said the man, smiling.

Lantry struck the man in the face. The man fell. Lantry bent quietly down and hit the man a killing blow across the neck with the side of his hand.

Dragging the body back into shadow, he stripped it and changed clothes with it. It wouldn't do for a fellow to go wandering about this future world with ancient clothing on. He found a small pocket knife in the man's coat; not much of a knife, but enough if you knew how to handle it properly. He knew how.

He rolled the body down into one of the already opened and exhumed graves. In a minute he had shoveled dirt down upon it, just enough to hide it. There was little chance of it being found. They wouldn't dig the same grave twice.

He adjusted himself in his new loose-fitting metallic suit. Fine, fine.

Hating, William Lantry walked down into town, to do battle with the Earth.

II

The Incinerator was open. It never closed. There was a wide entrance, all lighted up with hidden illumination, there was a helicopter landing table and a beetle drive. The town itself was dying down after another day of the dynamo. The lights were going dim, and the only quiet, lighted spot in the town now was the Incinerator. God, what a practical name, what an unromantic name.

William Lantry entered the wide, well-lighted door. It was an entrance, really; there were no doors to open or shut. People could go in and out, summer or winter, the inside was always warm. Warm from the fire that rushed whispering up the high round flue to where the whirlers, the propellors, the air jets pushed the leafy gray ashes on away for a ten-mile ride down the sky.

There was the warmth of the bakery here. The halls were floored with rubber parquet. You couldn't make a noise if you wanted to. Music played in hidden throats somewhere. Not music of death at all, but music of life and the way the sun lived inside the Incinerator; or the sun's brother, anyway. You could bear the flame floating inside the heavy brick wall.

William Lantry descended a ramp. Behind him he heard a whisper and turned in time to see a beetle stop before the entranceway. A bell rang. The music, as if at a signal, rose to ecstatic heights. There was joy in it.

From the beetle, which opened from the rear, some attendants stepped carrying a golden box. It was six feet long and there were sun symbols on it. From another beetle the relatives of the man in the box stepped and followed as the attendants took the golden box down a ramp to a kind of altar. On the side of the altar were the words, "WE THAT WERE BORN OF THE SUN RETURN TO THE SUN." The golden box was deposited upon the altar, the music leaped upward, the Guardian of this place spoke only a few words, then the attendants picked up the golden box, walked to a transparent wall, a safety lock, also transparent, and opened it. The box was shoved into the glass slot. A moment later an inner lock opened, the box was injected into the interior of the Flue, and vanished instantly in quick flame.

The attendants walked away. The relatives without a word turned and walked out. The music played.

William Lantry approached the glass fire lock. He peered through the wall at the vast, glowing, never-ceasing heart of the Incinerator. It burned steadily, without a flicker, singing to itself peacefully. It was so solid it was like a golden river flowing up out of the earth toward the sky. Anything you put into the river was borne upward, vanished.

Lantry felt again his unreasoning hatred of this thing, this monster, cleansing fire.

A man stood at his elbow. "May I help you, sir?"

"What?" Lantry turned abruptly. "What did you say?"

"May I be of service?"

"I—that is—" Lantry looked quickly at the ramp and the door. His hands trembled at his sides. "I've never been in here before."

"Never?" The Attendant was surprised.

That had been the wrong thing to say, Lantry realized. But it was said, nevertheless. "I mean," he said. "Not really. I mean, when you're a child, somehow, you don't pay attention. I suddenly realized tonight that I didn't really *know* the Incinerator."

The Attendant smiled. "We never know anything, do we, really? I'll be glad to show you around."

"Oh, no. Never mind. It—it's a wonderful place."

"Yes, it is." The Attendant took pride in it. "One of the finest in the world, I think."

"I—" Lantry felt he must explain further. "I haven't had many relatives die on me since I was a child. In fact, none. So, you see I haven't been here for many years."

"I see." The Attendant's face seemed to darken somewhat.

What've I said now, thought Lantry. What in God's name is wrong? What've I done? If I'm not careful I'll get myself shoved right into that monstrous firetrap. What's wrong with this fellow's face? He seems to be giving me more than the usual going-over.

"You wouldn't be one of the men who've just returned from Mars, would you?" asked the Attendant.

"No. Why do you ask?"

"No matter." The Attendant began to walk off. "If you want to know anything, just ask me."

"Just one thing," said Lantry.

"What's that?"

"This."

Lantry dealt him a stunning blow across the neck.

He had watched the fire-trap operator with expert eyes. Now, with the sagging body in his arms, he touched the button that opened the warm outer lock, placed the body in, heard the music rise, and saw the inner lock open. The body shot out into the river of fire. The music softened.

"Well done, Lantry, well done."

Barely an instant later another Attendant entered the room. Lantry was caught with an expression of pleased excitement on his face. The Attendant looked around as if expecting to find someone, then he walked toward Lantry. "May I help you?"

"Just looking," said Lantry.

"Rather late at night," said the Attendant.

"I couldn't sleep."

That was the wrong answer, too. Everybody slept in this world. Nobody had insomnia. If you did you simply turned on a hypno-ray, and, sixty seconds later, you were snoring. Oh, he was just *full* of wrong answers. First he had made the fatal error of saying he had never been in the Incinerator before, when he knew that all children were brought here on tours, every year, from the time they were four, to instill the idea of the clean fire death and the Incinerator in their minds. Death was a bright fire, death was warmth and the sun. It was not a dark, shadowed thing. That was important in their education. And he, pale, thoughtless fool, had immediately gabbled out his ignorance.

And another thing, this paleness of his. He looked at his hands and realized with growing terror that a pale man also was nonexistent in this world. They would suspect his paleness. That was why the first attendant had asked, "Are you one of those men newly returned from Mars?" Here, now, this new Attendant was clean and bright as a copper penny, his cheeks red with health and energy. Lantry hid his pale hands in his pockets. But he was fully aware of the searching the Attendant did on his face.

"I mean to say," said Lantry. "I didn't *want* to sleep. I wanted to think."

"Was there a service held here a moment ago?" asked the Attendant, looking about.

"I don't know, I just came in."

"I thought I heard the fire lock open and shut."

"I don't know," said Lantry.

The man pressed a wall button. "Anderson?"

A voice replied. "Yes."

"Locate Saul for me, will you?"

"I'll ring the corridors." A pause. "Can't find him."

"Thanks." The Attendant was puzzled. He was beginning to make little sniffing motions with his nose. "Do you—*smell* anything?"

Lantry sniffed. "No. Why?"

"I *smell* something."

Lantry took hold of the knife in his pocket. He waited.

"I remember once when I was a kid," said the man. "And we found a cow lying dead in the field. It had been there two days in the hot sun. That's what this smell is. I wonder what it's from?"

"Oh, I know what it is," said Lantry quietly. He held out his hand. "Here."

"What?"

"Me, of course."

"You?"

"Dead several hundred years."

"You're an odd joker." The Attendant was puzzled.

"Very." Lantry took out the knife. "Do you know what this is?"

"A knife."

"Do you ever use knives on people any more?"

"How do you mean?"

"I mean—killing them, with knives or guns or poison?"

"You *are* an odd joker!" The man giggled awkwardly.

"I'm going to kill you," said Lantry.

"Nobody kills anybody," said the man.

"Not any more they don't. But they used to, in the old days."

"I know they did."

"This will be the first murder in three hundred years.

I just killed your friend. I just shoved him into the fire lock."

That remark had the desired effect. It numbed the man so completely, it shocked him so thoroughly with its illogical aspects that Lantry had time to walk forward. He put the knife against the man's chest. "I'm going to kill you."

"That's silly," said the man, numbly. "People don't do that."

"Like this," said Lantry. "You see?"

The knife slid into the chest. The man stared at it for a moment. Lantry caught the falling body.

III

The Salem flue exploded at six that morning. The great fire chimney shattered into ten thousand parts and flung itself into the earth and into the sky and into the houses of the sleeping people. There was fire and sound, more fire than autumn made burning in the hills.

William Lantry was five miles away at the time of the explosion. He saw the town ignited by the great spreading cremation of it. And he shook his head and laughed a little bit and clapped his hands smartly together.

Relatively simple. You walked around killing people who didn't believe in murder, had only heard of it indirectly as some dim gone custom of the old barbarian races. You walked into the control room of the Incinerator and said, "How do you work this Incinerator?" and the control man told you, because everybody told the truth in this world of the future, nobody lied, there was no reason to lie, there was no danger to lie *against*. There was only one criminal in the world, and nobody knew HE existed yet.

Oh, it was an incredibly beautiful setup. The Control Man had told him just how the Incinerator worked, what pressure gauges controlled the flood of fire gases going up the flue, what levers were adjusted or readjusted. He and Lantry had had quite a talk. It was an easy, free world. People trusted people. A moment later Lantry had shoved a knife in the Control Man also and set the pressure gauges for an overload to occur half an hour later, and walked out of the Incinerator halls, whistling.

Now even the sky was palled with the vast black cloud of the explosion.

"This is only the first," said Lantry, looking at the sky. "I'll tear all the others down before they even suspect there's an unethical man loose in their society. They can't account for a variable like me. I'm beyond their understanding. I'm incomprehensible, impossible, therefore I do not exist. My God, I can kill hundreds of thousands of them before they even realize murder is out in the world again. I can make it look like an accident each time. Why, the idea is so huge, it's unbelievable!"

The fire burned the town. He sat under a tree for a long time, until morning. Then, he found a cave in the hills, and went in, to sleep.

He awoke at sunset with a sudden dream of fire. He saw himself pushed into the flue, cut into sections by flame, burned away to nothing. He sat up on the cave floor, laughing at himself. He had an idea.

He walked down into the town and stepped into an audio booth. He dialed OPERATOR. "Give me the Police Department," he said.

"I beg your pardon?" said the operator.

He tried again. "The Law Force," he said.

"I will connect you with the Peace Control," she said, at last.

A little fear began ticking inside him like a tiny watch. Suppose the operator recognized the term Police Department as an anachronism, took his audio number, and sent someone out to investigate? No, she wouldn't do that. Why should she suspect? Paranoids were non-existent in this civilization.

"Yes, the Peace Control," he said.

A buzz. A man's voice answered. "Peace Control. Stephens speaking."

"Give me the Homicide Detail," said Lantry, smiling.

"The *what?*"

"Who investigates murders?"

"I beg your pardon, what are you talking about?"

"Wrong number." Lantry hung up, chuckling. Ye gods, there was no such a thing as a Homicide Detail. There were no murders, therefore they needed no detectives. Perfect, perfect!

The audio rang back. Lantry hesitated, then answered.

"Say," said the voice on the phone. "Who *are* you?"

"The man just left who called," said Lantry, and hung up again.

He ran. They would recognize his voice and perhaps send someone out to check. People didn't lie. *He* had just lied. They knew his voice. He had lied. Anybody who lied needed a psychiatrist. They would come to pick him up to see why he was lying. For no *other* reason. They suspected him of nothing else. Therefore— he must run.

Oh, how very carefully he must act from now on. He knew nothing of this world, this odd straight truthful ethical world. Simply by looking pale you were suspect. Simply by not sleeping nights you were suspect. Simply by not bathing, by smelling like a—dead cow?—you were suspect. Anything.

He must go to a library. But that was dangerous, too. What were libraries like today? Did they have books or did they have film spools which projected books on a screen? Or did people have libraries at home, thus eliminating the necessity of keeping large main libraries?

He decided to chance it. His use of archaic terms might well make him suspect again, but now it was very important he learn all that could be learned of this foul world into which he had come again. He stopped a man on the street. "Which way to the library?"

The man was not surprised. "Two blocks east, one block north."

"Thank you."

Simple as that.

He walked into the library a few minutes later.

"May I help you?"

He looked at the librarian. May I help you, may I help you. What a world of helpful people! "I'd like to 'have' Edgar Allan Poe." His verb was carefully chosen. He didn't say 'read.' He was too afraid that books were passé, that printing itself was a lost art. Maybe all 'books' today were in the form of fully delineated three-dimensional motion pictures. How in blazes could you make a motion picture out of Socrates, Schopenhauer, Nietzsche, and Freud?

"What was that name again?"

"Edgar Allan Poe."

"There is no such author listed in our files."

"Will you please check?"

She checked. "Oh, yes. There's a red mark on the file card. He was one of the authors in the Great Burning of 2265."

"How ignorant of me."

"That's all right," she said. "Have you heard much of him?"

"He had some interesting barbarian ideas on death," said Lantry.

"Horrible ones," she said, wrinkling her nose. "Ghastly."

"Yes. Ghastly. Abominable, in fact. Good thing he was burned. Unclean. By the way, do you have any of Lovecraft?"

"Is that a sex book?"

Lantry exploded with laughter. "No, no. It's a man."

She riffled the file. "He was burned, too. Along with Poe."

"I suppose that applies to Machen and a man named Derleth and one named Ambrose Bierce, also?"

"Yes." She shut the file cabinet. "All burned. And good riddance." She gave him an odd warm look of interest. "I bet you've just come back from Mars."

"Why do you say that?"

"There was another explorer in here yesterday. He'd just made the Mars hop and return. He was interested in supernatural literature, also. It seems there are actually 'tombs' on Mars."

"What are 'tombs'?" Lantry was learning to keep his mouth closed.

"You know, those things they once buried people in."

"Barbarian custom. Ghastly!"

"*Isn't* it? Well, seeing the Martian tombs made this young explorer curious. He came and asked if we had any of those authors you mentioned. Of course we haven't even a smitch of their stuff." She looked at his pale face. "You *are* one of the Martian rocket men, aren't you?"

"Yes," he said. "Got back on the ship the other day."

"The other young man's name was Burke."

"Of course. Burke! Good friend of mine!"

"Sorry I can't help you. You'd best get yourself some vitamin shots and some sun lamps. You look terrible, Mr. ——?"

"Lantry. I'll be good. Thanks ever so much. See you next Hallows' Eve!"

"Aren't you the clever one." She laughed. "If there *were* a Hallows' Eve, I'd make it a date."

"But they burned *that*, too," he said.

"Oh, they burned everything," she said. "Good night."

"Good night." And he went on out.

Oh, how carefully he was balanced in this world! Like some kind of dark gyroscope, whirling with never a murmur, a very silent man. As he walked along the eight o'clock evening street he noticed with particular interest that there was not an unusual amount of lights about. There were the usual street lights at each corner, but the blocks themselves were only faintly illuminated. Could it be that these remarkable people were not *afraid of the dark*? Incredible nonsense! *Every one* was afraid of the dark. *Even he* himself had been afraid, as a child. It was as natural as eating.

A little boy ran by on pelting feet, followed by six others. They yelled and shouted and rolled on the dark cool October lawn, in the leaves. Lantry looked on for several minutes before addressing himself to one of the small boys who was for a moment taking a respite, gathering his breath into his small lungs, as a boy might blow to refill a punctured paper bag.

"Here, now," said Lantry. "You'll wear yourself out."

"Sure," said the boy.

"Could you tell me," said the man, "why there are no street lights in the middle of the blocks?"

"Why?" asked the boy.

"I'm a teacher, I thought I'd test your knowledge," said Lantry.

"Well," said the boy, "you don't need lights in the middle of the block, that's why."

"But it gets rather dark," said Lantry.

"So?" said the boy.

"Aren't you afraid?" asked Lantry.

"Of what?" asked the boy.

"The dark," said Lantry.

"Ho ho," said the boy. "Why should I be?"

"Well," said Lantry. "It's black, it's dark. And after all, street lights were invented to take away the dark and take away fear."

"That's silly. Street lights were made so you could see where you were walking. Outside of that there's nothing."

"You miss the whole point—" said Lantry. "Do you mean to say you would sit in the middle of an empty lot all night and not be afraid?"

"Of what?"

"Of what, of what, of what, you little ninny! Of the dark!"

"Ho ho."

"Would you go out in the hills and stay all night in the dark?"

"Sure."

"Would you stay in a deserted house alone?"

"Sure."

"And not be afraid?"

"Sure."

"You're a liar!"

"Don't you call me nasty names!" shouted the boy.

Liar was the improper noun, indeed. It seemed to be the worst thing you could call a person.

Lantry was completely furious with the little monster. "Look," he insisted. "Look into my eyes . . ."

The boy looked.

Lantry bared his teeth slightly. He put out his hands, making a clawlike gesture. He leered and gesticulated and wrinkled his face into a terrible mask of horror.

"Ho ho," said the boy. "You're funny."

"*What* did you say?"

"You're funny. Do it again. Hey, gang, c'mere! This man does funny things!"

"Never mind."

"Do it again, sir."

"Never mind, never mind. Good night!" Lantry ran off.

"Good night, sir. And mind the dark, sir!" called the little boy.

Of all the stupidity, of all the rank, gross, crawling, jelly-mouthed stupidity! He had never seen the like of it in his life! Bringing the children up without so much as an *ounce* of imagination! Where was the fun in being children if you didn't imagine things?

He stopped running. He slowed and for the first time began to appraise himself. He ran his hand over his face and bit his fingers and found that he himself was standing midway in the block and he felt uncomfortable. He moved up to the street corner where there was a glowing lantern. "That's better," he said, holding his hands out like a man to an open warm fire.

He listened. There was not a sound except the night breathing of the crickets. Finally there was a fire-hush as a rocket swept the sky. It was the sound a torch might make brandished gently on the dark air.

He listened to himself and for the first time he realized what there was so peculiar to himself. There was not a sound in him. The little nostril and lung noises were absent. His lungs did not take nor give oxygen or carbon dioxide; they did not move. The hairs on his nostrils did not quiver with warm combing air.

That faint purrling whisper of breathing did not sound
in his nose. Strange. Funny. A noise you never heard
when you were alive, the breath that fed your body,
and yet, once dead, oh how you missed it!

The only other time you ever heard it was on deep
dreamless awake nights when you wakened and listened
and heard first your nose taking and gently poking out
the air, and then the dull deep dim red thunder of the
blood in your temples, in your eardrums, in your
throat, in your aching wrists, in your warm loins, in
your chest. All of those little rhythms, gone. The wrist
beat gone, the throat pulse gone, the chest vibration
gone. The sound of the blood coming up down around
and through, up down around and through. Now it was
like listening to a statue.

And yet he *lived*. Or, rather, moved about. And how
was this done, over and above scientific explanations,
theories, doubts?

By one thing, and one thing alone.

Hatred.

Hatred was a blood in him, it went up down around
and through, up down around and through. It was a
heart in him, not beating, true, but warm. He was—
what? Resentment. Envy. They said he could not lie
any longer in his coffin in the cemetery. He had *wanted*
to. He had never had any particular desire to get up
and walk around. It had been enough, all these centuries, to lie in the deep box and feel but *not feel* the
ticking of the million insect watches in the earth
around, the moves of worms like so many deep
thoughts in the soil.

But then they had come and said, "Out you go and
into the furnace!" And that is the worst thing you can
say to any man. You cannot tell him what to do. If you
say you are dead, he will want not to be dead. If
you say there are no such things as vampires, by God,
that man will try to *be* one just for spite. If you say a
dead man cannot walk, he will test his limbs. If you say
murder is no longer occurring, he will make it occur.
He was, *in toto*, all the impossible things. They had
given birth to him with their practices and ignorances.
Oh, how wrong they were. They needed to be shown.

He would *show* them! Sun is *good*, so is *night*, there is nothing wrong with dark, *they* said.

Dark is horror, he shouted, silently, facing the little houses. It is *meant* for contrast. You must fear, you hear! That has always been the way of this world. You destroyers of Edgar Allan Poe and fine big-worded Lovecraft, you burner of Halloween masks and destroyer of pumpkin jack-o-lanterns! I will make night what it *once* was, the thing against which man built all his lanterned cities and his many children!

As if in answer to this, a rocket, flying low, trailing a long rakish feather of flame. It made Lantry flinch and draw back.

IV

It was but ten miles to the little town of Science Port. He made it by dawn, walking. But even this was not good. At four in the morning a silver beetle pulled up on the road beside him.

"Hello," called the man inside.

"Hello," said Lantry, wearily.

"Why are you walking?" asked the man.

"I'm going to Science Port."

"Why don't you ride?"

"I *like* to walk."

"*Nobody* likes to walk. Are you sick? May I give you a ride?"

"Thanks, but I like to walk."

The man hesitated, then closed the beetle door. "Good night."

When the beetle was gone over the hill, Lantry retreated into a nearby forest. A world full of bungling, helping people. By God, you couldn't even *walk* without being accused of sickness. That meant only one thing. He must not walk any longer, he had to ride. He should have accepted that fellow's offer.

The rest of the night he walked far enough off the highway so that if a beetle rushed by he had time to vanish in the underbrush. At dawn he crept into an empty dry water drain and closed his eyes.

The dream was as perfect as a rimed snowflake.

He saw the graveyard where he had lain deep and ripe over the centuries. He heard the early morning footsteps of the laborers returning to finish their work.

"Would you mind passing me the shovel, Jim?"

"Here you go."

"Wait a minute, wait a minute!"

"What's up?"

"Look here. We didn't finish last night, did we?"

"No."

"There was one more coffin, wasn't there?"

"Yes."

"Well, here it is, and open!"

"You've got the wrong hole."

"What's the name say on the gravestone?"

"Lantry. William Lantry."

"That's him, that's the one! Gone!"

"What could have happened to it?"

"How do I know. The body was here last night."

"We can't be sure, we didn't look."

"God man, people don't bury empty coffins. He was in his box. Now he isn't."

"Maybe this box was empty."

"Nonsense. Smell that smell? He was here all right."

A pause.

"Nobody would have taken the body, would they?"

"What for?"

"A curiosity, perhaps."

"Don't be ridiculous. People just don't steal. Nobody steals."

"Well, then, there's only one solution."

"And?"

"He got up and walked away."

A pause. In the dark dream, Lantry expected to hear laughter. There was none. Instead, the voice of the grave-digger, after a thoughtful pause, said, "Yes. That's it, indeed. He got up and walked away."

"That's interesting to think about," said the other.

"Isn't it, though!"

Silence.

Lantry awoke. It had all been a dream, but, how realistic. How strangely the two men had carried on. But not unnaturally, oh, no. That was exactly how you expected men of the future to talk. Men of the future. Lantry grinned wryly. That was an anachronism for you. This *was* the future. This was happening *now*. It wasn't three hundred years from now, it was now, not then, or any other time. This wasn't the twentieth century. Oh, how calmly those two men in the dream had said, "He got up and walked away." "—interesting to think about." "*Isn't* it, though?" With never a quaver in their voices. With not so much as a glance over their shoulders or a tremble of spade in hand. But, of course, with their perfectly honest, logical minds, there was but one explanation; certainly nobody had *stolen* the corpse. "*Nobody* steals." The corpse had simply got up and walked off. The corpse was the only one who could have *possibly* moved the corpse. By the few casual slow words of the gravediggers Lantry knew what they were thinking. Here was a man that had lain in suspended animation, not really dead, for hundreds of years. The jarring about, the activity, had brought him back.

Everyone had heard of those little green toads that are sealed for centuries inside mud rocks or in ice patties, alive, alive oh! And how when scientists chipped them out and warmed them like marbles in their hands the little toads leapt about and frisked and blinked. Then it was only logical that the gravediggers think of William Lantry in like fashion.

But what if the various parts were fitted together in the next day or so? If the vanished body and the shattered, exploded incinerator were connected? What if this fellow named Burke, who had returned pale from Mars, went to the library again and said to the young woman he wanted some books and she said, "Oh, your friend Lantry was in the other day." And he'd say, 'Lantry who? Don't know anyone by that name.' And she'd say, "Oh, he *lied*." And people in this time didn't lie. So it would all form and coalesce, item by item, bit by bit. A pale man who was pale and shouldn't be pale had lied and people don't lie, and a walking man on a lonely country road had walked and people don't walk any more, and a body was missing from a cemetery, and the Incinerator had blown up and and and—

They would come after him. They would find him. He would be easy to find. He walked. He lied. He was pale. They would find him and take him and stick him through the open fire lock of the nearest Burner and that would be your Mr. William Lantry, like a Fourth of July set-piece!

There was only one thing to be done efficiently and completely. He arose in violent moves. His lips were wide and his dark eyes were flared and there was a trembling and burning all through him. He must kill and kill and kill and kill and kill. He must make his enemies into friends, into people like himself who walked but shouldn't walk, who were pale in a land of pinks. He must kill and then kill and then kill again. He must make bodies and dead people and corpses. He must destroy Incinerator after Flue after Burner after Incinerator. Explosion on explosion. Death on death. Then, when the Incinerators were all in thrown ruin, and the hastily established morgues were jammed with the bodies of people shattered by the explosion, then he would begin his making of friends, his enrollment of the dead in his own cause.

Before they traced and found and killed him, they must be killed themselves. So far he was safe. He could kill and they would not kill back. People simply do not go around killing. That was his safety margin. He climbed out of the abandoned drain, stood in the road.

He took the knife from his pocket and hailed the next beetle.

It was like the Fourth of July! The biggest firecracker of them all. The Science Port Incinerator split down the middle and flew apart. It made a thousand small explosions that ended with a greater one. It fell upon the town and crushed houses and burned trees. It woke people from sleep and then put them to sleep again, forever, an instant later.

William Lantry, sitting in a beetle that was not his own, tuned idly to a station on the audio dial. The collapse of the Incinerator had killed some four hundred people. Many had been caught in flattened houses, others struck by flying metal. A temporary morgue was being set up at—

An address was given.

Lantry noted it with a pad and pencil.

He could go on this way, he thought, from town to town, from country to country, destroying the Burners, the Pillars of Fire, until the whole clean magnificent framework of flame and cauterization was tumbled. He made a fair estimate—each explosion averaged five hundred dead. You could work that up to a hundred thousand in no time.

He pressed the floor stud on the beetle. Smiling, he drove off through the dark streets of the city.

The city coroner had requisitioned an old warehouse. From midnight until four in the morning the gray beetles hissed down the rain-shiny streets, turned in, and the bodies were laid out on the cold concrete floors, with white sheets over them. It was a continuous flow until about four-thirty, then it stopped. There were about two hundred bodies there, white and cold.

The bodies were left alone; nobody stayed behind to tend them. There was no use tending the dead; it was a useless procedure; the dead could take care of themselves.

About five o'clock, with a touch of dawn in the east, the first trickle of relatives arrived to identify their sons or their fathers or their mothers or their uncles. The people moved quickly into the warehouse, made the identification, moved quickly out again. By six o'clock, with the sky still lighter in the east, this trickle had passed on, also.

William Lantry walked across the wide wet street and entered the warehouse.

He held a piece of blue chalk in one hand.

He walked by the coroner who stood in the entranceway talking to two others. " . . . drive the bodies to the Incinerator in Mellin Town, tomorrow . . ." The voices faded.

Lantry moved, his feet echoing faintly on the cool

concrete. A wave of sourceless relief came to him as he walked among the shrouded figures. He was among his own. And—better than that! He had *created* these! He had made them dead! He had procured for himself a vast number of recumbent friends!

Was the coroner watching? Lantry turned his head. No. The warehouse was calm and quiet and shadowed in the dark morning. The coroner was walking away now, across the street, with his two attendants; a beetle had drawn up on the other side of the street, and the coroner was going over to talk with whoever was in the beetle.

William Lantry stood and made a blue chalk pentagram on the floor by each of the bodies. He moved swiftly, swiftly, without a sound, without blinking. In a few minutes, glancing up now and then to see if the coroner was still busy, he had chalked the floor by a hundred bodies. He straightened up and put the chalk in his pocket.

Now is the time for all good men to come to the aid of their party, now is the time for all good men to come to the aid of their party, now is the time for all good men to come to the aid of their party, now is the time . . .

Lying in the earth, over the centuries, the processes and thoughts of passing peoples and passing times had seeped down to him, slowly, as into a deep-buried sponge. From some death-memory in him now, ironically, repeatedly, a black typewriter clacked out black even lines of pertinent words:

Now is the time for all good men, for all good men, to come to the aid of—

William Lantry.

Other words—

Arise my love, and come away—

The quick brown fox jumped over . . . *Paraphrase it.* The quick risen body jumped over the tumbled Incinerator . . .

Lazarus, come forth from the tomb . . .

He knew the right words. He need only speak them as they had been spoken over the centuries. He need only gesture with his hands and speak the words, the dark words that would cause these bodies to quiver, rise and walk!

And when they had risen he would take them through the town, they would kill others, and the others would rise and walk. By the end of the day there would be thousands of good friends, walking with him. And what of the naïve, living people of this year, this day, this hour? They would be completely unprepared for it. They would go down to defeat because they would not be expecting war of any sort. They wouldn't believe it possible, it would all be over before they could convince themselves that such an illogical thing could happen.

He lifted his hands. His lips moved. He said the words. He began in a chanting whisper and then raised his voice, louder. He said the words again and again. His eyes were closed tightly. His body swayed. He spoke faster and faster. He began to move forward among the bodies. The dark words flowed from his mouth. He was enchanted with his own formulae. He stooped and made further blue symbols on the concrete, in the fashion of long-dead sorcerers, smiling, confident. Any moment now the first tremor of the still bodies, any moment now the rising, the leaping up of the cold ones!

His hands lifted in the air. His head nodded. He spoke, he spoke, he spoke. He gestured. He talked loudly over the bodies, his eyes flaring, his body tensed. "Now!" he cried, violently. "Rise, *all* of you!"

Nothing happened.

"Rise!" he screamed, with a terrible torment in his voice.

The sheets lay in white blue-shadow folds over the silent bodies.

"Hear me, and act!" he shouted.

Far away, on the street, a beetle hissed along.

Again, again, again he shouted, pleaded. He got down by each body and asked of it his particular violent favor. No reply. He strode wildly between the even white rows, flinging his arms up, stooping again and again to make blue symbols!

Lantry was very pale. He licked his lips. "Come on,

get up," he said. "They have, they always have, for a
thousand years. When you make a mark—so! and
speak a word—so! they always rise! Why not now, why
not you! Come on, come *on,* before *they* come back!"

The warehouse went up into shadow. There were
steel beams across and down. In it, under the roof,
there was not a sound, except the raving of a lonely
man.

Lantry stopped.

Through the wide doors of the warehouse he caught
a glimpse of the last cold stars of morning.

This was the year 2349.

His eyes grew cold and his hands fell to his sides. He
did not move.

Once upon a time people shuddered when they heard
the wind about the house, once people raised crucifixes
and wolfbane, and believed in walking dead and bats
and loping white wolves. And as long as they believed,
then so long did the dead, the bats, the loping wolves
exist. The mind gave birth and reality to them.

But . . .

He looked at the white sheeted bodies.

These people did not believe.

They had never believed. They would never believe.
They had never imagined that the dead might walk.
The dead went up flues in flame. They had never heard
superstition, never trembled or shuddered or doubted in
the dark. Walking dead people could not exist, they
were illogical. This was the year 2349, man, after all!

Therefore, these people could not rise, could not
walk again. They were dead and flat and cold. Nothing,
chalk, imprecation, superstition, could wind them up
and set them walking. They were dead and *knew* they
were dead!

He was alone.

There were live people in the world who moved and
drove beetles and drank quiet drinks in little dimly
illumined bars by country roads, and kissed women and
talked much good talk all day and every day.

But he was not alive.

Friction gave him what little warmth he possessed.

There were two hundred dead people here in this warehouse now, cold upon the floor. The first dead people in a hundred years who were allowed to be corpses for an extra hour or more. The first not to be immediately trundled to the Incinerator and lit like so much phosphorus.

He should be happy with them, among them.

He was not.

They were completely dead. They did not know nor believe in walking once the heart had paused and stilled itself. They were deader than dead ever was.

He was indeed alone, more alone than any man had ever been. He felt the chill of his aloneness moving up into his chest, strangling him quietly.

William Lantry turned suddenly and gasped.

While he had stood there, someone had entered the warehouse. A tall man with white hair, wearing a light weight tan overcoat and no hat. How long the man had been nearby there was no telling.

There was no reason to stay here. Lantry turned and started to walk slowly out. He looked hastily at the man as he passed and the man with the white hair looked back at him, curiously. Had he heard? The imprecations, the pleadings, the shoutings? Did he suspect? Lantry slowed his walk. Had this man seen him make the blue chalk marks? But then, would he interpret them as symbols of an ancient superstition? Probably not.

Reaching the door, Lantry paused. For a moment he did not want to do anything but lie down and be coldly, really dead again and be carried silently down the street to some distant burning flue and there dispatched in ash and whispering fire. If he was indeed alone and there was no chance to collect an army to his cause, what, then, existed as a reason for going on? Killing? Yes, he'd kill a few thousand more. But that wasn't enough. You can only do so much of that before they drag you down.

He looked at the cold sky.

A rocket went across the black heaven, trailing fire.

Mars burned red among a million stars.

Mars. The library. The librarian. Talk. Returning rocket men. Tombs.

Lantry almost gave a shout. He restrained his hand, which wanted so much to reach up into the sky and touch Mars. Lovely red star on the sky. Good star that gave him sudden new hope. If he had a living heart now it would be thrashing wildly, and sweat would be breaking out of him and his pulses would be stammering, and tears would be in his eyes!

He would go down to wherever the rockets sprang up into space. He would go to Mars, one way or another. He would go to the Martian tombs. There, there were bodies, he would bet his last hatred on it, that would rise and walk and work with him! Theirs was an ancient culture, much different from that of Earth, patterned on the Egyptian, if what the librarian had said was true. And the Egyptian—what a crucible of dark superstition and midnight terror that culture had been. Mars it *was*, then. Beautiful Mars!

But he must not attract attention to himself. He must move carefully. He wanted to run, yes, to get away, but that would be the worst possible move he could make. The man with the white hair was glancing at Lantry from time to time, in the entranceway. There were too many people about. If anything happened he would be outnumbered. So far he had taken on only *one* man at a time.

Lantry forced himself to stop and stand on the steps before the warehouse. The man with the white hair came on onto the steps also and stood, looking at the sky. He looked as if he was going to speak at any moment. He fumbled in his pockets and took out a packet of cigarettes.

V

They stood outside the morgue together, the tall, pink, white-haired man, and Lantry, hands in their pockets. It was a cool night with a white shell of a moon that washed a house here, a road there, and farther on, parts of a river.

"Cigarette?" The man offered Lantry one.

"Thanks."

They lit up together. The man glanced at Lantry's mouth. "Cool night."

"Cool."

They shifted their feet. "Terrible accident."

"Terrible."

"So many dead."

"So many."

Lantry felt himself some sort of delicate weight upon a scale. The other man did not seem to be looking at him, but rather listening and feeling toward him. There was a feathery balance here that made for vast discomfort. He wanted to move away and get out from under this balancing, weighing. The tall white-haired man said, "My name's McClure."

"Did you have any friends inside?" asked Lantry.

"No. A casual acquaintance. Awful accident."

"Awful."

They balanced each other. A beetle hissed by on the road with its seventeen tires whirling quietly. The moon showed a little town farther over in the black hills.

"I say," said the man McClure.

"Yes."

"Could you answer me a question?"

"Be glad to." He loosened the knife in his coat pocket, ready.

"Is your name Lantry?" asked the man at last.

"Yes."

"*William* Lantry?"

"Yes."

"Then you're the man who came out of the Salem graveyard day before yesterday, aren't you?"

"Yes."

"Good Lord, I'm glad to meet you, Lantry! We've been trying to find you for the past twenty-four hours!"

The man seized his hand, pumped it, slapped him on the back.

"What, what?" said Lantry.

"Good Lord, man, why did you run off? Do you

realize what an instance this is? We want to talk to you!"

McClure was smiling, glowing. Another handshake, another slap. "I *thought* it was you!"

The man is mad, thought Lantry. Absolutely mad. Here I've toppled his incinerators, killed people, and he's shaking my hand. Mad, mad!

"Will you come along to the Hall?" said the man, taking his elbow.

"Wh-what hall?" Lantry stepped back.

"The Science Hall, of course. It isn't every year we get a real case of suspended animation. In small animals, yes, but in a man, hardly! Will you come?"

"What's the act!" demanded Lantry, glaring. "What's all this talk."

"My dear fellow, what do you mean?" the man was stunned.

"Never mind. Is that the only reason you want to see me?"

"What other reason would there be, Mr. Lantry? You don't know how glad I am to see you!" He almost did a little dance. "I suspected. When we were in there together. You being so pale and all. And then the way you smoked your cigarette, something about it, and a lot of other things, all subliminal. But it is you, isn't it, it *is* you!"

"It is I. William Lantry." Dryly.

"Good fellow! Come along!"

The beetle moved swiftly through the dawn streets. McClure talked rapidly.

Lantry sat, listening, astounded. Here was this fool, McClure, playing his cards for him! Here was this stupid scientist, or whatever, accepting him not as a suspicious baggage, a murderous item. Oh no! Quite the contrary! Only as a suspended animation case was he considered! Not as a dangerous man at all. Far from it!

"Of course," cried McClure, grinning. "You didn't know where to go, whom to turn to. It was all quite incredible to you."

"Yes."

"I had a feeling you'd be there at the morgue tonight," said McClure, happily.

"Oh?" Lantry stiffened.

"Yes. Can't explain it. But you, how shall I put it? Ancient Americans? You had funny ideas on death. And you were among the dead so long, I felt you'd be drawn back by the accident, by the morgue and all. It's not very logical. Silly, in fact. It's just a feeling. I hate feelings but there it was. I came on a, I guess you'd call it a hunch, wouldn't you?"

"You might call it that."

"And there you were!"

"There I was," said Lantry.

"Are you hungry?"

"I've eaten."

"How did you get around?"

"I hitchhiked."

"You *what?*"

"People gave me rides on the road."

"Remarkable."

"I imagine it sounds that way." He looked at the passing houses. "So this is the era of space travel, is it?"

"Oh, we've been traveling to Mars for some forty years now."

"Amazing. And those big funnels, those towers in the middle of every town?"

"Those. Haven't you heard? The Incinerators. Oh, of course, they hadn't anything of that sort in your time. Had some bad luck with them. An explosion in Salem and one here, all in a forty-eight-hour period. You looked as if you were going to speak; what is it?"

"I was thinking," said Lantry. "How fortunate I got out of my coffin when I did. I might well have been thrown into one of your Incinerators and burned up."

"Quite."

Lantry toyed with the dials on the beetle dash. He wouldn't go to Mars. His plans were changed. If this fool simply refused to recognize an act of violence when he stumbled upon it, then let him be a fool. If they didn't connect the two explosions with a man from the tomb, all well and good. Let them go on deluding themselves. If they couldn't imagine someone being mean and nasty and murderous, heaven help them. He rubbed his hands with satisfaction. No, no Martian trip for you, as yet, Lantry lad. First, we'll see what can be done boring from the inside. Plenty of time. The Incinerators can wait an extra week or so. One has to be subtle, you know. Any more immediate explosions might cause quite a ripple of thought.

McClure was gabbling wildly on.

"Of course, you don't have to be examined immediately. You'll want a rest. I'll put you up at my place."

"Thanks. I don't feel up to being probed and pulled. Plenty of time in a week or so."

They drew up before a house and climbed out.

"You want to sleep, naturally."

"I've been asleep for centuries. Be glad to stay awake. I'm not a bit tired."

"Good." McClure let them into the house. He headed for the drink bar. "A drink will fix us up."

"You have one," said Lantry. "Later for me. I just want to sit down."

"By all means sit." McClure mixed himself a drink. He looked around the room, looked at Lantry, paused for a moment with the drink in his hand, tilted his head to one side, and put his tongue in his cheek. Then he shrugged and stirred the drink. He walked slowly to a chair and sat, sipping the drink quietly. He seemed to be listening for something. "There are cigarettes on the table," he said.

"Thanks." Lantry took one and lit it and smoked it. He did not speak for some time.

Lantry thought, I'm taking this all too easily. Maybe I should kill and run. He's the only one that has found me, yet. Perhaps this is all a trap. Perhaps we're simply sitting here waiting for the police. Or whatever in blazes they use for police these days. He looked at McClure. No. They weren't waiting for police. They were waiting for something else.

McClure didn't speak. He looked at Lantry's face and he looked at Lantry's hands. He looked at Lantry's chest a long time, with easy quietness. He sipped his drink. He looked at Lantry's feet.

Finally he said, "Where'd you get the clothing?"

"I asked someone for clothes and they gave these things to me. Darned nice of them."

"You'll find that's how we are in this world. All you have to do is ask."

McClure shut up again. His eyes moved. Only his eyes and nothing else. Once or twice he lifted his drink.

A little clock ticked somewhere in the distance.

"Tell me about yourself, Mr. Lantry."

"Nothing much to tell."

"You're modest."

"Hardly. You know about the past. I know nothing of the future, or I should say 'today' and day before yesterday. You don't learn much in a coffin."

McClure did not speak. He suddenly sat forward in his chair and then leaned back and shook his head.

They'll never suspect me, thought Lantry. They aren't superstitious, they simply *can't* believe in a dead man walking. Therefore, I'll be safe. I'll keep putting off the physical checkup. They're polite. They won't force me. Then, I'll work it so I can get to Mars. After that, the tombs, in my own good time, and the plan. God, how simple. How naïve these people are.

McClure sat across the room for five minutes. A coldness had come over him. The color was very slowly going from his face, as one sees the color of medicine vanishing as one presses the bulb at the top of a dropper. He leaned forward, saying nothing, and offered another cigarette to Lantry.

"Thanks." Lantry took it. McClure sat deeply back into his easy chair, his knees folded one over the other. He did not look at Lantry, and yet somehow did. The feeling of weighing and balancing returned. McClure was like a tall thin master of hounds listening for something that nobody else could hear. There are little silver whistles you can blow that only dogs can hear. McClure seemed to be listening acutely, sensitively for such an invisible whistle, listening with his eyes and with his half-opened, dry mouth, and with his aching, breathing nostrils.

Lantry sucked the cigarette, sucked the cigarette,

sucked the cigarette, and, as many times, blew out,
blew out, blew out. McClure was like some lean red-
shagged hound listening and listening with a slick slide
of eyes to one side, with an apprehension in that hand
that was so precisely microscopic that one only sensed
it, as one sensed the invisible whistle, with some part of
the brain deeper than eyes or nostril or ear.

The room was so quiet the cigarette smoke made
some kind of invisible noise rising to the ceiling.
McClure was a thermometer, a chemist's scales, a listening hound, a litmus paper, an antennae; all these.
Lantry did not move. Perhaps the feeling would pass.
It had passed before. McClure did not move for a long
while and then, without a word, he nodded at the
sherry decanter, and Lantry refused as silently. They
sat looking but not looking at each other, again and
away, again and away.

McClure stiffened slowly. Lantry saw the color getting paler in those lean cheeks, and the hand tightening
on the sherry glass, and a knowledge come at last to
stay, never to go away, into the eyes.

Lantry did not move. He could not. All of this was
of such a fascination that he wanted only to see, to hear
what would happen next. It was McClure's show from
here on in.

McClure said, "At first I thought it was the first
psychosis I have ever seen. You, I mean. I thought,
he's convinced himself, Lantry's convinced himself,
he's quite insane, he's told himself to do all these little
things." McClure talked as if in a dream, and continued
talking and didn't stop.

"I said to myself, he purposely doesn't breathe
through his nose. I watched your nostrils, Lantry. The
little nostril hairs never once quivered in the last hour.
That wasn't enough. It was a fact I filed. It wasn't
enough. He breathes through his mouth, I said, on purpose. And then I gave you a cigarette and you sucked
and blew, sucked and blew. None of it ever came out
your nose. I told myself, well, that's all right. He
doesn't inhale. Is that terrible, is that suspect? All in
the mouth, all in the mouth. And then, I looked at
your chest. I watched. It never moved up or down, it

did nothing. He's convinced himself, I said to myself.
He's convinced himself about all this. He doesn't move
his chest, except slowly, when he thinks you're not
looking. That's what I told myself."

The words went on in the silent room, not pausing,
still in a dream. "And then I offered you a drink but
you don't drink and I thought, he doesn't drink, I
thought. Is *that* terrible? And I watched and watched
you all this time. Lantry holds his breath, he's fooling
himself. But now, yes, now, I understand it quite well.
Now I know everything the way it is. Do you know
how I know? I do not hear breathing in the room. I
wait and I hear nothing. There is no beat of heart or
intake of lung. The room is so silent. Nonsense, one
might say, but I know. At the Incinerator I know.
There is a difference. You enter a room where a man is
on a bed and you know immediately whether he will
look up and speak to you or whether he will not speak
to you ever again. Laugh if you will, but one can tell.
It is a subliminal thing. It is the whistle the dog hears
when no human hears. It is the tick of a clock that has
ticked so long one no longer notices. Something is in a
room when a man lives in it. Something is not in the
room when a man is dead in it."

McClure shut his eyes a moment. He put down his
sherry glass. He waited a moment. He took up his
cigarette and puffed it and then put it down in a black
tray.

"I am alone in this room," he said.

Lantry did not move.

"You are dead," said McClure. "My mind does not
know this. It is not a thinking thing. It is a thing of the
senses and the subconscious. At first I thought, this
man *thinks* he is dead. risen from the dead, a vampire.
Is that not logical? Would not any man, buried as many
centuries, raised in a superstitious, ignorant culture,
think likewise of himself once risen from the tomb?
Yes, that is logical. This man has hypnotized himself
and fitted his bodily functions so that they would in no
way interfere with his self-delusion, his great paranoia.
He governs his breathing. He tells himself, I cannot

hear my breathing, therefore I am dead. His inner mind censors the sound of breathing. He does not allow himself to eat or drink. These things he probably does in his sleep, with part of his mind, hiding the evidences of this humanity from his deluded mind at other times."

McClure finished it. "I was wrong. You are not insane. You are not deluding yourself. Nor me. This is all very illogical and—I must admit—almost frightening. Does that make you feel good, to think you frighten me? I have no label for you. You're a very odd man, Lantry. I'm glad to have met you. This will make an interesting report indeed."

"Is there anything wrong with me being dead?" said Lantry. "Is it a crime?"

"You must admit it's highly unusual."

"But, still now, is it a crime?" asked Lantry.

"We have no crime, no criminal court. We want to examine you, naturally, to find out how you have happened. It is like that chemical which, one minute is inert, the next is living cell. Who can say where what happened to what. You are that impossibility. It is enough to drive a man quite insane."

"Will I be released when you are done fingering me?"

"You will not be held. If you don't wish to be examined, you will not be. But I am hoping you will help by offering us your services."

"I might," said Lantry.

"But tell me," said McClure. "What were you doing at the morgue?"

"Nothing."

"I heard you talking when I came in."

"I was merely curious."

"You're lying. That is very bad, Mr. Lantry. The truth is far better. The truth is, is it not, that you are dead and, being the only one of your sort, were lonely. Therefore you killed people to have company."

"How does that follow?"

McClure laughed. "Logic, my dear fellow. Once I *knew* you were really dead, a moment ago, really a— what do you call it—a vampire (silly word!) I tied you immediately to the Incinerator blasts. Before that there was no reason to connect you. But once the one piece fell into place, the fact that you were dead, then it was simple to guess your loneliness, your hate, your envy, all of the tawdry motivations of a walking corpse. It took only an instant then to see the Incinerators blown to blazes, and then to think of you, among the bodies at the morgue, seeking help, seeking friends and people like yourself to work with—"

"Blast you!" Lantry was out of the chair. He was halfway to the other man when McClure rolled over and scuttled away, flinging the sherry decanter. With a great despair Lantry realized that, like an idiot, he had thrown away his one chance to kill McClure. He should have done it earlier. It had been Lantry's one weapon, his safety margin. If people in a society never *killed* each other, they never *suspected* one another. You could walk up to any one of them and kill him.

"Come back here!" Lantry threw the knife.

McClure got behind a chair. The idea of flight, of protection, of fighting, was still new to him. He had part of the idea, but there was still a bit of luck on Lantry's side if Lantry wanted to use it.

"Oh, no," said McClure, holding the chair between himself and the advancing man. "You want to kill me. It's odd, but true. I can't understand it. You want to cut me with that knife or something like that, and it's up to me to prevent you from doing such an odd thing."

"I *will* kill you!" Lantry let it slip out. He cursed himself. That was the worst possible thing to say.

Lantry lunged across the chair, clutching at McClure.

McClure was very logical. "It won't do you any good to kill me. You *know* that." They wrestled and held each other in a wild, toppling shuffle. Tables fell over, scattering articles. "You remember what happened in the morgue?"

"I don't care!" screamed Lantry.

"You didn't raise *those* dead, did you?"

"I don't care!" cried Lantry.

"Look here," said McClure, reasonably. "There will never be any more like you, ever, there's no use."

"Then I'll destroy all of you, all of you!" screamed Lantry.

"And then what? You'll still be alone, with no more like you about."

"I'll go to Mars. They have tombs there. I'll find more like myself!"

"No," said McClure. "The executive order went through yesterday. All of the tombs are being deprived of their bodies. They'll be burned in the next week."

They fell together to the floor. Lantry got his hands on McClure's throat.

"Please," said McClure. "Do you see, you'll *die*."

"What do you mean?" cried Lantry.

"Once you kill all of us, and you're alone, you'll die! The hate will die. That hate is what moved you, *nothing else*! That envy moves you. Nothing else! You'll die, inevitably. You're not immortal. You're not even alive, you're nothing but a moving hate."

"I don't care!" screamed Lantry, and began choking the man, beating his head with his fists, crouched on the defenseless body. McClure looked up at him with dying eyes.

The front door opened. Two men came in.

"I say," said one of them. "What's going on? A new game?"

Lantry jumped back and began to run.

"Yes, a new game!" said McClure, struggling up. "Catch him and you win!"

The two men caught Lantry. "We win," they said.

"Let me go!" Lantry thrashed, hitting them across their faces, bringing blood.

"Hold him tight!" cried McClure.

They held him.

"A rough game, what?" one of them said. "What do we do *now*?"

The beetle hissed along the shining road. Rain fell out of the sky and a wind ripped at the dark green wet trees. In the beetle, his hands on the half-wheel, McClure was talking. His voice was susurrant, a whispering, a hypnotic thing. The two other men sat in the back seat. Lantry sat, or rather lay, in the front seat, his head back, his eyes faintly open, the glowing green light of the dash dials showing on his cheeks. His mouth was relaxed. He did not speak.

McClure talked quietly and logically, about life and moving, about death and not moving, about the sun and the great sun Incinerator, about the emptied tombyard, about hatred and how hate lived and made a clay man live and move, and how illogical it all was, it all was, it all was. One was dead, was dead, was dead, that was all, all, all. One did not try to be otherwise. The car whispered on the moving road. The rain spattered gently on the windshield. The men in the back seat conversed quietly. Where were they going, going? To the Incinerator, of course. Cigarette smoke moved slowly up on the air, curling and tying into itself in gray loops and spirals. One was dead and must accept it.

Lantry did not move. He was a marionette, the strings cut. There was only a tiny hatred in his heart, in his eyes, like twin coals, feeble, glowing, fading.

I am Poe, he thought. I am all that is left of Edgar Allan Poe, and I am all that is left of Ambrose Bierce and all that is left of a man named Lovecraft. I am a gray night bat with sharp teeth, and I am a square black monolith monster. I am Osiris and Bal and Set. I am the Necronomicon, the Book of the Dead. I am the house of Usher, falling into flame. I am the Red Death. I am the man mortared into the catacomb with a cask of Amontillado . . . I am a dancing skeleton. I am a coffin, a shroud, a lightning bolt reflected in an old house window. I am an autumn-empty tree, I am a rapping, flinging shutter. I am a yellowed volume turned by a claw hand. I am an organ played in an attic at midnight. I am a mask, a skull mask behind an oak tree on the last day of October. I am a poison apple bobbling in a water tub for child noses to bump at, for child teeth to snap . . . I am a black candle lighted before an inverted cross. I am a coffin lid, a sheet with eyes, a foot-step on a black stairwell. I am Dunsany and Machen and I am the Legend of Sleepy Hollow. I am The Monkey's Paw and I am The Phantom Rickshaw. I am the Cat and the Canary, The Gorilla, the

Bat. I am the ghost of Hamlet's father on the castle wall.

All of these things am I. And now these last things will be burned. While I lived *they* still lived. While I moved and hated and existed, *they* still existed. I am *all* that remembers them. I am all of them that *still* goes on, and will *not* go on after tonight. Tonight, all of us, Poe and Bierce and Hamlet's father, we burn together. They will make a big heap of us and burn us like a bonfire, like things of Guy Fawkes' day, gasoline, torches, cries, and all!

And what a wailing will we put up. The world will be clean of us, but in our going we shall say, oh what is the world like, clean of fear, where is the dark imagination from the dark time, the thrill and the anticipation, the suspense of old October, gone, never more to come again, flattened and smashed and burned by the rocket people, by the Incinerator people, destroyed and obliterated, to be replaced by doors that open and close and lights that go on and off without fear. If only you could remember how once *we* lived, what Halloween was to us, and what Poe was, and how we gloried in the dark morbidities. One more drink, dear friends, of Amontillado, before the burning. All of this, all, exists but in one last brain on earth. A whole world dying tonight. One more drink, pray.

"Here we are," said McClure.

The Incinerator was brightly lighted. There was quiet music nearby. McClure got out of the beetle, came around to the other side. He opened the door. Lantry simply lay there. The talking and the logical talking had slowly drained him of life. He was no more than wax now, with a small glow in his eyes. This future world, how the men *talked* to you, how logically they reasoned away your life. They wouldn't believe in him. The force of their disbelief froze him. He could not move his arms or his legs. He could only mumble senselessly, coldly, eyes flickering.

McClure and the two others helped him out of the car, put him in a golden box, and rolled him on a roller table into the warm glowing interior of the building.

I am Edgar Allan Poe, I am Ambrose Bierce, I am Halloween, I am a coffin, a shroud, a Monkey's Paw, a Phantom, a Vampire . . .

"Yes, yes," said McClure, quietly, over him. "I know. I know."

The table glided. The walls swung over him and by him, the music played. You are dead, you are logically dead.

I am Usher, I am the Maelstrom, I am the MS Found In A Bottle, I am the Pit and I am the Pendulum, I am the Telltale Heart, I am the Raven nevermore, nevermore.

"Yes," said McClure, as they walked softly. "I know."

"I am in the catacomb," cried Lantry.

"Yes, the catacomb," said the walking man over him.

"I am being chained to a wall, and there is no bottle of Amontillado here!" cried Lantry weakly, eyes closed.

"Yes," someone said.

There was movement. The flame door opened.

"Now someone is mortaring up the cell, closing me in!"

"Yes, I *know*." A whisper.

The golden box slid into the flame lock.

"I'm being walled in! A very good joke indeed! Let us be gone!" A wild scream and much laughter.

"We know, we understand . . ."

The inner flame lock opened. The golden coffin shot forth into flame.

"For the love of God, Montresor! For the love of God!"

ZERO HOUR

Oh, it was to be so jolly! What a game! Such excitement they hadn't known in years. The children catapulted this way and that across the green lawns, shouting at each other, holding hands, flying in circles, climbing trees, laughing. Overhead the rockets flew, and beetle cars whispered by on the streets, but the children played on. Such fun, such tremulous joy, such tumbling and hearty screaming.

Mink ran into the house, all dirt and sweat. For her seven years she was loud and strong and definite. Her mother, Mrs. Morris, hardly saw her as she yanked out drawers and rattled pans and tools into a large sack.

"Heavens, Mink, what's going on?"

"The most exciting game ever!" gasped Mink, pink-faced.

"Stop and get your breath," said the mother.

"No, I'm all right," gasped Mink. "Okay I take these things, Mom?"

"But don't dent them," said Mrs. Morris.

"Thank you, thank you!" cried Mink, and boom! she was gone, like a rocket.

Mrs. Morris surveyed the fleeing tot. "What's the name of the game?"

"Invasion!" said Mink. The door slammed.

In every yard on the street children brought out knives and forks and pokers and old stovepipes and can openers.

It was an interesting fact that this fury and bustle occurred only among the younger children. The older ones, those ten years and more, disdained the affair and

69

marched scornfully off on hikes or played a more dignified version of hide-and-seek on their own.

Meanwhile, parents came and went in chromium
beetles. Repairmen came to repair the vacuum elevators
in houses, to fix fluttering television sets, or hammer
upon stubborn food-delivery tubes. The adult civilization passed and repassed the busy youngsters, jealous of
the fierce energy of the wild tots, tolerantly amused at
their flourishings, longing to join in themselves.

"This and this and *this*," said Mink, instructing the
others with their assorted spoons and wrenches. "Do
that, and bring *that* over here. No! *Here,* ninny! Right.
Now get back while I fix this." Tongue in teeth, face
wrinkled in thought. "Like that. See?"

"Yayyyy!" shouted the kids.

Twelve-year-old Joseph Connors ran up.

"Go away," said Mink straight at him.

"I wanna play," said Joseph.

"Can't!" said Mink.

"Why not?"

"You'd just make fun of us."

"Honest, I wouldn't."

"No. We know *you.* Go away or we'll kick you."

Another twelve-year-old boy whirred by on little
motor skates. "Hey, Joe! Come on! Let them sissies
play!"

Joseph showed reluctance and a certain wistfulness.
"I *want* to play," he said.

"You're old," said Mink firmly.

"Not *that* old," said Joe sensibly.

"You'd only laugh and spoil the Invasion."

The boy on the motor skates made a rude lip noise.
"Come on, Joe! Them and their fairies! Nuts!"

Joseph walked off slowly. He kept looking back, all
down the block.

Mink was already busy again. She made a kind of
apparatus with her gathered equipment. She had ap-
pointed another little girl with a pad and pencil to take
down notes in painful slow scribbles. Their voices rose
and fell in the warm sunlight.

All around them the city hummed. The streets were
lined with good green and peaceful trees. Only the wind

made a conflict across the city, across the country, across the continent. In a thousand other cities there were trees and children and avenues, businessmen in their quiet offices taping their voices, or watching televisors. Rockets hovered like darning needles in the blue sky. There was the universal, quiet conceit and easiness of men accustomed to peace, quite certain there would never be trouble again. Arm in arm, men all over earth were a united front. The perfect weapons were held in equal trust by all nations. A situation of incredibly beautiful balance had been brought about. There were no traitors among men, no unhappy ones, no disgruntled ones; therefore the world was based upon a stable ground. Sunlight illumined half the world and the trees drowsed in a tide of warm air.

Mink's mother, from her upstairs window, gazed down.

The children. She looked upon them and shook her head. Well, they'd eat well, sleep well, and be in school on Monday. Bless their vigorous little bodies. She listened.

Mink talked earnestly to someone near the rose bush—though there was no one there.

These odd children. And the little girl, what was her name? Anna? Anna took notes on a pad. First, Mink asked the rosebush a question, then called the answer to Anna.

"Triangle," said Mink.

"What's a tri," said Anna with difficulty, "angle?"

"Never mind," said Mink.

"How you spell it?" asked Anna.

"T-r-i——" spelled Mink slowly, then snapped, "Oh, spell it yourself!" She went on to other words. "Beam," she said.

"I haven't got tri," said Anna, "angle down yet!"

"Well, hurry, hurry!" cried Mink.

Mink's mother leaned out the upstairs window. "A-n-g-l-e," she spelled down at Anna.

"Oh, thanks, Mrs. Morris," said Anna.

"Certainly," said Mink's mother and withdrew, laughing, to dust the hall with an electro-duster magnet.

The voices wavered on the shimmery air. "Beam," said Anna. Fading.

"Four-nine-seven-A-and-B-and-X," said Mink, far away, seriously. "And a fork and a string and a—hex-hex-agony—hexagonal!"

At lunch Mink gulped milk at one tosss and was at the door. Her mother slapped the table.

"You sit right back down," commanded Mrs. Morris. "Hot soup in a minute." She poked a red button on the kitchen butler, and ten seconds later something landed with a bump in the rubber receiver. Mrs. Morris opened it, took out a can with a pair of aluminum holders, unsealed it with a flick, and poured hot soup into a bowl.

During all this Mink fidgeted. "Hurry, Mom! This is a matter of life and death! Aw——"

"I was the same way at your age. Always life and death. I know."

Mink banged away at the soup.

"Slow down," said Mom.

"Can't," said Mink. "Drill's waiting for me."

"Who's Drill? What a peculiar name," said Mom.

"You don't know him," said Mink.

"A new boy in the neighborhood?" asked Mom.

"He's new all right," said Mink. She started on her second bowl.

"Which one is Drill?" asked Mom.

"He's around," said Mink evasively. "You'll make fun. Everybody pokes fun. Gee, darn."

"Is Drill shy?"

"Yes. No. In a way. Gosh, Mom, I got to run if we want to have the Invasion!"

"Who's invading what?"

"Martians invading Earth. Well, not exactly Martians. They're—I don't know. From up." She pointed her spoon.

"And *inside*," said Mom, touching Mink's feverish brow.

Mink rebelled. "You're laughing! You'll kill Drill and everybody."

"I didn't mean to," said Mom. "Drill's a Martian?"

"No. He's—well—maybe from Jupiter or Saturn or Venus. Anyway, he's had a hard time."

"I imagine." Mrs. Morris hid her mouth behind her hand.

"They couldn't figure a way to attack Earth."

"We're impregnable," said Mom in mock seriousness.

"That's the word Drill used! Impreg—— That was the word, Mom."

"My, my, Drill's a brilliant little boy. Two-bit words."

"They couldn't figure a way to attack, Mom. Drill says—he says in order to make a good fight you got to have a new way of surprising people. That way you win. And he says also you got to have help from your enemy."

"A fifth column," said Mom.

"Yeah. That's what Drill said. And they couldn't figure a way to surprise Earth or get help."

"No wonder. We're pretty darn strong." Mom laughed, cleaning up. Mink sat there, staring at the table, seeing what she was talking about.

"Until, one day," whispered Mink melodramatically, "they thought of children!"

"*Well!*" said Mrs. Morris brightly.

"And they thought of how grownups are so busy they never look under rosebushes or on lawns!"

"Only for snails and fungus."

"And then there's something about dim-dims."

"Dim-dims?"

"Dimens-shuns."

"Dimensions?"

"Four of 'em! And there's something about kids under nine and imagination. It's real funny to hear Drill talk."

Mrs. Morris was tired. "Well, it must be funny. You're keeping Drill waiting now. It's getting late in the day and, if you want to have your Invasion before your supper bath, you'd better jump."

"Do I have to take a bath?" growled Mink.

"You do. Why is it children hate water? No matter

what age you live in children hate water behind the ears!"

"Drill says I won't have to take baths," said Mink.

"Oh, he does, does he?"

"He told all the kids that. No more baths. And we can stay up till ten o'clock and go to two televisor shows on Saturday 'stead of one!"

"Well, Mr. Drill better mind his p's and q's. I'll call up his mother and——"

Mink went to the door. "We're having trouble with guys like Pete Britz and Dale Jerrick. They're growing up. They make fun. They're worse than parents. They just won't believe in Drill. They're so snooty, 'cause they're growing up. You'd think they'd know better. They were little only a coupla years ago. I hate them worst. We'll kill them *first*."

"Your father and I last?"

"Drill says you're dangerous. Know why? 'Cause you don't believe in Martians! They're going to let *us* run the world. Well, not just us, but the kids over in the next block, too. I might be queen." She opened the door.

"Mom?"

"Yes?"

"What's lodge-ick?"

"Logic? Why, dear, logic is knowing what things are true and not true."

"He *mentioned* that," said Mink. "And what's impres-sion-able?" It took her a minute to say it.

"Why, it means——" Her mother looked at the floor, laughing gently. "It means—to be a child, dear."

"Thanks for lunch!" Mink ran out, then stuck her head back in. "Mom, I'll be sure you won't be hurt much, really!"

"Well, thanks," said Mom.

Slam went the door.

At four o'clock the audiovisor buzzed. Mrs. Morris flipped the tab. "Hello, Helen!" she said in welcome.

"Hello Mary. How are things in New York?"

"Fine. How are things in Scranton? You look tired."

"So do you. The children. Underfoot," said Helen.

Mrs. Morris sighed. "My Mink too. The super-Invasion."

Helen laughed. "Are your kids playing that game too?"

"Lord, yes. Tomorrow it'll be geometrical jacks and motorized hopscotch. Were we this bad when we were kids in '48?"

"Worse. Japs and Nazis. Don't know how my parents put up with me. Tomboy."

"Parents learn to shut their ears."

A silence.

"What's wrong, Mary?" asked Helen.

Mrs. Morris's eyes were half closed; her tongue slid slowly, thoughtfully, over her lower lip. "Eh?" She jerked. "Oh, nothing. Just thought about *that*. Shutting ears and such. Never mind. Where were we?"

"My boy Tim's got a crush on some guy named—*Drill*, I think it was."

"Must be a new password. Mink likes him too."

"Didn't know it had got as far as New York. Word of mouth, I imagine. Looks like a scrap drive. I talked to Josephine and she said her kids—that's in Boston—are wild on this new game. It's sweeping the country."

At that moment Mink trotted into the kitchen to gulp a glass of water. Mrs. Morris turned. "How're things going?"

"Almost finished," said Mink.

"Swell," said Mrs. Morris. "What's *that*?"

"A yo-yo," said Mink. "Watch."

She flung the yo-yo down its string. Reaching the end it—

It vanished.

"See?" said Mink. "Ope!" Dibbling her finger, she made the yo-yo reappear and zip up the string.

"Do that again," said her mother.

"Can't. Zero hour's five o'clock! 'By." Mink exited, zipping her yo-yo.

On the audiovisor, Helen laughed. "Tim brought one of those yo-yos in this morning, but when I got curious he said he wouldn't show it to me, and when I tried to work it, finally, it wouldn't work."

"You're not *impressionable*," said Mrs. Morris.

"What?"

"Never mind. Something I thought of. Can I help you, Helen?"

"I wanted to get that black-and-white cake recipe——"

The hour drowsed by. The day waned. The sun lowered in the peaceful blue sky. Shadows lengthened on the green lawns. The laughter and excitement continued. One little girl ran away, crying. Mrs. Morris came out the front door.

"Mink, was that Peggy Ann crying?"

Mink was bent over in the yard, near the rosebush. "Yeah. She's a scarebaby. We won't let her play, now. She's getting too old to play. I guess she grew up all of a sudden."

"Is that why she cried? Nonsense. Give me a civil answer, young lady, or inside you come!"

Mink whirled in consternation, mixed with irritation. "I can't quit now. It's almost time. I'll be good. I'm sorry."

"Did you hit Peggy Ann?"

"No, honest. You ask her. It was something—well, she's just a scaredy pants."

The ring of children drew in around Mink where she scowled at her work with spoons and a kind of square-shaped arrangement of hammers and pipes. "There and there," murmured Mink.

"What's wrong?" said Mrs. Morris.

"Drill's stuck. Halfway. If we could only get him all the way through, it'd be easier. Then all the others could come through after him."

"Can I help?"

"No'm, thanks. I'll fix it."

"All right. I'll call you for your bath in half an hour. I'm tired of watching you."

She went in and sat in the electric relaxing chair, sipping a little beer from a half-empty glass. The chair massaged her back. Children, children. Children love and hate, side by side. Sometimes children loved you, hated you—all in half a second. Strange children, did they ever forget or forgive the whippings and the harsh, strict words of command? She wondered. How can you ever forget or forgive those over and above you, those tall and silly dictators?

Time passed. A curious, waiting silence came upon the street, deepening.

Five o'clock. A clock sang softly somewhere in the house in a quiet, musical voice: "Five o'clock—five o'clock. Time's a-wasting. Five o'clock," and purred away into silence.

Zero hour.

Mrs. Morris chuckled in her throat. Zero hour.

A beetle car hummed into the driveway. Mr. Morris. Mrs. Morris smiled. Mr. Morris got out of the beetle, locked it and called hello to Mink at her work. Mink ignored him. He laughed and stood for a moment watching the children. Then he walked up the front steps.

"Hello, darling."

"Hello, Henry."

She strained forward on the edge of the chair, listening. The children were silent. Too silent.

He emptied his pipe, refilled it. "Swell day. Makes you glad to be alive."

Buzz.

"What's that?" asked Henry.

"I don't know." She got up suddenly, her eyes widening. She was going to say something. She stopped it. Ridiculous. Her nerves jumped. "Those children haven't anything dangerous out there, have they?" she said.

"Nothing but pipes and hammers. Why?"

"Nothing electrical?"

"Heck, no," said Henry. "I looked."

She walked to the kitchen. The buzzing continued. "Just the same, you'd better go tell them to quit. It's after five. Tell them——" Her eyes widened and narrowed. "Tell them to put off their Invasion until tomorrow." She laughed, nervously.

The buzzing grew louder.

"What are they up to? I'd better go look, all right."

The explosion!

The house shook with dull sound. There were other explosions in other yards on other streets.

Involuntarily, Mrs. Morris screamed. "Up this way!" she cried senselessly, knowing no sense, no reason. Perhaps she saw something from the corners of her eyes; perhaps she smelled a new odor or heard a new noise. There was no time to argue with Henry to convince him. Let him think her insane. Yes, insane! Shrieking, she ran upstairs. He ran after her to see what she was up to. "In the attic!" she screamed. "That's where it is!" It was only a poor excuse to get him in the attic in time. Oh, God—in time!

Another explosion outside. The children screamed with delight, as if at a great fireworks display.

"It's not in the attic!" cried Henry. "It's outside!"

"No, no!" Wheezing, gasping, she fumbled at the attic door. "I'll show you. Hurry! I'll show you!"

They tumbled into the attic. She slammed the door, locked it, took the key, threw it into a far, cluttered corner.

She was babbling wild stuff now. It came out of her. All the subconscious suspicion and fear that had gathered secretly all afternoon and fermented like a wine in her. All the little revelations and knowledges and sense that had bothered her all day and which she had logically and carefully and sensibly rejected and censored. Now it exploded in her and shook her to bits.

"There, there," she said, sobbing against the door. "We're safe until tonight. Maybe we can sneak out. Maybe we can escape!"

Henry blew up too, but for another reason. "Are you crazy? Why'd you throw that key away? Blast it!"

"Yes, yes, I'm crazy, if it helps, but stay here with me!"

"I don't know how I can get out!"

"Quiet. They'll hear us. Oh, God, they'll find us soon enough——"

Below them, Mink's voice. The husband stopped. There was a great universal humming and sizzling, a screaming and giggling. Downstairs the audio-televisor buzzed and buzzed insistently, alarmingly, violently. *Is that Helen calling?* thought Mrs. Morris. *And is she calling about what I think she's calling about?*

Footsteps came into the house. Heavy footsteps.

"Who's coming in my house?" demanded Henry angrily. "Who's tramping around down there?"

Heavy feet. Twenty, thirty, forty, fifty of them. Fifty persons crowding into the house. The humming. The giggling of the children. "This way!" cried Mink, below.

"Who's downstairs?" roared Henry. "Who's there!"

"Hush. Oh, nonononononono!" said his wife, weakly, holding him. "Please, be quiet. They might go away."

"Mom?" called Mink. "Dad?" A pause. "Where are you?"

Heavy footsteps, heavy, heavy, *very heavy* footsteps, came up the stairs. Mink leading them.

"Mom?" A hesitation. "Dad?" A waiting, a silence.

Humming. Footsteps toward the attic. Mink's first.

They trembled together in silence in the attic, Mr. and Mrs. Morris. For some reason the electric humming, the queer cold light suddenly visible under the door crack, the strange odor, and the alien sound of eagerness in Mink's voice finally got through to Henry Morris too. He stood, shivering, in the dark silence, his wife beside him.

"Mom! Dad!"

Footsteps. A little humming sound. The attic lock melted. The door opened. Mink peered inside, tall blue shadows behind her.

"Peekaboo," said Mink.

THE MAN

Captain Hart stood in the door of the rocket. "Why don't they come?" he said.

"Who knows?" said Martin, his lieutenant. "Do I know, Captain?"

"What kind of a place is this, anyway?" The captain lighted a cigar. He tossed the match out into the glittering meadow. The grass started to burn.

Martin moved to stamp it out with his boot.

"No," ordered Captain Hart, "let it burn. Maybe they'll come see what's happening then, the ignorant fools."

Martin shrugged and withdrew his foot from the spreading fire.

Captain Hart examined his watch. "An hour ago we landed here, and does the welcoming committee rush out with a brass band to shake our hands? No indeed! Here we ride millions of miles through space and the fine citizens of some silly town on some unknown planet ignore us!" He snorted, tapping his watch. "Well, I'll just give them five more minutes, and then——"

"And then what?" asked Martin, ever so politely, watching the captain's jowls shake.

"We'll fly over their blasted city again and scare blazes out of them." His voice grew quieter. "Do you think, Martin, maybe they didn't see us land?"

"They saw us. They looked up as we flew over."

"Then why aren't they running across the field? Are they hiding? Are they yellow?"

Martin shook his head. "No. Take these binoculars, sir. See for yourself. Everybody's walking around.

81

They're not frightened. They—well, they don't seem to care."

Captain Hart placed the binoculars to his tired eyes. Martin looked up and had time to observe the lines and the grooves of irritation, tiredness, nervousness there. Hart looked a million years old; he never slept, he ate little, and drove himself on, on. Now his mouth moved, aged and drear, but sharp, under the held binoculars.

"Really, Martin, I don't know why we bother. We build rockets, we go to all the trouble of crossing space, searching for them, and this is what we get. Neglect. Look at those idiots wander about in there. Don't they realize how big this is? The first space flight to touch their provincial land. How many times does that happen? Are they that blasé?"

Martin didn't know.

Captain Hart gave him back the binoculars wearily. "Why do we do it, Martin? This space travel, I mean. Always on the go. Always searching. Our insides always tight, never any rest."

"Maybe we're looking for peace and quiet. Certainly there's none on Earth," said Martin.

"No, there's not, is there?" Captain Hart was thoughtful, the fire damped down. "Not since Darwin, eh? Not since everything went by the board, everything we used to believe in, eh? Divine power and all that. And so you think maybe that's why we're going out to the stars, eh, Martin? Looking for our lost souls, is that it? Trying to get away from our evil planet to a good one?"

"Perhaps, sir. Certainly we're looking for something."

Captain Hart cleared his throat and tightened back into sharpness. "Well, right now we're looking for the mayor of that city there. Run in, tell them who we are, the first rocket expedition to Planet Forty-three in Star System Three. Captain Hart sends his salutations and desires to meet the mayor. On the double!"

"Yes, sir." Martin walked slowly across the meadow.

"Hurry!" snapped the captain.

"Yes, sir!" Martin trotted away. Then he walked again, smiling to himself.

The captain had smoked two cigars before Martin returned.

Martin stopped and looked up into the door of the rocket, swaying, seemingly unable to focus his eyes or think.

"Well?" snapped Hart. "What happened? Are they coming to welcome us?"

"No." Martin had to lean dizzily against the ship.

"Why not?"

"It's not important," said Martin. "Give me a cigarette, please, Captain." His fingers groped blindly at the rising pack, for he was looking at the golden city and blinking. He lighted one and smoked quietly for a long time.

"Say something!" cried the captain. "Aren't they interested in our rocket?"

Martin said, "What? Oh. The rocket?" He inspected his cigarette. "No, they're not interested. Seems we came at an inopportune time."

"Inopportune time!"

Martin was patient. "Captain, listen. Something big happened yesterday in that city. It's so big, so important that we're second-rate—second fiddle. I've got to sit down." He lost his balance and sat heavily, gasping for air.

The captain chewed his cigar angrily. "What happened?"

Martin lifted his head, smoke from the burning cigarette in his fingers, blowing in the wind. "Sir, yesterday, in that city, a remarkable man appeared—good, intelligent, compassionate, and infinitely wise!"

The captain glared at his lieutnant. "What's that to do with us?"

"It's hard to explain. But he was a man for whom they'd waited a long time—a million years maybe. And yesterday he walked into their city. That's why today, sir, our rocket landing means nothing."

The captain sat down violently. "Who was it? Not Ashley? He didn't arrive in his rocket before us and steal my glory, did he?" He seized Martin's arm. His face was pale and dismayed.

"Not Ashley, sir."

"Then it was Burton! I knew it. Burton stole in ahead of us and ruined my landing! You can't trust anyone any more."

"Not Burton, either, sir," said Martin quietly.

The captain was incredulous. "There were only three rockets. We were in the lead. This man who got here ahead of us? What was his name!"

"He didn't have a name. He doesn't need one. It would be different on every planet, sir."

The captain stared at his lieutenant with hard, cynical eyes.

"Well, what did he do that was so wonderful that nobody even looks at our ship?"

"For one thing," said Martin steadily, "he healed the sick and comforted the poor. He fought hypocrisy and dirty politics and sat among the people, talking, through the day."

"Is that so wonderful?"

"Yes, Captain."

"I don't get this." The captain confronted Martin, peered into his face and eyes. "You been drinking, eh?" He was suspicious. He backed away. "I don't understand."

Martin looked at the city. "Captain, if you don't understand, there's no way of telling you."

The captain followed his gaze. The city was quiet and beautiful and a great peace lay over it. The captain stepped forward, taking his cigar from his lips. He squinted first at Martin, then at the golden spires of the buildings.

"You don't mean—you *can't* mean—— That man you're talking about couldn't be——"

Martin nodded. "That's what I mean, sir."

The captain stood silently, not moving. He drew himself up.

"I don't believe it," he said at last.

At high noon Captain Hart walked briskly into the city, accompanied by Lieutenant Martin and an assistant who was carrying some electrical equipment. Every once in a while the captain laughed loudly, put his hands on his hips, and shook his head.

The mayor of the town confronted him. Martin set up a tripod, screwed a box onto it, and switched on the batteries.

"Are you the mayor?" The captain jabbed a finger out.

"I am," said the mayor.

The delicate apparatus stood between them, controlled and adjusted by Martin and the assistant. Instantaneous translations from any language were made by the box. The words sounded crisply on the mild air of the city.

"About this occurrence yesterday," said the captain. "It occurred?"

"It did."

"You have witnesses?"

"We have."

"May we talk to them?"

"Talk to any of us," said the mayor. "We are all witnesses."

In an aside to Martin the captain said, "Mass hallucination." To the mayor, "What did this man—this stranger—look like?"

"That would be hard to say," said the mayor, smiling a little.

"Why would it?"

"Opinions might differ slightly."

"I'd like your opinion, sir, anyway," said the captain. "Record this," he snapped to Martin over his shoulder. The lieutenant pressed the button of a hand recorder.

"Well," said the mayor of the city, "he was a very gentle and kind man. He was of a great and knowing intelligence."

"Yes, yes, I know, I know." The captain waved his fingers. "Generalizations. I want something specific. What did he look like?"

"I don't believe that is important," replied the mayor.

"It's very important," said the captain sternly. "I want a description of this fellow. If I can't get it from you, I'll get it from others." To Martin, "I'm sure it must have been Burton, pulling one of his practical jokes."

Martin would not look him in the face. Martin was coldly silent.

The captain snapped his fingers. "There was something or other—a healing?"

"Many healings," said the mayor.

"May I see one?"

"You may," said the mayor. "My son." He nodded at a small boy who stepped forward. "He was afflicted with a withered arm. Now, look upon it."

At this the captain laughed tolerantly. "Yes, yes. This isn't even circumstantial evidence, you know. I didn't see the boy's withered arm. I see only his arm whole and well. That's no proof. What proof have you that the boy's arm was withered yesterday and today is well?"

"My word is my proof," said the mayor simply.

"My dear man!" cried the captain. "You don't expect me to go on hearsay, do you? Oh no!"

"I'm sorry," said the mayor, looking upon the captain with what appeared to be curiosity and pity.

"Do you have any pictures of the boy before today?" asked the captain.

After a moment a large oil portrait was carried forth, showing the son with a withered arm.

"My dear fellow!" The captain waved it away. "Anybody can paint a picture. Paintings lie. I want a photograph of the boy."

There was no photograph. Photography was not a known art in their society.

"Well," sighed the captain, face twitching, "let me talk to a few other citizens. We're getting nowhere." He pointed at a woman. "You." She hesitated. "Yes, you; come here," ordered the captain. "Tell me about this *wonderful* man you saw yesterday."

The woman looked steadily at the captain. "He walked among us and was very fine and good."

"What color were his eyes?"

"The color of the sun, the color of the sea, the color of a flower, the color of the mountains, the color of the night."

"That'll do." The captain threw up his hands. "See, Martin? Absolutely nothing. Some charlatan wanders through whispering sweet nothings in their ears and——"

"Please, stop it," said Martin.

The captain stepped back. "What?"

"You heard what I said," said Martin. "I like these people. I believe what they say. You're entitled to your opinion, but keep it to yourself, sir."

"You can't talk to me this way," shouted the captain.

"I've had enough of your high-handedness," replied Martin. "Leave these people alone. They've got something good and decent, and you come and foul up the nest and sneer at it. Well, I've talked to them too. I've gone through the city and seen their faces, and they've got something you'll never have—a little simple faith, and they'll move mountains with it. You, you're boiled because someone stole your act, got here ahead and made you unimportant!"

"I'll give you five seconds to finish," remarked the captain. "I understand. You've been under a strain, Martin. Months of traveling in space, nostalgia, loneliness. And now, with this thing happening, I sympathize, Martin. I overlook your petty insubordination."

"I don't overlook your petty tyranny," replied Martin. "I'm stepping out. I'm staying here."

"You can't do that!"

"Can't I? Try and stop me. This is what I came looking for. I didn't know it, but this is it. This is for me. Take your filth somewhere else and foul up other nests with your doubt and your—scientific method!" He looked swiftly about. "These people have had an experience, and you can't seem to get it through your head that it's really happened and we were lucky enough to almost arrive in time to be in on it.

"People on Earth have talked about this man for twenty centuries after he walked through the old world. We've all wanted to see him and hear him, and never had the chance. And now, today, we just missed seeing him by a few hours."

Captain Hart looked at Martin's cheeks. "You're crying like a baby. Stop it."

"I don't care."

"Well, I do. In front of these natives we're to keep up a front. You're overwrought. As I said, I forgive you."

"I don't want your forgiveness."

"You idiot. Can't you see this is one of Burton's tricks, to fool these people, to bilk them, to establish his oil and mineral concerns under a religious guise! You fool, Martin. You absolute fool! You should know Earthmen by now. They'll do anything—blaspheme, lie, cheat, steal, kill, to get their ends. Anything is fine if it works; the true pragmatist, that's Burton. You know him!"

The captain scoffed heavily. "Come off it, Martin, admit it; this is the sort of scaly thing Burton might carry off, polish up these citizens and pluck them when they're ripe."

"No," said Martin, thinking of it.

The captain put his hand up. "That's Burton. That's him. That's his dirt, that's his criminal way. I have to admire the old dragon. Flaming in here in a blaze and a halo and a soft word and a loving touch, with a medicated salve here and a healing ray there. That's Burton all right!"

"No." Martin's voice was dazed. He covered his eyes. "No, I won't believe it."

"You don't want to believe." Captain Hart kept at it. "Admit it now. Admit it! It's just the thing Burton would do. Stop daydreaming, Martin. Wake up! It's morning. This is a real world and we're real, dirty people—Burton the dirtiest of us all!"

Martin turned away.

"There, there, Martin," said Hart, mechanically patting the man's back. "I understand. Quite a shock for you. I know. A rotten shame, and all that. That Burton is a rascal. You go take it easy. Let me handle this."

Martin walked off slowly toward the rocket.

Captain Hart watched him go. Then, taking a deep breath, he turned to the woman he had been questioning. "Well. Tell me some more about this man. As you were saying, madam?"

Later the officers of the rocket ship ate supper on card tables outside. The captain correlated his data to a silent Martin who sat red-eyed and brooding over his meal.

"Interviewed three dozen people, all of them full of the same milk and hogwash," said the captain. "It's Burton's work all right, I'm positive. He'll be spilling back in here tomorrow or next week to consolidate his miracles and beat us out in our contracts. I think I'll stick on and spoil it for him."

Martin glanced up sullenly. "I'll kill him," he said.

"Now, now, Martin! There, there, boy."

"I'll kill him—so help me, I will."

"We'll put an anchor on his wagon. You have to admit he's clever. Unethical but clever."

"He's dirty."

"You must promise not to do anything violent." Captain Hart checked his figures. "According to this, there were thirty miracles of healing performed, a blind man restored to vision, a leper cured. Oh, Burton's efficient, give him that."

A gong sounded. A moment later a man ran up. "Captain, sir. A report! Burton's ship is coming down. Also the Ashley ship, sir!"

"See!" Captain Hart beat the table. "Here come the jackals to the harvest! They can't wait to feed. Wait till I confront them. I'll make them cut me in on this feast—I will!"

Martin looked sick. He stared at the captain.

"Business, my dear boy, business," said the captain.

Everybody looked up. Two rockets swung down out of the sky.

When the rockets landed they almost crashed.

"What's wrong with those fools?" cried the captain, jumping up. The men ran across the meadowlands to the steaming ships. The captain arrived. The airlock door popped open on Burton's ship.

A man fell out into their arms.

"What's wrong?" cried Captain Hart.

The man lay on the ground. They bent over him and he was burned, badly burned. His body was covered with wounds and scars and tissue that was inflamed and smoking. He looked up out of puffed eyes and his thick tongue moved in his split lips.

"What happened?" demanded the captain, kneeling down, shaking the man's arm.

"Sir, sir," whispered the dying man. "Forty-eight hours ago, back in Space Sector Seventy-nine DFS, off Planet One in this system, our ship, and Ashley's ship, ran into a cosmic storm, sir." Blood trickled from his mouth. "Wiped out. All crew. Burton dead. Ashley died an hour ago. Only three survivals."

"Listen to me!" shouted Hart, bending over the bleeding man. "You didn't come to this planet before this very hour?"

Silence.

"Answer me!" cried Hart.

The dying man said, "No. Storm. Burton dead two days ago. This first landing on any world in six months."

"Are you sure?" shouted Hart, shaking violently, gripping the man in his hands. "Are you sure?"

"Sure, sure," mouthed the dying man.

"Burton died two days ago? You're positive?"

"Yes, yes," whispered the man. His head fell forward. The man was dead.

The captain knelt beside the silent body. The captain's face twitched, the muscles jerking involuntarily. The other members of the crew stood back of him looking down. Martin waited. The captain asked to be helped to his feet, finally, and this was done. They stood looking at the city. "That means—"

"That means?" said Martin.

"We're the only ones who've been here," whispered Captain Hart. "And that man——"

"What about that man, Captain?" asked Martin.

The captain's face twitched senselessly. He looked very old indeed, and gray. His eyes were glazed. He moved forward in the dry grass.

"Come along, Martin. Come along. Hold me up; for

my sake, hold me. I'm afraid I'll fall. And hurry. We can't waste time—"

They moved, stumbling, toward the city, in the long dry grass, in the blowing wind.

Several hours later they were sitting in the mayor's auditorium. A thousand people had come and talked and gone. The captain had remained seated, his face haggard, listening, listening. There was so much light in the faces of those who came and testified and talked he could not bear to see them. And all the while his hands traveled, on his knees, together; on his belt, jerking and quivering.

When it was over, Captain Hart turned to the mayor and with strange eyes said:

"But you must know where he went?"

"He didn't say where he was going," replied the mayor.

"To one of the other nearby worlds?" demanded the captain.

"I don't know."

"You must know."

"Do you see him?" asked the mayor, indicating the crowd.

The captain looked. "No."

"Then he is probably gone," said the mayor.

"Probably, probably!" cried the captain weakly. "I've made a horrible mistake, and I want to see him now. Why, it just came to me, this is a most unusual thing in history. To be in on something like this. Why, the chances are one in billions we'd arrived at one certain planet among millions of planets the day after *he* came! You must know where he's gone!"

"Each finds him in his own way," replied the mayor gently.

"You're hiding him." The captain's face grew slowly ugly. Some of the old hardness returned in stages. He began to stand up.

"No," said the mayor.

"You know where he is then?" The captain's fingers twitched at the leather holster on his right side.

"I couldn't tell you where he is, exactly," said the mayor.

"I advise you to start talking," and the captain took out a small steel gun.

"There's no way," said the mayor, "to tell you anything."

"Liar!"

An expression of pity came into the mayor's face as he looked at Hart.

"You're very tired," he said. "You've traveled a long way and you belong to a tired people who've been without faith a long time, and you want to believe so much now that you're interfering with yourself. You'll only make it harder if you kill. You'll never find him that way."

"Where'd he go? He told you; you know. Come on, tell me!" The captain waved the gun.

The mayor shook his head.

"Tell me! Tell me!"

The gun cracked once, twice. The mayor fell, his arm wounded.

Martin leaped forward. "Captain!"

The gun flashed at Martin. "Don't interfere."

On the floor, holding his wounded arm, the mayor looked up. "Put down your gun. You're hurting yourself. You've never believed, and now that you think you believe, you hurt people because of it."

"I don't need you," said Hart, standing over him. "If I missed him by one day here, I'll go on to another world. And another and another. I'll miss him by half a day on the next planet, maybe, and a quarter of a day on the third planet, and two hours on the next, and an hour on the next, and half an hour on the next, and a minute on the next. But after that, one day I'll catch up with him! Do you hear that?" He was shouting now, leaning wearily over the man on the floor. He staggered with exhaustion. "Come along, Martin." He let the gun hang in his hand.

"No," said Martin. "I'm staying here."

"You're a fool. Stay if you like. But I'm going on, with the others, as far as I can go."

The mayor looked up at Martin. "I'll be all right. Leave me. Others will tend my wounds."

"I'll be back," said Martin. "I'll walk as far as the rocket."

They walked with vicious speed through the city. One could see with what effort the captain struggled to show all the old iron, to keep himself going. When he reached the rocket he slapped the side of it with a trembling hand. He holstered his gun. He looked at Martin.

"Well, Martin?"

Martin looked at him. "Well, Captain?"

The captain's eyes were on the sky. "Sure you won't—come with—with me, eh?"

"No, sir."

"It'll be a great adventure, by God. I know I'll find him."

"You are set on it now, aren't you, sir?" asked Martin.

The captain's face quivered and his eyes closed. "Yes."

"There's one thing I'd like to know."

"What?"

"Sir, when you find him—*if* you find him," asked Martin, "what will you ask of him?"

"Why——" The captain faltered, opening his eyes. His hands clenched and unclenched. He puzzled a moment and then broke into a strange smile. "Why, I'll ask him for a little—peace and quiet." He touched the rocket. "It's been a long time, a long, long time since—since I relaxed."

"Did you ever just try, Captain?"

"I don't understand," said Hart.

"Never mind. So long, Captain?"

"Good-bye, Mr. Martin."

The crew stood by the port. Out of their number only three were going on with Hart. Seven others were remaining behind, they said, with Martin.

Captain Hart surveyed them and uttered his verdict: "Fools!"

He, last of all, climbed into the airlock, gave a brisk salute, and laughed sharply. The door slammed.

The rocket lifted into the sky on a pillar of fire.

Martin watched it go far away and vanish.

At the meadow's edge the mayor, supported by several men, beckoned.

"He's gone," said Martin, walking up.

"Yes, poor man, he's gone," said the mayor. "And he'll go on, planet after planet, seeking and seeking, and always and always he will be an hour late, or a half hour late, or ten minutes late, or a minute late. And finally he will miss out by only a few seconds. And when he has visited three hundred worlds and is seventy or eighty years old he will miss out by only a fraction of a second, and then a smaller fraction of a second. And he will go on and on, thinking to find that very thing which he left behind here, on this planet, in this city——"

Martin looked steadily at the mayor.

The mayor put out his hand. "Was there ever any doubt of it?" He beckoned to the others and turned. "Come along now. We mustn't keep him waiting."

They walked into the city.

TIME IN THY FLIGHT

A wind blew the long years away past their hot faces.

The Time Machine stopped.

"Nineteen hundred and twenty-eight," said Janet. The two boys looked past her.

Mr. Fields stirred. "Remember, you're here to observe the behavior of these ancient people. Be inquisitive, be intelligent, observe."

"Yes," said the girl and the two boys in crisp khaki uniforms. They wore identical haircuts, had identical wristwatches, sandals, and coloring of hair, eyes, teeth, and skin, though they were not related.

"Shh!" said Mr. Fields.

They looked out at a little Illinois town in the spring of the year. A cool mist lay on the early morning streets.

Far down the street a small boy came running in the last light of the marble-cream moon. Somewhere a great clock struck 5 A.M. far away. Leaving tennis-shoe prints softly in the quiet lawns, the boy stepped near the invisible Time Machine and cried up to a high dark house window.

The house window opened. Another boy crept down the roof to the ground. The two boys ran off with banana-filled mouths into the dark cold morning.

"Follow them," whispered Mr. Fields. "Study their life patterns. Quick!"

Janet and William and Robert ran on the cold pavements of spring, visible now, through the slumbering town, through a park. All about, lights flickered, doors clicked, and other children rushed alone or in gasping pairs down a hill to some gleaming blue tracks.

"Here it comes!" The children milled about before dawn. Far down the shining tracks a small light grew seconds later into steaming thunder.

"What is it?" screamed Janet.

"A train, silly, you've seen pictures of them!" shouted Robert.

And as the Time Children watched, from the train stepped gigantic gray elephants, steaming the pavements with their mighty waters, lifting question-mark nozzles to the cold morning sky. Cumbrous wagons rolled from the long freight flats, red and gold. Lions roared and paced in boxed darkness.

"Why—*this* must be a—circus!" Janet trembled.

"You think so? Whatever happened to them?"

"Like Christmas, I guess. Just vanished, long ago."

Janet looked around. "Oh, it's awful, isn't it."

The boys stood numbed. "It sure is."

Men shouted in the first faint gleam of dawn. Sleeping cars drew up, dazed faces blinked out at the children. Horses clattered like a great fall of stones on the pavement.

Mr. Fields was suddenly behind the children. "Disgusting, barbaric, keeping animals in cages. If I'd known this was here, I'd never let you come see. This is a terrible ritual."

"Oh, yes." But Janet's eyes were puzzled. "And yet, you know, it's like a nest of maggots. I want to study it."

"I don't know," said Robert, his eyes darting, his fingers trembling. "It's pretty crazy. We might try writing a thesis on it if Mr. Fields says it's all right . . ."

Mr. Fields nodded. "I'm glad you're digging in here, finding motives, studying this horror. All right—we'll see the circus this afternoon."

"I think I'm going to be sick," said Janet.

The Time Machine hummed.

"So that was a circus," said Janet, solemnly.

The trombone circus died in their ears. The last thing they saw was candy-pink trapeze people whirling while baking powder clowns shrieked and bounded.

"You must admit psychovision's better," said Robert slowly.

"All those nasty animal smells, the excitement." Janet blinked. "That's bad for children, isn't it? And those older people seated with the children. Mothers, fathers, they called them. Oh, that *was* strange."

Mr. Fields put some marks in his class grading book.

Janet shook her head numbly. "I want to see it all again. I've missed the motives somewhere. I want to make that run across town again in the early morning. The cold air on my face—the sidewalk under my feet— the circus train coming in. Was it the air and the early hour that made the children get up and run to see the train come in? I want to retrace the entire pattern. Why should they be excited? I feel I've missed out on the answer."

"They all smiled so much," said William.

"Manic-depressives," said Robert.

"What are summer vacations? I heard them talk about it." Janet looked at Mr. Fields.

"They spent their summers racing about like idiots, beating each other up," replied Mr. Fields seriously.

"I'll take our State Engineered summers of work for children anytime," said Robert, looking at nothing, his voice faint.

The Time Machine stopped again.

"The Fourth of July," announced Mr. Fields. "Nineteen hundred and twenty-eight. An ancient holiday when people blew each other's fingers off."

They stood before the same house on the same street but on a soft summer evening. Fire wheels hissed, on front porches laughing children tossed things out that went bang!

"Don't run!" cried Mr. Fields. "It's not war, don't be afraid!"

But Janet's and Robert's and William's faces were pink, now blue, now white with fountains of soft fire.

"We're all right," said Janet, standing very still.

"Happily," announced Mr. Fields, "they prohibited fireworks a century ago, did away with the whole messy explosion."

Children did fairy dances, weaving their names and destinies on the dark summer air with white sparklers.

"I'd like to do that," said Janet, softly. "Write my name on the air. See? I'd like that."

"What?" Mr. Fields hadn't been listening.

"Nothing," said Janet.

"Bang!" whispered William and Robert, standing under the soft summer trees, in shadow, watching, watching the red, white, and green fires on the beautiful summer night lawns. "Bang!"

October.

The Time Machine paused for the last time, an hour later in the month of burning leaves. People bustled into dim houses carrying pumpkins and corn shocks. Skeletons danced, bats flew, candles flamed, apples swung in empty doorways.

"Halloween," said Mr. Fields. "The acme of horror. This was the age of superstition, you know. Later they banned the Grimm Brothers, ghosts, skeletons, and all that claptrap. You children, thank God, were raised in an antiseptic world of no shadows or ghosts. You had decent holidays like William C. Chatterton's Birthday, Work Day, and Machine Day."

They walked by the same house in the empty October night, peering in at the triangle-eyed pumpkins, the masks leering in black attics and damp cellars. Now, inside the house, some party children squatted telling stories, laughing!

"I want to be inside with them," said Janet at last.

"Sociologically, of course," said the boys.

"No," she said.

"What?" asked Mr. Fields.

"No, I just want to be inside, I just want to stay here, I want to see it all and be here and never be anywhere else, I want firecrackers and pumpkins and circuses, I want Christmases and Valentines and Fourths, like we've seen."

"This is getting out of hand . . ." Mr. Fields started to say.

But suddenly Janet was gone. "Robert, William, come on!" She ran. The boys leaped after her.

"Hold on!" shouted Mr. Fields. "Robert! William,

I've got you!" He seized the last boy, but the other escaped. "Janet, Robert—come back here! You'll never pass into the seventh grade! You'll fail, Janet, Bob—*Bob!*"

An October wind blew wildly down the street, vanishing with the children off among moaning trees.

William twisted and kicked.

"No, not you, too, William, you're coming home with me. We'll teach those other two a lesson they won't forget. So they want to stay in the past, do they?" Mr. Fields shouted so everyone could hear. "All right, Janet, Bob, stay in this horror, in this chaos! In a few weeks you'll come sniveling back here to me. But I'll be gone! I'm leaving you here to go mad in this world!"

He hurried William to the Time Machine. The boy was sobbing. "Don't make me come back here on any more Field Excursions ever again, please, Mr. Fields, please—"

"Shut up!"

Almost instantly the Time Machine whisked away toward the future, toward the underground hive cities. the metal buildings, the metal flowers, the metal lawns.

"Good-bye, Janet, Bob!"

A great cold October wind blew through the town like water. And when it had ceased blowing it had carried all the children, whether invited or uninvited, masked or unmasked, to the doors of houses which closed upon them. There was not a running child anywhere in the night. The wind whined away in the bare treetops.

And inside the big house, in the candlelight, someone was pouring cold apple cider all around, to everyone, no matter *who* they were.

HEMET HIGH SCHOOL

THE PEDESTRIAN

To enter out into that silence that was the city at eight o'clock of a misty evening in November, to put your feet upon that buckling concrete walk, to step over grassy seams and make your way, hands in pockets, through the silences, that was what Mr. Leonard Mead most dearly loved to do. He would stand upon the corner of an intersection and peer down long moonlit avenues of sidewalk in four directions, deciding which way to go, but it really made no difference; he was alone in this world of A.D. 2053, or as good as alone, and with a final decision made, a path selected, he would stride off, sending patterns of frosty air before him like the smoke of a cigar.

Sometimes he would walk for hours and miles and return only at midnight to his house. And on his way he would see the cottages and homes with their dark windows, and it was not unequal to walking through a graveyard where only the faintest glimmers of firefly light appeared in flickers behind the windows. Sudden gray phantoms seemed to manifest upon inner room walls where a curtain was still undrawn against the night, or there were whisperings and murmurs where a window in a tomb-like building was still open.

Mr. Leonard Mead would pause, cock his head, listen, look, and march on, his feet making no noise on the lumpy walk. For long ago he had wisely changed to sneakers when strolling at night, because the dogs in intermittent squads would parallel his journey with barkings if he wore hard heels, and lights might click on and faces appear and an entire street be startled by the passing of a lone figure, himself, in the early November evening.

On this particular evening he began his journey in a westerly direction, toward the hidden sea. There was a good crystal frost in the air; it cut the nose and made the lungs blaze like a Christmas tree inside; you could feel the cold light going on and off, all the branches filled with invisible snow. He listened to the faint push of his soft shoes through autumn leaves with satisfaction, and whistled a cold quiet whistle between his teeth, occasionally picking up a leaf as he passed, examining its skeletal pattern in the infrequent lamplights as he went on, smelling its rusty smell.

"Hello, in there," he whispered to every house on every side as he moved. "What's up tonight on Channel 4, Channel 7, Channel 9? Where are the cowboys rushing, and do I see the United States Cavalry over the next hill to the rescue?"

The street was silent and long and empty, with only his shadow moving like the shadow of a hawk in midcountry. If he closed his eyes and stood very still, frozen, he could imagine himself upon the center of a plain, a wintry, windless American desert with no house in a thousand miles, and only dry river beds, the streets, for company.

"What is it now?" he asked the houses, noticing his wrist watch. "Eighty-thirty P.M.? Time for a dozen assorted murders? A quiz? A revue? A comedian falling off the stage?"

Was that a murmur of laughter from within a moon-white house? He hesitated, but went on when nothing more happened. He stumbled over a particularly uneven section of sidewalk. The cement was vanishing under flowers and grass. In ten years of walking by night or day, for thousands of miles, he had never met another person walking, not once in all that time.

He came to a cloverleaf intersection which stood silent where two main highways crossed the town. During the day it was a thunderous surge of cars, the gas stations open, a great insect rustling and a ceaseless jockeying for position as the scarab-beetles, a faint incense puttering from their exhausts, skimmed homeward to the far directions. But now these highways, too, were like streams in a dry season, all stone and bed and moon radiance.

He turned back on a side street, circling around toward his home. He was within a block of his destination when the lone car turned a corner quite suddenly and flashed a fierce white cone of light upon him. He stood entranced, not unlike a night moth, stunned by the illumination, and then drawn toward it.

A metallic voice called to him:

"Stand still. Stay where you are! Don't move!"

He halted.

"Put up your hands!"

"But—" he said.

"Your hands up! Or we'll shoot!"

The police, of course, but what a rare, incredible thing; in a city of three million, there was only *one* police car left, wasn't that correct? Ever since a year ago, 2052, the election year, the force had been cut down from three cars to one. Crime was ebbing; there was no need now for the police, save for this one lone car wandering and wandering the empty streets.

"Your name?" said the police car in a metallic whisper. He couldn't see the men in it for the bright light in his eyes.

"Leonard Mead," he said.

"Speak up!"

"Leonard Mead!"

"Business or profession?"

"I guess you'd call me a writer."

"No profession," said the police car, as if talking to itself. The light held him fixed, like a museum specimen, needle thrust through chest.

"You might say that," said Mr. Mead. He hadn't written in years. Magazines and books didn't sell any more. Everything went on in the tomblike houses at night now, he thought, continuing his fancy. The tombs, ill-lit by television light, where the people sat like the dead, the gray or multicolored lights touching their faces, but never really touching *them*.

"No profession," said the phonograph voice, hissing. "What are you doing out?"

"Walking," said Leonard Mead.

"Walking!"

"Just walking," he said simply, but his face felt cold.

"Walking, just walking, walking?"

"Yes, sir."

"Walking where? For what?"

"Walking for air. Walking to see."

"Your address!"

"Eleven South Saint James Street."

"And there is air *in* your house, you have an *air conditioner*, Mr. Mead?"

"Yes."

"And you have a viewing screen in your house to see with?"

"No."

"No?" There was a crackling quiet that in itself was an accusation.

"Are you married, Mr. Mead?"

"No."

"Not married," said the police voice behind the fiery beam. The moon was high and clear among the stars and the houses were gray and silent.

"Nobody wanted me," said Leonard Mead with a smile.

"Don't speak unless you're spoken to!"

Leonard Mead waited in the cold night.

"Just *walking*, Mr. Mead?"

"Yes."

"But you haven't explained for what purpose."

"I explained; for air, and to see, and just to walk."

"Have you done this often?"

"Every night for years."

The police car sat in the center of the street with its radio throat faintly humming.

"Well, Mr. Mead," it said.

"Is that all?" he asked politely.

"Yes," said the voice. "Here." There was a sigh, a pop. The back door of the police car sprang wide. "Get in."

"Wait a minute, I haven't done anything!"

"Get in."

"I protest!"

"Mr. Mead."

He walked like a man suddenly drunk. As he passed the front window of the car he looked in. As he had expected there was no one in the front seat, no one in the car at all.

"Get in."

He put his hand to the door and peered into the back seat, which was a little cell, a little black jail with bars. It smelled of riveted steel. It smelled of harsh antiseptic; it smelled too clean and hard and metallic. There was nothing soft there.

"Now if you had a wife to give you an alibi," said the iron voice. "But——"

"Where are you taking me?"

The car hesitated, or rather gave a faint whirring click, as if information, somewhere, was dropping card by punch-slotted card under electric eyes. "To the Psychiatric Center for Research on Regressive Tendencies."

He got in. The door shut with a soft thud. The police car rolled through the night avenues, flashing its dim lights ahead.

They passed one house on one street a moment later, one house in an entire city of houses that were dark, but this one particular house had all of its electric lights brightly lit, every window a loud yellow illumination, square and warm in the cool darkness.

"That's *my* house," said Leonard Mead.

No one answered him.

The car moved down the empty river-bed streets and off away, leaving the empty streets with the empty sidewalks, and no sound and no motion all the rest of the chill November night.

HAIL AND FAREWELL

But of course he was going away, there was nothing else to do, the time was up, the clock had run out, and he was going very far away indeed. His suitcase was packed, his shoes were shined, his hair was brushed, he had expressly washed behind his ears, and it remained only for him to go down the stairs, out the front door, and up the street to the small-town station where the train would make a stop for him alone. Then Fox Hill, Illinois would be left far off in his past. And he would go on, perhaps to Iowa, perhaps to Kansas, perhaps even to California; a small boy, twelve years old, with a birth certificate in his valise to show he had been born forty-three years ago.

"Willie!" called a voice belowstairs.

"Yes!" He hoisted his suitcase. In his bureau mirror he saw a face made of June dandelions and July apples and warm summer-morning milk. There, as always, was his look of the angel and the innocent, which might never, in the years of his life, change.

"Almost time," called the woman's voice.

"All right!" And he went down the stairs, grunting and smiling. In the living room sat Anna and Steve, their clothes painfully neat.

"Here I am!" cried Willie in the parlor door.

Anna looked like she was going to cry. "Oh, good Lord, you can't really be leaving us, can you, Willie?"

"People are beginning to talk," said Willie quietly. "I've been here three years now. But when people begin to talk, I know it's time to put on my shoes and buy a railway ticket."

"It's all so strange. I don't understand. It's so sudden," Anna said. "Willie, we'll miss you."

"I'll write you every Christmas, so help me. Don't you write me."

"It's been a great pleasure and satisfaction," said Steve, sitting there, his words the wrong size in his mouth. "It's a shame it had to stop. It's a shame you had to tell us about yourself. It's an awful shame you can't stay on."

"You're the nicest folks I ever had," said Willie, four feet high, in no need of a shave, the sunlight on his face.

And then Anna *did* cry. "Willie, Willie." And she sat down and looked as if she wanted to hold him but was afraid to hold him now; she looked at him with shock and amazement and her hands empty, not knowing what to do with him now.

"It's not easy to go," said Willie. "You get used to things. You want to stay. But it doesn't work. I tried to stay on once after people began to suspect. 'How horrible!' people said. 'All these years, playing with our innocent children,' they said, 'and us not guessing! Awful!' they said. And finally I had to just leave town one night. It's not easy. You know darned well how much I love both of you. Thanks for three swell years."

They all went to the front door. "Willie, where're you going?"

"I don't know. I just start traveling. When I see a town that looks green and nice, I settle in."

"Will you ever come back?"

"Yes," he said earnestly with his high voice. "In about twenty years it should begin to show in my face. When it does, I'm going to make a grand tour of all the mothers and fathers I've ever had."

They stood on the cool summer porch, reluctant to say the last words. Steve was looking steadily at an elm tree. "How many other folks've you stayed with, Willie? How many adoptions?"

Willie figured it, pleasantly enough. "I guess it's about five towns and five couples and over twenty years gone by since I started my tour."

"Well, we can't holler," said Steve. "Better to've had a son thirty-six months than none whatever."

"Well," said Willie, and kissed Anna quickly, seized at his luggage, and was gone up the street in the green noon light, under the trees, a very young boy indeed, not looking back, running steadily.

The boys were playing on the green park diamond when he came by. He stood a little while among the oak-tree shadows, watching them hurl the white, snowy baseball into the warm summer air, saw the baseball shadow fly like a dark bird over the grass, saw their hands open in mouths to catch this swift piece of summer that now seemed most especially important to hold onto. The boys' voices yelled. The ball lit on the grass near Willie.

Carrying the ball forward from under the shade trees, he thought of the last three years now spent to the penny, and the five years before that, and so on down the line to the year when he was really eleven and twelve and fourteen and the voices saying: "What's wrong with Willie, missus?" "Mrs. B., is Willie late a-growin'?" "Willie, you smokin' cigars lately?" The echoes died in summer light and color. His mother's voice: "Willie's twenty-one today!" And a thousand voices saying: "Come back, son, when you're fifteen; then maybe we'll give you a job."

He stared at the baseball in his trembling hand, as if it were his life, an interminable ball of years strung around and around and around, but always leading back to his twelfth birthday. He heard the kids walking toward him; he felt them blot out the sun, and they were older, standing around him.

"Willie! Where you goin'?" They kicked his suitcase.

How tall they stood to the sun. In the last few months it seemed the sun had passed a hand above their heads, beckoned, and they were warm metal drawn melting upwards; they were golden taffy pulled by an immense gravity to the sky, thirteen, fourteen years old, looking down upon Willie, smiling, but already beginning to neglect him. It had started four months ago:

"Choose up sides! Who wants Willie?"

"Aw, Willie's too little; we don't play with 'kids.' "

And they raced ahead of him, drawn by the moon and the sun and the turning seasons of leaf and wind, and he was twelve years old and not of them any more. And the other voices beginning again on the old, the dreadfully familiar, the cool refrain: "Better feed that boy vitamins, Steve." "Anna, does shortness *run* in your family?" And the cold fist kneading at your heart again and knowing that the roots would have to be pulled up again after so many good years with the "folks."

"Willie, where are you goin'?"

He jerked his head. He was back among the towering, shadowing boys who milled around him like giants at a drinking fountain bending down.

"Goin' a few days visitin' a cousin of mine."

"Oh." There was a day, a year ago, when they would have cared very much indeed. But now there was only curiosity for his luggage, their enchantment with trains and trips and far places.

"How about a coupla fast ones?" said Willie.

They looked doubtful, but, considering the circumstances, nodded. He dropped his bag and ran out; the white baseball was up in the sun, away to their burning white figures in the far meadow, up in the sun again, rushing, life coming and going in a pattern. Here, *there*! Mr. and Mrs. Robert Hanlon, Creek Bend, Wisconsin, 1932, the first couple, the first year! Here, there! Henry and Alice Boltz, Limeville, Iowa, 1935! The baseball flying. The Smiths, the Eatons, the Robinsons! 1939! 1945! Husband and wife, husband and wife, husband and wife, no children, no children, no children! A knock on this door, a knock on that.

"Pardon me. My name is William. I wonder if——"

"A sandwich? Come in, sit down. Where you *from*, son?"

The sandwich, a tall glass of cold milk, the smiling, the nodding, the comfortable, leisurely talking.

"Son, you look like you been traveling. You run *off* from somewhere?"

"No."

"Boy, are you an orphan?"

Another glass of milk.

"We always wanted kids. It never worked out. Never knew why. One of those things. Well, well. It's getting late, son. Don't you think you better hit for home?"

"Got no home."

"A boy like you? Not dry behind the ears? Your mother'll be worried."

"Got no home and no folks anywhere in the world. I wonder if—I wonder—could I sleep here tonight?"

"Well, now, son, I don't just know. We never considered taking in——" said the husband.

"We got chicken for supper tonight," said the wife, "enough for extras, enough for company. . . ."

And the years turning and flying away, the voices, and the faces, and the people, and always the same first conversations. The voice of Emily Robinson, in her rocking chair, in summer-night darkness, the last night he stayed with her, the night she discovered his secret, her voice saying:

"I look at all the little children's faces going by. And I sometimes think, What a shame, what a shame, that all these flowers have to be cut, all these bright fires have to be put out. What a shame these, all of these you see in schools or running by, have to get tall and unsightly and wrinkle and turn gray or get bald and finally, all bone and wheeze, be dead and buried off away. When I hear them laugh I can't believe they'll ever go the road I'm going. Yet here they *come*! I still remember Wordsworth's poem: 'When all at once I saw a crowd, A host of golden daffodils; Beside the lake, beneath the trees, Fluttering and dancing in the breeze.' That's how I think of children, cruel as they sometimes are, mean as I know they can be, but not yet showing the meanness around their eyes or *in* their eyes, not yet full of tiredness. They're so eager for everything! I guess that's what I miss most in older folks, the eagerness gone nine times out of ten, the freshness gone, so much of the drive and life down the drain. I like to watch school let out each day. It's like someone threw a bunch of flowers out the school front doors. How does it feel, Willie? How does it feel to be young forever? To look like a silver dime new from the mint? Are you happy? Are you as fine as you *seem*?"

The baseball whizzed from the blue sky, stung his hand like a great pale insect. Nursing it, he heard his memory say:

"I worked with what I had. After my folks died, after I found I couldn't get man's work anywhere, I tried carnivals, but they only laughed. 'Son,' they said, 'you're not a midget, and even if you are, you look like a *boy*! We want midgets with midgets' *faces*! Sorry, son, sorry.' So I left home, started out, thinking: What was I? A boy. I looked like a boy, sounded like a boy, so I might as well go on being a boy. No use fighting it. No use screaming. So what could I do? What job was handy? And then one day I saw this man in a restaurant looking at another man's pictures of his children. 'Sure wish I had kids,' he said. 'Sure wish I had kids.' He kept shaking his head. And me sitting a few seats away from him, a hamburger in my hands. I sat there, *frozen*! At that very instant I knew what my job would be for most of my life. There was work for me, after all. Making lonely people happy. Keeping myself busy. Playing forever. I knew I had to play forever. Deliver a few papers, run a few errands, mow a few lawns, maybe. But *hard* work? No. All I had to do was be a mother's son and a father's pride: I turned to the man down the counter from me. 'I beg your pardon,' I said. I *smiled* at him. . . ."

"But, Willie," said Mrs. Emily long ago, "didn't you ever get lonely? Didn't you ever want—*things*—that grownups wanted?"

"I fought that out alone," said Willie. "I'm a boy, I told myself, I'll have to live in a boy's world, read boys' books, play boys' games, cut myself off from everything else. I can't be both. I got to be only one thing—young. And so I played that way. Oh, it wasn't easy. There were times——" He lapsed into silence.

"And the family you lived with, they never knew?"

"No. Telling them would have spoiled everything. I told them I was a runaway; I let them check through official channels, police. Then, when there was no record, let them put in to adopt me. That was best of all; as long as they never guessed. But then, after three years, or five years, they guessed, or a traveling man came through, or a carnival man saw me, and it was over. It always had to end."

"And you're very happy and it's *nice* being a child for over forty years?"

"It's a living, as they say. And when you make other people happy, then you're almost happy too. I got my job to do and I do it. And anyway, in a few years now I'll be in my second childhood. All the fevers will be out of me and all the unfulfilled things and most of the dreams. Then I can relax, maybe, and play the role all the way."

He threw the baseball one last time and broke the reverie. Then he was running to seize his luggage. Tom, Bill, Jamie, Bob, Sam—their names moved on his lips. They were embarrassed at his shaking hands.

"After all, Willie, it ain't as if you're going to China or Timbuktu."

"That's right, isn't it?" Willie did not move.

"So long, Willie. See you next week!"

"So long, so long!"

And he was walking off with his suitcase again looking at the trees, going away from the boys and the street where he had lived, and as he turned the corner a train whistle screamed, and he began to run.

The last thing he saw and heard was a white ball tossed at a high roof, back and forth, back and forth, and two voices crying out as the ball pitched now up, down, and back through the sky, "Annie, annie, over! Annie, annie, over!" like the crying of birds flying off to the far south.

In the early morning, with the smell of the mist and the cold metal, with the iron smell of the train around him and a full night of traveling shaking his bones and his body, and a smell of the sun beyond the horizon, he awoke and looked out upon a small town just arising from sleep. Lights were coming on, soft voices muttered, a red signal bobbed back and forth, back and forth in the cold air. There was that sleeping hush in which echoes are dignified by clarity, in which echoes stand nakedly alone and sharp. A porter moved by, a shadow in shadows.

"Sir," said Willie.

The porter stopped.

"What town's this?" whispered the boy in the dark.

"Valleyville."

"How many people?"

"Ten thousand. Why? This your stop?"

"It looks green." Willie gazed out at the cold morning town for a long time. "It looks nice and quiet," said Willie.

"Son," said the porter, "you know where you *going*?"

"Here," said Willie, and got up quietly in the still, cool, iron-smelling morning, in the train dark, with a rustling and stir.

"I hope you know what you're doing, boy," said the porter.

"Yes, sir," said Willie. "I know what I'm doing." And he was down the dark aisle, luggage lifted after him by the porter, and out in the smoking, steaming-cold, beginning-to-lighten morning. He stood looking up at the porter and the black metal train against the few remaining stars. The train gave a great wailing blast of whistle, the porters cried out all along the line, the cars jolted, and his special porter waved and smiled down at the boy there, the small boy there with the big luggage who shouted up to him, even as the whistle screamed again.

"What?" shouted the porter, hand cupped to ear.

"Wish me luck!" cried Willie.

"Best of luck, son," called the porter, waving, smiling. "Best of luck, boy!"

"Thanks!" said Willie, in the great sound of the train, in the steam and roar.

He watched the black train until it was completely gone away and out of sight. He did not move all the time it was going. He stood quietly, a small boy twelve years old, on the worn wooden platform, and only after three entire minutes did he turn at last to face the empty streets below.

Then, as the sun was rising, he began to walk very fast, so as to keep warm, down into the new town.

INVISIBLE BOY

She took the great iron spoon and the mummified frog and gave it a bash and made dust of it, and talked to the dust while she ground it in her stony fists quickly. Her beady gray bird-eyes flickered at the cabin. Each time she looked, a head in the small thin window ducked as if she'd fired off a shotgun.

"Charlie!" cried Old Lady. "You come outa there! I'm fixing a lizard magic to unlock that rusty door! You come out now and I won't make the earth shake or the trees go up in fire or the sun set at high noon!"

The only sound was the warm mountain light on the high turpentine trees, a tufted squirrel chittering around and around on a green-furred log, the ants moving in a fine brown line at Old Lady's bare, blue-veined feet.

"You been starving in there two days, darn you!" she panted, chiming the spoon against a flat rock, causing the plump gray miracle bag to swing at her waist. Sweating sour, she rose and marched at the cabin, bearing the pulverized flesh. "Come out, now!" She flicked a pinch of powder inside the lock. "All right, I'll come get you!" she wheezed.

She spun the knob with one walnut-colored hand, first one way, then the other. "O Lord," she intoned "fling this door wide!"

When nothing flung, she added yet another philter and held her breath. Her long blue untidy skirt rustled as she peered into her bag of darkness to see if she had any scaly monsters there, any charm finer than the frog she'd killed months ago for such a crisis as this.

She heard Charlie breathing against the door. His

folks had pranced off into some Ozark town early this
week, leaving him, and he'd run almost six miles to Old
Lady for company—she was by way of being an aunt
or cousin or some such, and he didn't mind her fash-
ions.

But then, two days ago, Old Lady, having gotten
used to the boy around, decided to keep him for conve-
nient company. She pricked her thin shoulder bone,
drew out three blood pearls, spat wet over her right
elbow, tromped on a crunch-cricket, and at the same
instant clawed her left hand at Charlie, crying, "My son
you are, you are my son, for all eternity!"

Charlie, bounding like a startled hare, had crashed
off into the bush, heading for home.

But Old Lady, skittering quick as a gingham lizard,
cornered him in a dead end, and Charlie holed up in
this old hermit's cabin and wouldn't come out, no
matter how she whammed door, window, or knothole
with amber-colored fist or trounced her ritual fires,
explaining to him that he was certainly her son *now*, all
right.

"Charlie, you *there?*" she asked, cutting holes in the
door planks with her bright little slippery eyes.

"I'm all of me here," he replied finally, very tired.

Maybe he would fall out on the ground any moment.
She wrestled the knob hopefully. Perhaps a pinch too
much frog powder had grated the lock wrong. She
always overdid or underdid her miracles, she mused
angrily, never doing them just *exact*, Devil take it!

"Charlie, I only wants someone to night-prattle to,
someone to warm hands with at the fire. Someone to
fetch kindling for me mornings, and fight off the spunks
that come creeping of early fogs! I ain't got no fetchings
on you for myself, son, just for your company." She
smacked her lips. "Tell you what, Charles, you come
out and I *teach* you things!"

"What things?" he suspicioned.

"Teach you how to buy cheap, sell high. Catch a
snow weasel, cut off its head, carry it warm in your
hind pocket. There!"

"Aw," said Charlie.

She made haste. "Teach you to make yourself shot-proof. So if anyone bangs at you with a gun, nothing happens."

When Charlie stayed silent, she gave him the secret in a high, fluttering whisper. "Dig and stitch mouse-ear roots on Friday during full moon, and wear 'em around your neck in a white silk."

"You're *crazy*," Charlie said.

"Teach you how to stop blood or make animals stand frozen or make blind horses see, all them things I'll teach you! Teach you to cure a swelled-up cow and unbewitch a goat. Show you how to make yourself invisible!"

"Oh," said Charlie.

Old Lady's heart beat like a Salvation tambourine.

The knob turned from the other side.

"You," said Charlie, "are funning me."

"No, I'm not," exclaimed Old Lady. "Oh, Charlie, why, I'll make you like a window, see right through you. Why, child, you'll be surprised!"

"Real invisible?"

"Real invisible!"

"You won't fetch onto me if I walk out?"

"Won't touch a bristle of you, son."

"Well," he drawled reluctantly, "all right."

The door opened. Charlie stood in his bare feet, head down, chin against chest. "Make me invisible," he said.

"First we got to catch us a bat," said Old Lady. "Start lookin'!"

She gave him some jerky beef for his hunger and watched him climb a tree. He went high up and high up and it was nice seeing him there and it was nice having him here and all about after so many years alone with nothing to say good morning to but bird-droppings and silvery snail tracks.

Pretty soon a bat with a broken wing fluttered down out of the tree. Old Lady snatched it up, beating warm and shrieking between its porcelain white teeth, and Charlie dropped down after it, hand upon clenched hand, yelling.

That night, with the moon nibbling at the spiced pine cones, Old Lady extracted a long silver needle from under her wide blue dress. Gumming her excitement and secret anticipation, she sighted up the dead bat and held the cold needle steady-steady.

She had long ago realized that her miracles, despite all perspirations and salts and sulphurs, failed. But she had always dreamt that one day the miracles might start functioning, might spring up in crimson flowers and silver stars to prove that God had forgiven her for her pink body and her pink thoughts and her warm body and her warm thoughts as a young miss. But so far God had made no sign and said no word, but nobody knew this except Old Lady.

"Ready?" she asked Charlie, who crouched cross-kneed, wrapping his pretty legs in long goose-pimpled arms, his mouth open, making teeth. "Ready," he whispered, shivering.

"There!" She plunged the needle deep in the bat's right eye. "So!"

"Oh!" screamed Charlie, wadding up his face.

"Now I wrap it in gingham, and here, put it in your pocket, keep it there, bat and all. Go on!"

He pocketed the charm.

"Charlie!" she shrieked fearfully. "Charlie, where *are* you? I can't *see* you, child!"

"Here!" he jumped so the light ran in red streaks up his body. "I'm here, Old Lady!" He stared wildly at his arms, legs, chest, and toes. "I'm here!"

Her eyes looked as if they were watching a thousand fireflies crisscrossing each other in the wild night air.

"Charlie, oh, you went *fast!* Quick as a humming-bird! Oh, Charlie, come *back* to me!"

"But I'm *here!*" he wailed.

"Where?"

"By the fire, the fire! And—and I can see myself. I'm not invisible at all!"

Old Lady rocked on her lean flanks. "Course *you* can see *you!* Every invisible person knows himself. Otherwise, how could you eat, walk, or get around places? Charlie, touch me. Touch me so I *know* you."

Uneasily he put out a hand.

She pretended to jerk, startled, at his touch. *"Ah!"*

"You mean to say you can't *find* me?" he asked. "Truly?"

"Not the least half rump of you!"

She found a tree to stare at, and stared at it with shining eyes, careful not to glance at him. "Why, I sure *did* a trick *that* time!" She sighed with wonder. "Whooeee. Quickest invisible I *ever* made! Charlie. Charlie, how you *feel?*"

"Like creek water—all stirred."

"You'll settle."

Then after a pause she added, "Well, what you going to do now, Charlie, since you're invisible?"

All sorts of things shot through his brain, she could tell. Adventures stood up and danced like fire in his eyes, and his mouth, just hanging, told what it meant to be a boy who imagined himself like the mountain winds. In a cold dream he said, "I'll run across wheat fields, climb snow mountains, steal white chickens off'n farms. I'll kick pink pigs when they ain't looking. I'll pinch pretty girls' legs when they sleep, snap their garters in schoolrooms." Charlie looked at Old Lady, and from the shiny tips of her eyes she saw something wicked shape his face. "And other things I'll do, I'll do, I will," he said.

"Don't try nothing on me," warned Old Lady. "I'm brittle as spring ice and I don't take handling." Then: "What about your folks?"

"My folks?"

"You can't fetch yourself home looking like that. Scare the inside ribbons out of them. Your mother'd faint straight back like timber falling. Think they want you about the house to stumble over and your ma have to call you every three minutes, even though you're in the room next her elbow?"

Charlie had not considered it. He sort of simmered down and whispered out a little "Gosh," and felt of his long bones carefully.

"You'll be mighty lonesome. People looking through you like a water glass, people knocking you aside because they didn't reckon you to be underfoot. And women, Charlie, *women*—"

He swallowed. "What about women?"

"No woman will be giving you a second stare. And no woman wants to be kissed by a boy's mouth they can't even *find!*"

Charlie dug his bare toe in the soil contemplatively. He pouted. "Well, I'll stay invisible, anyway, for a spell. I'll have me some fun. I'll just be pretty careful, is all. I'll stay out from in front of wagons and horses and Pa. Pa shoots at the nariest sound." Charlie blinked. "Why, with me invisible, someday Pa might just up and fill me with buckshot, thinkin' I was a hill squirrel in the dooryard. Oh ..."

Old Lady nodded at a tree. "That's likely."

"Well," he decided slowly, "I'll stay invisible for tonight, and tomorrow you can fix me back all whole again, Old Lady."

"Now if that ain't just like a critter, always wanting to be what he can't be," remarked Old Lady to a beetle on a log.

"What you mean?" said Charlie.

"Why," she explained, "it was real hard work, fixing you up. It'll take a little *time* for it to wear off. Like a coat of paint wears off, boy."

"You!" he cried. "You did this to me! Now you make me back, you make me seeable!"

"Hush," she said. "It'll wear off, a hand or a foot at a time."

"How'll it look, me around the hills with just one hand showing!"

"Like a five-winged bird hopping on the stones and bramble."

"Or a foot showing!"

"Like a small pink rabbit jumping thicket."

"Or my head floating!"

"Like a hairy balloon at the carnival!"

"How long before I'm *whole?*" he asked.

She deliberated that it might pretty well be an entire year.

He groaned. He began to sob and bite his lips and make fists. "You magicked me, you did this, you did this thing to me. Now I won't be able to run home!"

She winked. "But you *can* stay here, child, stay on

with me real comfort-like, and I'll keep you fat and saucy."

He flung it out: "You did this on purpose! You mean old hag, you want to keep me here!"

He ran off through the shrubs on the instant.

"Charlie, come back!"

No answer but the patter of his feet on the soft dark turf, and his wet choking cry which passed swiftly off and away.

She waited and then kindled herself a fire. "He'll be back," she whispered. And thinking inward on herself, she said, "And now I'll have me my company through spring and into late summer. Then, when I'm tired of him and want a silence, I'll send him home."

Charlie returned noiselessly with the first gray of dawn, gliding over the rimed turf to where Old Lady sprawled like a bleached stick before the scattered ashes.

He sat on some creek pebbles and stared at her.

She didn't dare look at him or beyond. He had made no sound, so how could she know he was anywhere about? She couldn't.

He sat there, tear marks on his cheeks.

Pretending to be just waking—but she had found no sleep from one end of the night to the other—Old Lady stood up, grunting and yawning, and turned in a circle to the dawn.

"Charlie?"

Her eyes passed from pines to soil, to sky, to the far hills. She called out his name, over and over again, and she felt like staring plumb straight at him, but she stopped herself. "Charlie? Oh, Charles!" she called, and heard the echoes say the very same.

He sat, beginning to grin a bit, suddenly, knowing he was close to her, yet she must feel alone. Perhaps he felt the growing of a secret power, perhaps he felt secure from the world, certainly he was *pleased* with his invisibility.

She said aloud, "Now where *can* that boy be? If he only made a noise so I could tell just where he is, maybe I'd fry him a breakfast."

She prepared the morning victuals, irritated at his

continuous quiet. She sizzled bacon on a hickory stick. "The smell of it will draw his nose," she muttered.

While her back was turned he swiped all the frying bacon and devoured it tastily.

She whirled, crying out, "Lord!"

She eyed the clearing suspiciously. "Charlie, that *you?*"

Charlie wiped his mouth clean on his wrists.

She trotted about the clearing, making like she was trying to locate him. Finally, with a clever thought, acting blind, she headed straight for him, groping. "Charlie, where *are* you?"

A lightning streak, he evaded her, bobbing, ducking.

It took all her will power not to give chase; but you can't chase invisible boys, so she sat down, scowling, sputtering, and tried to fry more bacon. But every fresh strip she cut he would steal bubbling off the fire and run away far. Finally, cheeks burning, she cried, "I know where you are! Right *there!* I hear you run!" She pointed to one side of him, not too accurate. He ran again. "Now you're there!" she shouted. "There, and there!" pointing to all the places he was in the next five minutes. "I hear you press a grass blade, knock a flower, snap a twig. I got fine shell ears, delicate as roses. They can hear the stars moving!"

Silently he galloped off among the pines, his voice trailing back, "Can't hear me when I'm set on a rock. I'll just *set!*"

All day he sat on an observatory rock in the clear wind, motionless and sucking his tongue.

Old Lady gathered wood in the deep forest, feeling his eyes weaseling on her spine. She wanted to babble: "Oh, I see you, I see you! I was only fooling about invisible boys! You're right there!" But she swallowed her gall and gummed it tight.

The following morning he did the spiteful things. He began leaping from behind trees. He made toad-faces, frog-faces, spider-faces at her, clenching down his lips with his fingers, popping his raw eyes, pushing up his nostrils so you could peer in and see his brain thinking.

Once she dropped her kindling. She pretended it was a blue jay startled her.

He made a motion as if to strangle her.

She trembled a little.

He made another move as if to bang her shins and spit on her cheek.

These motions she bore without a lid-flicker or a mouth-twitch.

He stuck out his tongue, making strange bad noises. He wiggled his loose ears so she wanted to laugh, and finally she did laugh and explained it away quickly by saying, "Sat on a salamander! Whew, how it poked!"

By high noon the whole madness boiled to a terrible peak.

For it was at that exact hour that Charlie came racing down the valley stark boy-naked!

Old Lady nearly fell flat with shock!

"Charlie!" she almost cried.

Charlie raced naked up one side of a hill and naked down the other—naked as day, naked as the moon, raw as the sun and a newborn chick, his feet shimmering and rushing like the wings of a low-skimming hummingbird.

Old Lady's tongue locked in her mouth. What could she say? Charlie, go dress? For *shame? Stop* that? *Could* she? Oh, Charlie, Charlie, God! Could she say that now? *Well?*

Upon the big rock, she witnessed him dancing up and down, naked as the day of his birth, stomping bare feet, smacking his hands on his knees and sucking in and out his white stomach like blowing and deflating a circus balloon.

She shut her eyes tight and prayed.

After three hours of this she pleaded, "Charlie, Charlie, come here! I got something to *tell* you!"

Like a fallen leaf he came, dressed again, praise the Lord.

"Charlie," she said, looking at the pine trees, "I see your right toe. *There* it is."

"You do?" he said.

"Yes," she said very sadly. "There it is like a horny toad on the grass. And there, up there's your left ear hanging on the air like a pink butterfly."

Charlie danced. "I'm forming in, I'm forming in!"

Old Lady nodded. "Here comes your ankle!"

"Gimme *both* my feet!" ordered Charlie.

"You got 'em."

"How about my hands?"

"I see one crawling on your knee like a daddy long-legs."

"How about the other one?"

"It's crawling too."

"I got a body?"

"Shaping up fine."

"I'll need my head to go home, Old Lady."

To go home, she thought wearily. "No!" she said, stubborn and angry. "No, you ain't got no head. No head at all," she cried. She'd leave that to the very last. "No head, no head," she insisted.

"No head?" he wailed.

"Yes, oh my God, yes, yes, you got your blamed head!" she snapped, giving up. "Now, fetch me back my bat with the needle in his eye!"

He flung it at her. "Haaaa-yoooo!" His yelling went all up the valley, and long after he had run toward home she heard his echoes, racing.

Then she plucked up her kindling with a great dry weariness and started back toward her shack, sighing, talking. And Charlie followed her all the way, *really* invisible now, so she couldn't see him, just hear him, like a pine cone dropping or a deep underground stream trickling, or a squirrel clambering a bough; and over the fire at twilight she and Charlie sat, him so invisible, and her feeding him bacon he wouldn't take, so she ate it herself, and then she fixed some magic and fell asleep with Charlie, made out of sticks and rags and pebbles, but still warm and her very own son, slumbering and nice in her shaking mother arms . . . and they talked about golden things in drowsy voices until dawn made the fire slowly, slowly wither out. . . .

COME INTO MY CELLAR

Hugh Fortnum woke to Saturday's commotions, and lay, eyes shut, savoring each in its turn.

Below, bacon in a skillet; Cynthia waking him with fine cookings instead of cries.

Across the hall, Tom *actually* taking a shower.

Far off in the bumble-bee dragon-fly light, whose voice was already cursing the weather, the time, and the tides? Mrs. Goodbody? Yes. That Christian giantess, six feet tall with her shoes off, the gardener extraordinary, the octogenarian-dietitian and town philosopher.

He rose, unhooked the screen, and leaned out to hear her cry:

"There! Take *that!* *This'll* fix you! Hah!"

"Happy Saturday, Mrs. Goodbody!"

The old woman froze in clouds of bug spray pumped from an immense gun.

"Nonsense!" she shouted. "With these fiends and pests to watch for?"

"What kind *this* time?" called Fortnum.

"I don't want to shout it to the jaybirds, but—" she glanced suspiciously around—"what would you say if I told you I was the first line of defense concerning Flying Saucers?"

"Fine," replied Fortnum. "There'll be rockets between the worlds any year now."

"There already *are!*" She pumped, aiming the spray under the hedge. "There! Take that!"

He pulled his head back in from the fresh day, somehow not as high-spirited as his first response had indicated. Poor soul, Mrs. Goodbody. Always the very essence of reason. And now what? Old age?

The doorbell rang.

He grabbed his robe and was half down the stairs when he heard a voice say, "Special Delivery. Fortnum?" and saw Cynthia turn from the front door, a small packet in her hand.

He put his hand out, but she shook her head.

"Special Delivery Air Mail for your son."

Tom was downstairs like a centipede.

"Wow! That must be from the Great Bayou Novelty Greenhouse!"

"I wish I were as excited about ordinary mail," observed Fortnum.

"Ordinary?!" Tom ripped the cord and paper wildly. "Don't you read the back pages of *Popular Mechanics?* Well, here *they* are!"

Everyone peered into the small open box.

"Here," said Fortnum, "*what* are?"

"The Sylvan Glade Jumbo-Giant Guaranteed Growth Raise-Them-in-Your-Cellar-for-Big-Profit Mushrooms!"

"Oh, of course," said Fortnum. "How silly of me."

Cynthia squinted. "Those little teeny bits—?"

" 'Fabulous growth in twenty-four hours,' " Tom quoted from memory. " 'Plant them in your own cellar—' "

Fortnum and wife exchanged glances.

"Well," she admitted, "it's better than frogs and green snakes."

"Sure is!" Tom ran.

"Oh, Tom," said Fortnum, lightly.

Tom paused at the cellar door.

"Tom," said his father. "Next time, fourth-class mail would do fine."

"Heck," said Tom. "They must've made a mistake, thought I was some rich company. Air mail special, who can afford *that?*"

The cellar door slammed.

Fortnum, bemused, scanned the wrapper a moment, then dropped it into the wastebasket. On his way to the kitchen, he opened the cellar door.

Tom was already on his knees, digging with a hand-rake in the dirt of the back part of the cellar.

He felt his wife beside him, breathing softly, looking down into the cool dimness.

"Those *are* mushrooms, I hope. Not . . . toadstools?"

Fortnum laughed. "Happy harvest, farmer!"

Tom glanced up and waved.

Fortnum shut the door, took his wife's arm, and walked her out to the kitchen, feeling fine.

Toward noon, Fortnum was driving toward the nearest market when he saw Roger Willis, a fellow Rotarian, and teacher of biology at the town high school, waving urgently from the sidewalk.

Fortnum pulled his car up and opened the door.

"Hi, Roger, give you a lift?"

Willis responded all too eagerly, jumping in and slamming the door.

"Just the man I want to see. I've put off calling for days. Could you play psychiatrist for five minutes, God help you?"

Fortnum examined his friend for a moment as he drove quietly on.

"God help you, yes. Shoot."

Willis sat back and studied his fingernails. "Let's just drive a moment. There. Okay. Here's what I want to say: something's wrong with the world."

Fortnum laughed easily. "Hasn't there always been?"

"No, no, I mean . . . something strange—something unseen—is happening."

"Mrs. Goodbody," said Fortnum, half to himself, and stopped.

"Mrs. Goodbody?"

"This morning. Gave me a talk on flying saucers."

"No." Willis bit the knuckle of his forefinger nervously. "Nothing like saucers. At least I don't think. Tell me, what is intuition?"

"The conscious recognition of something that's been subconscious for a long time. But don't quote this amateur psychologist!" He laughed again.

"Good, good!" Willis turned, his face lighting. He

readjusted himself in the seat. "That's it! Over a long period, things gather, right? All of a sudden, you have to spit, but you don't remember saliva collecting. Your hands are dirty, but you don't know how they got that way. Dust falls on you every day and you don't feel it. But when you get enough dust collected up, there it is, you see and name it. That's intuition, as far as I'm concerned. Well, what kind of dust has been falling on *me*? A few meteors in the sky at night? Funny weather just before dawn? I don't know. Certain colors, smells, the way the house creaks at three in the morning? Hair prickling on my arms? All I know is, the dust *has* collected. Quite suddenly I *know*."

"Yes," said Fortnum, disquieted. "But what *is* it you know?"

Willis looked at his hands in his lap.

"I'm afraid. I'm not afraid. Then I'm afraid again, in the middle of the day. Doctor's checked me. I'm A-1. No family problems. Joe's a fine boy, a good son. Dorothy? She's remarkable. With her, I'm not afraid of growing old or dying."

"Lucky man."

"But beyond my luck now. Scared stiff, really, for myself, my family; even, right now, for *you*."

"Me?" said Fortnum.

They had stopped now by an empty lot near the market. There was a moment of great stillness, in which Fortnum turned to survey his friend. Willis's voice had suddenly made him cold.

"I'm afraid for everybody," said Willis. "Your friends, mine, and their friends, on out of sight. Pretty silly, eh?"

Willis opened the door, got out, and peered in at Fortnum. Fortnum felt he had to speak.

"Well—what do we *do* about it?"

Willis looked up at the sun burning blind in the great, remote sky.

"Be aware," he said, slowly. "Watch everything for a few days."

"Everything?"

"We don't use half what God gave us, 10 per cent of the time. We ought to hear more, feel more, smell

more, taste more. Maybe there's something wrong with
the way the wind blows these weeds there in the lot.
Maybe it's the sun up on those telephone wires or the
cicadas singing in the elm trees. If only we could stop,
look, listen, a few days, a few nights, and compare
notes. Tell me to shut up then, and I will."

"Good enough," said Fortnum, playing it lighter
than he felt. "I'll look around. But how do I know the
thing I'm looking for when I *see* it?"

Willis peered in at him sincerely. "You'll know.
You've got to know. Or we're done for, all of us," he
said quietly.

Fortnum shut the door, and didn't know what to
say. He felt a flush of embarrassment creeping up his
face. Willis sensed this.

"Hugh, do you think I'm—off my rocker?"

"Nonsense!" said Fortnum, too quickly. "You're just
nervous, is all. You should take a couple of weeks off."

Willis nodded. "See you Monday night?"

"Any time. Drop around."

"I hope I will, Hugh. I really hope I will."

Then Willis was gone, hurrying across the dry
weed-grown lot, toward the side entrance of the market.

Watching him go, Fortnum suddenly did not want to
move. He discovered that very slowly he was taking
deep breaths, weighing the silence. He licked his lips,
tasting the salt. He looked at his arm on the doorsill,
the sunlight burning the golden hairs. In the empty lot
the wind moved all alone to itself. He leaned out to
look at the sun, which stared back with one massive
stunning blow of intense power that made him jerk his
head in.

He exhaled. Then he laughed out loud. Then he
drove away.

The lemonade glass was cool and deliciously sweaty.
The ice made music inside the glass, and the lemonade
was just sour enough, just sweet enough on his tongue.
He sipped, he savored, he tilted back in the wicker
rocking chair on the twilight front porch, his eyes
closed. The crickets were chirping out on the lawn.
Cynthia, knitting across from him on the porch, eyed

him curiously. He could feel the pressure of her attention.

"What are you up to?" she said at last.

"Cynthia," he said, "is your intuition in running order? Is this earthquake weather? Is the land going to sink? Will war be declared? Or is it only that our delphinium will die of the blight?"

"Hold on. Let me feel my bones."

He opened his eyes and watched Cynthia in turn closing hers and sitting absolutely statue-still, her hands on her knees. Finally she shook her head and smiled.

"No. No war declared. No land sinking. Not even a blight. Why?"

"I've met a lot of Doom Talkers today. Well, two, anyway, and—"

The screen door burst wide. Fortnum's body jerked as if he had been struck. "What!"

Tom, a gardener's wooden flat in his arms, stepped out on the porch.

"Sorry," he said. "What's wrong, Dad?"

"Nothing," Fortnum stood up, glad to be moving. "Is that the crop?"

Tom moved forward, eagerly. "Part of it. Boy, they're doing great. In just seven hours, with lots of water, look how big the darn things are!" He set the flat on the table between his parents.

The crop was indeed plentiful. Hundreds of small grayish brown mushrooms were sprouting up in the damp soil.

"I'll be...." said Fortnum, impressed.

Cynthia put out her hand to touch the flat, then took it away uneasily.

"I hate to be a spoilsport, but ... there's no way for these to be anything else but mushrooms, is there?"

Tom looked as if he had been insulted. "What do you think I'm going to feed you? Poison fungoids?"

"That's just it," said Cynthia quickly. "How do you tell them apart?"

"Eat 'em," said Tom. "If you live, they're mushrooms. If you drop dead—*well!*"

He gave a great guffaw, which amused Fortnum, but only made his mother wince. She sat back in her chair.

"I—I don't like them," she said.

"Boy, oh, boy." Tom seized the flat angrily. "When are we going to have the next Wet Blanket Sale in *this* house!?"

He shuffled morosely away.

"Tom—" said Fortnum.

"Never mind," said Tom. "Everyone figures they'll be ruined by the boy entrepreneur. To heck with it!"

Fortnum got inside just as Tom heaved the mushrooms, flat and all, down the cellar stairs. He slammed the cellar door and ran angrily out the back door.

Fortnum turned back to his wife, who, stricken, glanced away.

"I'm sorry," she said. "I don't know why, I just *had* to say that to Tom."

The phone rang. Fortnum brought the phone outside on its extension cord.

"Hugh?" It was Dorothy Willis's voice. She sounded suddenly very old and very frightened. "Hugh . . . Roger isn't there, is he?"

"Dorothy? No."

"He's gone!" said Dorothy. "All his clothes were taken from the closet." She began to cry softly.

"Dorothy, hold on, I'll be there in a minute."

"You must help, oh, you must. Something's happened to him, I know it," she wailed. "Unless you do something, we'll never see him alive again."

Very slowly, he put the receiver back on its hook, her voice weeping inside it. The night crickets, quite suddenly, were very loud. He felt the hairs, one by one, go up on the back of his neck.

Hair can't do that, he thought. Silly, silly. It can't do that, not in *real* life, it can't!

But, one by slow pricking one, his hair did.

The wire hangers were indeed empty. With a clatter, Fortnum shoved them aside and down along the rod, then turned and looked out of the closet at Dorothy Willis and her son Joe.

"I was just walking by," said Joe, "and saw the closet empty, all Dad's clothes gone!"

"Everything was fine," said Dorothy. "We've had a wonderful life. I don't understand it, I don't, I don't!" She began to cry again, putting her hands to her face.

Fortnum stepped out of the closet.

"You didn't hear him leave the house?"

"We were playing catch out front," said Joe. "Dad said he had to go in for a minute. I went around back. Then—he was gone!"

"He must have packed quickly and walked wherever he was going, so we wouldn't hear a cab pull up front of the house."

They were moving out through the hall now.

"I'll check the train depot and the airport." Fortnum hesitated. "Dorothy, is there anything in Roger's background—"

"It wasn't insanity took him." She hesitated. "I feel—somehow—he was kidnapped."

Fortnum shook his head. "It doesn't seem reasonable he would arrange to pack, walk out of the house, and go meet his abductors."

Dorothy opened the door as if to let the night or the night wind move down the hall as she turned to stare back through the rooms, her voice wandering.

"No. Somehow they came into the house. Right in front of us, they stole him away."

And then:

" . . . a terrible thing has happened."

Fortnum stepped out into the night of crickets and rustling trees. The Doom Talkers, he thought, talking their Dooms. Mrs. Goodbody. Roger. And now Roger's wife. Something terrible *has* happened. But *what,* in God's name? And *how?*

He looked from Dorothy to her son. Joe, blinking the wetness from his eyes, took a long time to turn, walk along the hall, and stop, fingering the knob of the cellar door.

Fortnum felt his eyelids twitch, his iris flex, as if he were snapping a picture of something he wanted to remember.

Joe pulled the cellar door wide, stepped down out of sight, gone. The door tapped shut.

Fortnum opened his mouth to speak, but Dorothy's hand was taking his now, he had to look at her.

"Please," she said. "Find him for me."

He kissed her cheek. "If it's humanly possible . . ."

If it's humanly possible. Good Lord, why had he picked those words?

He walked off into the summer night.

A gasp, an exhalation, a gasp, an exhalation, an asthmatic insuck, a vaporing sneeze. Someone dying in the dark? No.

Just Mrs. Goodbody, unseen beyond the hedge, working late, her hand pump aimed, her bony elbow thrusting. The sick-sweet smell of bug spray enveloped Fortnum heavily as he reached his house.

"Mrs. Goodbody? Still at it?!"

From the black hedge, her voice leapt:

"Blast it, yes! Aphids, waterbugs, woodworms, and now the *marasmius oreades*. Lord, it grows fast!"

"What does?"

"The *marasmius oreades*, of course! It's me against them, and I intend to win. There! There! There!"

He left the hedge, the gasping pump, the wheezing voice, and found his wife waiting for him on the porch almost as if she were going to take up where Dorothy had left off at her door a few minutes ago.

Fortnum was about to speak, when a shadow moved inside. There was a creaking noise. A knob rattled.

Tom vanished into the basement.

Fortnum felt as if someone had set off an explosion in his face. He reeled. Everything had the numbed familiarity of those waking dreams where all motions are remembered before they occur, all dialogue known before it fell from the lips.

He found himself staring at the shut basement door. Cynthia took him inside, amused.

"What? Tom? Oh, I relented. The darn mushrooms meant so much to him. Besides, when he threw them into the cellar, they did nicely, just lying in the dirt."

"Did they?" Fortnum heard himself say.

Cynthia took his arm. "What about Roger?"

"He's gone, yes."

"Men, men, men," she said.

"No, you're wrong," he said. "I saw Roger every day for the last ten years. When you know a man that well, you can tell how things are at home, whether things are in the oven or the mixmaster. Death hadn't breathed down his neck yet. He wasn't running scared after his immortal youth, picking peaches in someone else's orchards. No, no, I swear, I'd bet my last dollar on it, Roger—"

The doorbell rang behind him. The delivery boy had come up quietly onto the porch and was standing there with a telegram in his hand.

"Fortnum?"

Cynthia snapped on the hall light as he ripped the envelope open and smoothed it out for reading.

"TRAVELING NEW ORLEANS. THIS TELE-GRAM POSSIBLE OFF-GUARD MOMENT. YOU MUST REFUSE, REPEAT REFUSE, ALL SPE-CIAL DELIVERY PACKAGES! ROGER."

Cynthia glanced up from the paper.

"I don't understand. What does he mean?"

But Fortnum was already at the telephone, dialing swiftly, once. "Operator? The police, and hurry!"

At ten-fifteen that night, the phone rang for the sixth time during the evening. Fortnum got it, and immediately gasped. "Roger! Where are you?"

"Where am I?" said Roger lightly, almost amused. "You know very well where I am. You're responsible for this. I should be angry!"

Cynthia, at his nod, had hurried to take the extension phone in the kitchen. When he heard the soft click, he went on.

"Roger, I swear I don't know. I got that telegram from you—"

"What telegram?" said Roger, jovially. "I sent no telegram. Now, of a sudden, the police come pouring onto the southbound train, pull me off in some jerk-water, and I'm calling you to get them off my neck. Hugh, if this is some joke—"

"But, Roger, you just vanished!"

"On a business trip. If you can call that vanishing. I told Dorothy about this, and Joe."

"This is all very confusing, Roger. You're in no danger? Nobody's blackmailing you, forcing you into this speech?"

"I'm fine, healthy, free, and unafraid."

"But, Roger, your premonitions . . . ?"

"Poppycock! Now, look, I'm being very good about this, aren't I?"

"Sure, Roger."

"Then play the good father and give me permission to go. Call Dorothy and tell her I'll be back in five days. How *could* she have forgotten?"

"She did, Roger. See you in five days, then?"

"Five days, I swear."

The voice was indeed winning and warm, the old Roger again. Fortnum shook his head, more bewildered than before.

"Roger," he said, "this is the craziest day I've ever spent. You're not running off from Dorothy? Good Lord, you can tell *me*."

"I love her with all my heart. Now, here's Lieutenant Parker of the Ridgetown police. Good-by, Hugh."

"Good—"

But the lieutenant was on the line, talking angrily. What had Fortnum meant putting them to this trouble? What was going on? Who did he think he was? Did or didn't he want this so-called friend held or released?

"Released," Fortnum managed to say somewhere along the way, and hung up the phone and imagined he heard a voice call all aboard and the massive thunder of the train leaving the station two hundred miles south in the somehow increasingly dark night.

Cynthia walked very slowly into the parlor.

"I feel so foolish," she said.

"How do you think I feel?"

"Who could have sent that telegram? And why?"

He poured himself some Scotch and stood in the middle of the room looking at it.

"I'm glad Roger is all right," his wife said, at last.

"He isn't," said Fortnum.

"But you just said—"

"I said nothing. After all, we couldn't very well drag him off that train and truss him up and send him home, could we, if he insisted he was okay? No. He sent that telegram, but he changed his mind after sending it. Why, why, why?" Fortnum paced the room, sipping the drink. "Why warn us against special delivery packages? The only package we've got this *year* which fits that description is the one Tom got this morning—" His voice trailed off.

Before he could move, Cynthia was at the wastepaper basket taking out the crumpled wrapping paper with the special-delivery stamps on it.

The postmark read: NEW ORLEANS, LA.

Cynthia looked up from it. "New Orleans. Isn't that where Roger is heading right *now?*"

A doorknob rattled, a door opened and closed in Fortnum's mind. Another doorknob rattled, another door swung wide and then shut. There was a smell of damp earth.

He found his hand dialing the phone. After a long while, Dorothy Willis answered at the other end. He could imagine her sitting alone in a house with too many lights on. He talked quietly with her awhile, then cleared his throat and said, "Dorothy, look. I know it sounds silly. Did any special delivery air mail packages arrive at your house the last few days?"

Her voice was faint. "No." Then: "No, wait. Three days ago. But I thought you *knew!* All the boys on the block are going in for it."

Fortnum measured his words carefully.

"Going in for what?"

"But why ask?" she said. "There's nothing wrong with raising mushrooms, is there?"

Fortnum closed his eyes.

"Hugh? Are you still there?" asked Dorothy. "I said: there's nothing wrong with—"

"—raising mushrooms?" said Fortnum, at last. "No. Nothing wrong. Nothing wrong."

And slowly he put down the phone.

The curtains blew like veils of moonlight. The clock

ticked. The after-midnight world flowed into and filled
the bedroom. He heard Mrs. Goodbody's clear voice on
this morning's air, a million years gone now. He heard
Roger putting a cloud over the sun at noon. He heard
the police cursing him by phone from downstate. Then
Roger's voice again, with the locomotive thunder hurrying him away and away, fading. And finally, Mrs.
Goodbody's voice behind the hedge:

"Lord, it grows fast!"

"What does?"

"*Marasmius oreades!*"

He snapped his eyes open. He sat up.

Downstairs, a moment later, he flicked through the
unabridged dictionary.

His forefinger underlined the words:

"*Marasmius oreades*: a mushroom commonly found
on lawns in summer and early autumn."

He let the book fall shut.

Outside, in the deep summer night, he lit a cigarette
and smoked quietly.

A meteor fell across space, burning itself out quickly. The trees rustled softly.

The front door tapped shut.

Cynthia moved toward him in her robe.

"Can't sleep?"

"Too warm, I guess."

"It's not warm."

"No," he said, feeling his arms. "In fact, it's cold."
He sucked on the cigarette twice, then, not looking at
her, said, "Cynthia . . . What if. . . ?" He snorted and
had to stop. "Well, what if Roger was right this morning? Mrs. Goodbody, what if she's right, too? Something terrible *is* happening. Like—well—" he nodded
at the sky and the million stars—"Earth being invaded
by things from other worlds, maybe."

"Hugh!"

"No, let me run wild."

"It's quite obvious we're not being invaded or we'd
notice."

"Let's say we've only half-noticed, become uneasy

about something. What? How could we be invaded? By what means would creatures invade?"

Cynthia looked at the sky and was about to try something when he interrupted.

"No, not meteors or flying saucers. Not things we can see. What about bacteria? That comes from outer space, too, doesn't it?"

"I read once, yes—"

"Spores, seeds, pollens, viruses probably bombard our atmosphere by the billions every second and have done so for millions of years. Right now we're sitting out under an invisible rain. It falls all over the country, the cities, the towns, and right now . . . our lawn."

"*Our* lawn?"

"*And* Mrs. Goodbody's But people like her are always pulling weeds, spraying poison, kicking toadstools off their grass. It would be hard for any strange life form to survive in cities. Weather's a problem, too. Best climate might be South: Alabama, Georgia, Louisiana. Back in the damp bayous, they could grow to a fine size."

But Cynthia was beginning to laugh now.

"Oh, really, you don't believe, do you, that this Great Bayou or whatever Greenhouse Novelty Company that sent Tom his package is owned and operated by six-foot-tall mushrooms from another planet?"

"If you put it that way, it sounds funny," he admitted.

"Funny! It's hilarious!" She threw her head back deliciously.

"Good grief!" he cried, suddenly irritated. "*Something's* going on! Mrs. Goodbody is rooting out and killing *marasmius oreades*. What is *marasmius oreades*? A certain kind of mushroom. Simultaneously, and I suppose you'll call it coincidence, by special delivery, what arrives the same day? Mushrooms for Tom! What else happens? Roger fears he may soon cease to be! Within hours, he vanishes, then telegraphs us, warning us not to accept what? The special delivery mushrooms for Tom! Has Roger's son got a similar package in the last few days? He has! Where do the packages come from? New Orleans! And where is Roger going when he vanishes? New Orleans! Do you see, Cynthia, do you see? I wouldn't be upset if all these separate things didn't lock together! Roger, Tom, Joe, mushrooms, Mrs. Goodbody, packages, destinations, everything in one pattern!"

She was watching his face now, quieter, but still amused. "Don't get angry."

"I'm not!" Fortnum almost shouted. And then he simply could not go on. He was afraid that if he did, he would find himself shouting with laughter, too, and somehow he did not want that. He stared at the surrounding houses up and down the block and thought of the dark cellars and the neighbor boys who read *Popular Mechanics* and sent their money in by the millions to raise the mushrooms hidden away. Just as he, when a boy, had mailed off for chemicals, seeds, turtles, numberless salves and sickish ointments. In how many million American homes tonight were billions of mushrooms rousing up under the ministrations of the innocent?

"Hugh?" His wife was touching his arm now. "Mushrooms, even big ones, can't think. They can't move. They don't have arms and legs. How could they run a mail-order service and 'take over' the world? Come on, now. Let's look at your terrible fiends and monsters!"

She pulled him toward the door. Inside, she headed for the cellar, but he stopped, shaking his head, a foolish smile shaping itself somehow to his mouth. "No, no, I know what we'll find. You win. The whole thing's silly. Roger will be back next week and we'll all get drunk together. Go on up to bed now and I'll drink a glass of warm milk and be with you in a minute . . . well, a couple of minutes . . ."

"That's better!" She kissed him on both cheeks, squeezed him, and went away up the stairs.

In the kitchen, he took out a glass, opened the refrigerator, and was pouring the milk when he stopped suddenly.

Near the front of the top shelf was a small yellow

dish. It was not the dish that held his attention, however. It was what lay in the dish.

The fresh-cut mushrooms.

He must have stood there for half a minute, his breath frosting the refrigerated air, before he reached out, took hold of the dish, sniffed it, felt the mushrooms, then at last, carrying the dish, went out into the hall. He looked up the stairs, hearing Cynthia moving about in the bedroom, and was about to call up to her, "Cynthia, did you put *these* in the refrigerator!?"

Then he stopped. He knew her answer. She had not.

He put the dish of mushrooms on the newel at the bottom of the stairs and stood looking at them. He imagined himself, in bed later, looking at the walls, the open windows, watching the moonlight sift patterns on the ceiling. He heard himself saying, Cynthia? And her answering, yes? And him saying, there *is* a way for mushrooms to grow arms and legs . . . What? she would say, silly, silly man, what? And he would gather courage against her hilarious reaction and go on, what if a man wandered through the swamp, picked the mushrooms, and *ate* them. . . ?

No response from Cynthia.

Once inside the man, would the mushrooms spread through his blood, take over every cell, and change the man from a man to a—Martian? Given this theory, would the mushroom *need* its own arms and legs? No, not when it could borrow people, live inside and become them. Roger ate mushrooms given him by his son. Roger became "something else." He kidnaped himself. And in one last flash of sanity, of being "himself," he telegraphed us, warning us not to accept the special delivery mushrooms. The "Roger" that telephoned later was no longer Roger but a captive of what he had eaten! Doesn't that figure, Cynthia? Doesn't it, doesn't it?

No, said the imagined Cynthia, no, it doesn't figure, no, no, no . . .

There was the faintest whisper, rustle, stir from the

cellar. Taking his eyes from the bowl, Fortnum walked to the cellar door and put his ear to it.

"Tom?"

No answer.

"Tom, are you down there?"

No answer.

"Tom?"

After a long while, Tom's voice came up from below.

"Yes, Dad?"

"It's after midnight," said Fortnum, fighting to keep his voice from going high. "What are you doing down there?"

No answer.

"I said—"

"Tending to my crop," said the boy at last, his voice cold and faint.

"Well, get up out of there! You hear me?!"

Silence.

"Tom? Listen! Did you put some mushrooms in the refrigerator tonight? If so, why?"

Ten seconds must have ticked by before the boy replied from below. "For you and Mom to eat, of course."

Fortnum heard his heart moving swiftly, and had to take three deep breaths before he could go on.

"Tom? You didn't . . . that is . . . you haven't by any chance eaten some of the mushrooms yourself, have you?"

"Funny you ask that," said Tom. "Yes. Tonight. On a sandwich after supper. Why?"

Fortnum held to the doorknob. Now it was his turn not to answer. He felt his knees beginning to melt and he fought the whole silly senseless fool thing. No reason, he tried to say, but his lips wouldn't move.

"Dad?" called Tom softly from the cellar. "Come on down." Another pause. "I want you to see the harvest."

Fortnum felt the knob slip in his sweaty hand. The knob rattled. He gasped.

"Dad?" called Tom softly.

Fortnum opened the door.

The cellar was completely black below.

He stretched his hand in toward the light switch. As if sensing this intrusion, from somewhere Tom said:

"Don't. Light's bad for the mushrooms."

Fortnum took his hand off the switch.

He swallowed. He looked back at the stair leading up to his wife. I suppose, he thought, I should go say good-by to Cynthia. But why should I think that! Why should I think that at *all*? No reason, is there?

None.

"Tom?" he said, affecting a jaunty air. "Ready or not, here I come!"

And stepping down in darkness, he shut the door.

THE MILLION-YEAR PICNIC

Somehow the idea was brought up by Mom that perhaps the whole family would enjoy a fishing trip. But
they weren't Mom's words; Timothy knew that. They
were Dad's words, and Mom used them for him somehow.

Dad shuffled his feet in a clutter of Martian pebbles
and agreed. So immediately there was a tumult and a
shouting, and very quickly the camp was tucked into
capsules and containers, Mom slipped into traveling
jumpers and blouse, Dad stuffed his pipe full with
trembling hands, his eyes on the Martian sky, and the
three boys piled yelling into the motorboat, none of
them really keeping an eye on Mom and Dad, except
Timothy.

Dad pushed a stud. The water boat sent a humming
sound up into the sky. The water shook back and the
boat nosed ahead, and the family cried, "Hurrah!"

Timothy sat in the back of the boat with Dad, his
small fingers atop Dad's hairy ones, watching the canal
twist, leaving the crumbled place behind where they
had landed in their small family rocket all the way
from Earth. He remembered the night before they left
Earth, the hustling and hurrying, the rocket that Dad
had found somewhere, somehow, and the talk of a
vacation on Mars. A long way to go for a vacation, but
Timothy said nothing because of his younger brothers.
They came to Mars and now, first thing, or so they
said, they were going fishing.

Dad had a funny look in his eyes as the boat went
up-canal. A look that Timothy couldn't figure. It was

made of strong light and maybe a sort of relief. It made the deep wrinkles laugh instead of worry or cry.

So there went the cooling rocket, around a bend, gone.

"How far are we going?" Robert splashed his hand. It looked like a small crab jumping in the violet water.

Dad exhaled. "A million years."

"Gee," said Robert.

"Look, kids." Mother pointed one soft long arm. "There's a dead city."

They looked with fervent anticipation, and the dead city lay dead for them alone, drowsing in a hot silence of summer made on Mars by a Martian weatherman.

And Dad looked as if he was pleased that it was dead.

It was a futile spread of pink rocks sleeping on a rise of sand, a few tumbled pillars, one lonely shrine, and then the sweep of sand again. Nothing else for miles. A white desert around the canal and a blue desert over it.

Just then a bird flew up. Like a stone thrown across a blue pond, hitting, falling deep, and vanishing.

Dad got a frightened look when he saw it. "I thought it was a rocket."

Timothy looked at the deep ocean sky, trying to see Earth and the war and the ruined cities and the men killing each other since the day he was born. But he saw nothing. The war was as removed and far off as two flies battling to the death in the arch of a great high and silent cathedral. And just as senseless.

William Thomas wiped his forehead and felt the touch of his son's hand on his arm, like a young tarantula, thrilled. He beamed at his son. "How goes it, Timmy?"

"Fine, Dad."

Timothy hadn't quite figured out what was ticking inside the vast adult mechanism beside him. The man with the immense hawk nose, sunburned, peeling—and the hot blue eyes like agate marbles you play with after school in summer back on Earth, and the long thick columnar legs in the loose riding breeches.

"What are you looking at so hard, Dad?"

"I was looking for Earthian logic, common sense, good government, peace, and responsibility."

"All that up there?"

"No. I didn't find it. It's not there any more. Maybe it'll never be there again. Maybe we fooled ourselves that it was ever there."

"Huh?"

"See the fish," said Dad, pointing.

There rose a soprano clamor from all three boys as they rocked the boat in arching their tender necks to see. They *oohed* and *aahed*. A silver ring fish floated by them, undulating, and closing like an iris, instantly, around food particles, to assimilate them.

Dad looked at it. His voice was deep and quiet.

"Just like war. War swims along, sees food, contracts. A moment later—Earth is gone."

"William," said Mom.

"Sorry," said Dad.

They sat still and felt the canal water rush, cool, swift, and glassy. The only sound was the motor hum, the glide of water, the sun expanding the air.

"When do we see the Martians?" cried Michael.

"Quite soon, perhaps," said Father. "Maybe tonight."

"Oh, but the Martians are a dead race now," said Mom.

"No, they're not. I'll show you some Martians, all right," Dad said presently.

Timothy scowled at that but said nothing. Everything was odd now. Vacations and fishing and looks between people.

The other boys were already engaged making shelves of their small hands and peering under them toward the seven-foot stone banks of the canal, watching for Martians.

"What do they look like?" demanded Michael.

"You'll know them when you see them." Dad sort of laughed, and Timothy saw a pulse beating time in his cheek.

Mother was slender and soft, with a woven plait of spun-gold hair over her head in a tiara, and eyes the

color of the deep cool canal water where it ran in
shadow, almost purple, with flecks of amber caught in
it. You could see her thoughts swimming around in her
eyes, like fish—some bright, some dark, some fast,
quick, some slow and easy, and sometimes, like when
she looked up where Earth was, being nothing but color
and nothing else. She sat in the boat's prow, one hand
resting on the side lip, the other on the lap of her dark
blue breeches, and a line of sun-burned soft neck
showing where her blouse opened like a white flower.

She kept looking ahead to see what was there, and,
not being able to see it clearly enough, she looked
backward toward her husband, and through his eyes,
reflected then, she saw what was ahead; and since he
added part of himself to this reflection, a determined
firmness, her face relaxed and she accepted it and she
turned back, knowing suddenly what to look for.

Timothy looked too. But all he saw was a straight
pencil line of canal going violet through a wide shallow
valley penned by low, eroded hills, and on until it fell
over the sky's edge. And this canal went on and on,
through cities that would have rattled like beetles in a
dry skull if you shook them. A hundred or two hundred cities dreaming hot summer-day dreams and cool
summer-night dreams . . .

They had come millions of miles for this outing—to
fish. But there had been a gun on the rocket. This was
a vacation. But why all the food, more than enough to
last them years and years, left hidden back there near
the rocket? Vacation. Just behind the veil of the vacation was not a soft face of laughter, but something hard
and bony and perhaps terrifying. Timothy could not lift
the veil, and the two other boys were busy being ten
and eight years old, respectively.

"No Martians yet. Nuts." Robert put his V-shaped
chin on his hands and glared at the canal.

Dad had brought an atomic radio along, strapped to
his wrist. It functioned on an old-fashioned principle:
you held it against the bones near your ear and it
vibrated singing or talking to you. Dad listened to it
now. His face looked like one of those fallen Martian
cities, caved in, sucked dry, almost dead.

Then he gave it to Mom to listen. Her lips dropped open.

"What——" Timothy started to question, but never finished what he wished to say.

For at that moment there were two titanic, marrow-jolting explosions that grew upon themselves, followed by a half-dozen minor concussions.

Jerking his head up, Dad notched the boat speed higher immediately. The boat leaped and jounced and spanked. This shook Robert out of his funk and elicited yelps of frightened but ecstatic joy from Michael, who clung to Mom's legs and watched the water pour by his nose in a wet torrent.

Dad swerved the boat, cut speed, and ducked the craft into a little branch canal and under an ancient, crumbling stone wharf that smelled of crab flesh. The boat rammed the wharf hard enough to throw them all forward, but no one was hurt, and Dad was already twisted to see if the ripples on the canal were enough to map their route into hiding. Water lines went across, lapped the stones, and rippled back to meet each other, settling, to be dappled by the sun. It all went away.

Dad listened. So did everybody.

Dad's breathing echoed like fists beating against the cold wet wharf stones. In the shadow, Mom's cat eyes just watched Father for some clue to what next.

Dad relaxed and blew out a breath, laughing at himself.

"The rocket, of course. I'm getting jumpy. The rocket."

Michael said, "What happened, Dad, what happened?"

"Oh, we just blew up our rocket, is all," said Timothy, trying to sound matter-of-fact. "I've heard rockets blown up before. Ours just blew."

"Why did we blow up our rocket?" asked Michael. Huh, Dad?"

"It's part of the game, silly!" said Timothy.

"A game!" Michael and Robert loved the word.

"Dad fixed it so it would blow up and no one'd know where we landed or went! In case they ever came looking, see?"

"Oh boy, a secret!"

"Scared by my own rocket," admitted Dad to Mom. "I *am* nervous. It's silly to think there'll ever be any more rockets. Except *one,* perhaps, if Edwards and his wife get through with *their* ship."

He put his tiny radio to his ear again. After two minutes he dropped his hand as you would drop a rag.

"It's over at last," he said to Mom. "The radio just went off the atomic beam. Every other world station's gone. They dwindled down to a couple in the last few years. Now the air's completely silent. It'll probably remain silent."

"For how long?" asked Robert.

"Maybe—your great-grandchildren will hear it again," said Dad. He just sat there, and the children were caught in the center of his awe and defeat and resignation and acceptance.

Finally he put the boat out into the canal again, and they continued in the direction in which they had originally started.

It was getting late. Already the sun was down the sky, and a series of dead cities lay ahead of them.

Dad talked very quietly and gently to his sons. Many times in the past he had been brisk, distant, removed from them, but now he patted them on the head with just a word and they felt it.

"Mike, pick a city."

"What, Dad?"

"Pick a city, Son. Any one of these cities we pass."

"All right," said Michael. "How do I pick?"

"Pick the one you like the most. You, too, Robert and Tim. Pick the city you like best."

"I want a city with Martians in it," said Michael.

"You'll have that," said Dad. "I promise." His lips were for the children, but his eyes were for Mom.

They passed six cities in twenty minutes. Dad didn't say anything more about the explosions; he seemed much more interested in having fun with his sons, keeping them happy, than anything else.

Michael liked the first city they passed, but this was vetoed because everyone doubted quick first judgments. The second city nobody liked. It was an Earth man's settlement, built of wood and already rotting into saw-dust. Timothy liked the third city because it was large. The fourth and fifth were too small and the sixth brought acclaim from everyone, including Mother, who joined in the Gees, Goshes, and Look-at-thats!

There were fifty or sixty huge structures still standing, streets were dusty but paved, and you could see one or two old centrifugal fountains still pulsing wetly in the plazas. That was the only life—water leaping in the late sunlight.

"This is the city," said everybody.

Steering the boat to a wharf, Dad jumped out.

"Here we are. This is ours. This is where we live from now on!"

"From now on?" Michael was incredulous. He stood up, looking, and then turned to blink back at where the rocket used to be. "What about the rocket? What about Minnesota?"

"Here," said Dad.

He touched the small radio to Michael's blond head. "Listen."

Michael listened.

"Nothing," he said.

"That's right. Nothing. Nothing at all any more. No more Minneapolis, no more rockets, no more Earth."

Michael considered the lethal revelation and began to sob little dry sobs.

"Wait a moment," said Dad the next instant. "I'm giving you a lot more in exchange, Mike!"

"What?" Michael held off the tears, curious, but quite ready to continue in case Dad's further revelation was as disconcerting as the original.

"I'm giving you this city, Mike. It's yours."

"Mine?"

"For you and Robert and Timothy, all three of you, to own for yourselves."

Timothy bounded from the boat. "Look, guys, all for *us!* All of *that!*" He was playing the game with Dad, playing it large and playing it well. Later, after it was all over and things had settled, he could go off by himself and cry for ten minutes. But now it was still a game, still a family outing, and the other kids must be kept playing.

Mike jumped out with Robert. They helped Mom.

"Be careful of your sister," said Dad, and nobody knew what he meant until later.

They hurried into the great pink-stoned city, whispering among themselves, because dead cities have a way of making you want to whisper, to watch the sun go down.

"In about five days," said Dad quietly, "I'll go back down to where our rocket was and collect the food hidden in the ruins there and bring it here; and I'll hunt for Bert Edwards and his wife and daughters there."

"Daughters?" asked Timothy. "How many?"

"Four."

"I can see that'll cause trouble later." Mom nodded slowly.

"Girls." Michael made a face like an ancient Martian stone image. "Girls."

"Are they coming in a rocket too?"

"Yes. If they make it. Family rockets are made for travel to the Moon, not Mars. We were lucky we got through."

"Where did you get the rocket?" whispered Timothy, for the other boys were running ahead.

"I saved it. I saved it for twenty years, Tim. I had it hidden away, hoping I'd never have to use it. I suppose I should have given it to the government for the war, but I kept thinking about Mars. . . ."

"And a picnic!"

"Right. This is between you and me. When I saw everything was finishing on Earth, after I'd waited until the last moment, I packed us up. Bert Edwards had a ship hidden, too, but we decided it would be safer to take off separately, in case anyone tried to shoot us down."

"Why'd you blow up the rocket, Dad?"

"So we can't go back, ever. And so if any of those evil men ever come to Mars they won't know we're here."

"Is that why you look up all the time?"

"Yes, it's silly. They won't follow us, ever. They haven't anything to follow with. I'm being too careful, is all."

Michael came running back. "Is this really *our* city, Dad?"

"The whole darn planet belongs to us, kids. The whole darn planet."

They stood there, King of the Hill, Top of the Heap, Ruler of All They Surveyed, Unimpeachable Monarchs and Presidents, trying to understand what it meant to own a world and how big a world really was.

Night came quickly in the thin atmosphere, and Dad left them in the square by the pulsing fountain, went down to the boat, and came walking back carrying a stack of paper in his big hands.

He laid the papers in a clutter in an old courtyard and set them afire. To keep warm, they crouched around the blaze and laughed, and Timothy saw the little letters leap like frightened animals when the flames touched and engulfed them. The papers crinkled like an old man's skin, and the cremation surrounded innumerable words:

"GOVERNMENT BONDS; Business Graph, 1999; Religious Prejudice: An Essay; The Science of Logistics; Problems of the Pan-American Unity; Stock Report for July 3, 1998; The War Digest . . ."

Dad had insisted on bringing these papers for this purpose. He sat there and fed them into the fire, one by one, with satisfaction, and told his children what it all meant.

"It's time I told you a few things. I don't suppose it was fair, keeping so much from you. I don't know if you'll understand, but I have to talk, even if only part of it gets over to you."

He dropped a leaf in the fire.

"I'm burning a way of life, just like that way of life is being burned clean of Earth right now. Forgive me if I talk like a politician. I am, after all, a former state governor, and I was honest and they hated me for it. Life on Earth never settled down to doing anything very good. Science ran too far ahead of us too quickly, and the people got lost in a mechanical wilderness, like children making over pretty things, gadgets, helicopters, rockets; emphasizing the wrong items, emphasizing machines instead of how to run the machines. Wars got bigger and bigger and finally killed Earth. That's what the silent radio means. That's what we ran away from.

"We were lucky. There aren't any more rockets left. It's time you knew this isn't a fishing trip at all. I put off telling you. Earth is gone. Interplanetary travel won't be back for centuries, maybe never. But that way of life proved itself wrong and strangled itself with its own hands. You're young. I'll tell you this again every day until it sinks in."

He paused to feed more papers to the fire.

"Now we're alone. We and a handful of others who'll land in a few days. Enough to start over. Enough to turn away from all that back on Earth and strike out on a new line——"

The fire leaped up to emphasize his talking. And then all the papers were gone except one. All the laws and beliefs of Earth were burnt into small hot ashes which soon would be carried off in a wind.

Timothy looked at the last thing that Dad tossed in the fire. It was a map of the World, and it wrinkled and distorted itself hotly and went—flimpf—and was gone like a warm, black butterfly. Timothy turned away.

Now I'm going to show you the Martians," said Dad. "Come on, all of you. Here, Alice." He took her hand.

Michael was crying loudly, and Dad picked him up and carried him, and they walked down through the ruins toward the canal.

The canal. Where tomorrow or the next day their future wives would come up in a boat, small laughing girls now, with their father and mother.

The night came down around them, and there were stars. But Timothy couldn't find Earth. It had already set. That was something to think about.

A night bird called among the ruins as they walked. Dad said, "Your mother and I will try to teach you. Perhaps we'll fail. I hope not. We've had a good lot to see and learn from. We planned this trip years ago, before you were born. Even if there hadn't been a war

we would have come to Mars, I think, to live and form
our own standard of living. It would have been another
century before Mars would have been really poisoned
by the Earth civilization. Now, of course—"

They reached the canal. It was long and straight and
cool and wet and reflective in the night.

"I've always wanted to see a Martian," said Michael.
"Where are they, Dad? You promised."

"There they are," said Dad, and he shifted Michael
on his shoulder and pointed straight down.

The Martians were there. Timothy began to shiver.

The Martians were there—in the canal—reflected in
the water. Timothy and Michael and Robert and Mom
and Dad.

The Martians stared back up at them for a long, long
silent time from the rippling water. . . .

THE SCREAMING WOMAN

My name is Margaret Leary and I'm ten years old and in the fifth grade at Central School. I haven't any brothers or sisters, but I've got a nice father and mother except they don't pay much attention to me. And anyway, we never thought we'd have anything to do with a murdered woman. Or almost, anyway.

When you're just living on a street like we live on, you don't think awful things are going to happen, like shooting or stabbing or burying people under the ground, practically in your back yard. And when it does happen you don't believe it. You just go on buttering your toast or baking a cake.

I got to tell you how it happened. It was a noon in the middle of July. It was hot and Mama said to me, "Margaret, you go to the store and buy some ice cream. It's Saturday, Dad's home for lunch, so we'll have a treat."

I ran out across the empty lot behind our house. It was a big lot, where kids had played baseball, and broken glass and stuff. And on my way back from the store with the ice cream I was just walking along, minding my own business, when all of a sudden it happened.

I heard the Screaming Woman.

I stopped and listened.

It was coming up out of the ground.

A woman was buried under the rocks and dirt and glass, and she was screaming, all wild and horrible, for someone to dig her out.

I just stood there, afraid. She kept screaming, muffled.

Then I started to run. I fell down, got up, and ran some more. I got in the screen door of my house and there was Mama, calm as you please, not knowing what I knew, that there was a real live woman buried out in back of our house, just a hundred yards away, screaming bloody murder.

"Mama," I said.

"Don't stand there with the ice cream," said Mama.

"But, Mama," I said.

"Put it in the icebox," she said.

"Listen, Mama, there's a Screaming Woman in the empty lot."

"And wash your hands," said Mama.

"She was screamin' and screamin' . . ."

"Let's see now, salt and pepper," said Mama, far away.

"Listen to me," I said, loud. "We got to dig her out. She's buried under tons and tons of dirt and if we don't dig her out, she'll choke up and die."

"I'm certain she can wait until after lunch," said Mama.

"Mama, don't you believe me?"

"Of course, dear. Now wash your hands and take this plate of meat in to your father."

"I don't even know who she is or how she got there," I said. "But we got to help her before it's too late."

"Good gosh," said Mama. "Look at this ice cream. What did you do, just stand in the sun and let it melt?"

"Well, the empty lot . . ."

"Go on, now, scoot."

I went into the dining room.

"Hi, Dad, there's a Screaming Woman in the empty lot."

"I never knew a woman who didn't," said Dad.

"I'm serious," I said.

"You look very grave," said Father.

"We've got to get picks and shovels and excavate, like for an Egyptian mummy," I said.

"I don't feel like an archaeologist, Margaret," said

Father. "Now, some nice cool October day, I'll take you up on that."

"But we can't wait that long," I almost screamed. My heart was bursting in me. I was excited and scared and afraid and here was Dad, putting meat on his plate, cutting and chewing and paying me no attention.

"Dad?" I said.

"Mmmm?" he said, chewing.

"Dad, you just gotta come out after lunch and help me," I said. "Dad, Dad, I'll give you all the money in my piggy bank!"

"Well," said Dad, "So it's a business proposition, is it? It must be important for you to offer your perfectly good money. How much money will you pay, by the hour?"

"I got five whole dollars it took me a year to save, and it's all yours."

Dad touched my arm. "I'm touched. I'm really touched. You want me to play with you and you're willing to pay for my time. Honest, Margaret, you make your old Dad feel like a piker. I don't give you enough time. Tell you what, after lunch, I'll come out and listen to your screaming woman, free of charge."

"Will you, oh, will you, really?"

"Yes, ma'am, that's what I'll do," said Dad. "But you must promise me one thing?"

"What?"

"If I come out, you must eat all of your lunch first."

"I promise," I said.

"Okay."

Mother came in and sat down and we started to eat.

"Not so fast," said Mama.

I slowed down. Then I started eating fast again.

"You heard your mother," said Dad.

"The Screaming Woman," I said. "We got to hurry."

"I," said Father, "intend sitting here quietly and judiciously giving my attention first to my steak, then to my potatoes, and my salad, of course, and then to my ice cream, and after that to a long drink of iced coffee, if you don't mind. I may be a good hour at it. And another thing, young lady, if you mention her name, this Screaming What-sis, once more at this table during lunch, I won't go out with you to hear her recital."

"Yes, sir."

"Is that understood?"

"Yes, sir," I said.

Lunch was a million years long. Everybody moved in slow motion, like those films you see at the movies. Mama got up slow and got down slow and forks and knives and spoons moved slow. Even the flies in the room were slow. And Dad's cheek muscles moved slow. It was so slow. I wanted to scream, "Hurry! Oh, please, rush, get up, run around, come on out, run!"

But no, I had to sit, and all the while we sat there slowly, slowly eating our lunch, out there in the empty lot (I could hear her screaming in my mind. *Scream!*) was the Screaming Woman, all alone, while the world ate its lunch and the sun was hot and the lot was empty as the sky.

"There we are," said Dad, finished at last.

"Now will you come out to see the Screaming Woman?" I said.

"First a little more iced coffee," said Dad.

"Speaking of Screaming Women," said Mother. "Charlie Nesbitt and his wife Helen had another fight last night."

"That's nothing new," said Father. "They're always fighting."

"If you ask me, Charlie's no good," said Mother. "Or her, either."

"Oh, I don't know," said Dad. "I think she's pretty nice."

"You're prejudiced. After all, you almost married her."

"You going to bring that up again?" he said. "After all, I was only engaged to her six weeks."

"You showed some sense when you broke it off."

"Oh, you know Helen. Always stagestruck. Wanted to travel in a trunk. I just couldn't see it. That broke it up. She was sweet, though. Sweet and kind."

"What did it get her? A terrible brute of a husband like Charlie."

"Dad," I said.

"I'll give you that. Charlie has got a terrible temper," said Dad. "Remember when Helen had the lead in our high school graduation play? Pretty as a picture. She wrote some songs for it herself. That was the summer she wrote that song for me."

"Ha," said Mother.

"Don't laugh. It was a good song."

"You never told me about that song."

"It was between Helen and me. Let's see, how *did* it go?"

"Dad," I said.

"You'd better take your daughter out in the back lot," said Mother, "before she collapses. You can sing me that wonderful song later."

"Okay, come on you," said Dad, and I ran him out of the house.

The empty lot was still empty and hot and the glass sparkled green and white and brown all around where the bottles lay.

"Now, where's this Screaming Woman?" laughed Dad.

"We forgot the shovels," I cried.

"We'll get them later, after we hear the soloist," said Dad.

I took him over to the spot. "Listen," I said.

We listened.

"I don't hear anything," said Dad, at last.

"Shh," I said. "Wait."

We listened some more. "Hey, there, Screaming Woman!" I cried.

We heard the sun in the sky. We heard the wind in the trees, real quiet. We heard a bus, far away, running along. We heard a car pass.

That was all.

"Margaret," said Father. "I suggest you go lie down and put a damp cloth on your forehead."

"But she was here," I shouted. "I heard her, screaming and screaming and screaming. See, here's where the ground's been dug up." I called frantically at the earth. "Hey there, you down there!"

"Margaret," said Father. "This is the place where

Mr. Kelly dug yesterday, a big hole, to bury his trash and garbage in."

"But during the night," I said, "someone else used Mr. Kelly's burying place to bury a woman. And covered it all over again."

"Well, I'm going back in and take a cool shower," said Dad.

"You won't help me dig?"

"Better not stay out here too long," said Dad. "It's hot."

Dad walked off. I heard the back door slam.

I stamped on the ground. "Darn," I said.

The screaming started again.

She screamed and screamed. Maybe she had been tired and was resting and now she began it all over, just for me.

I stood in the empty lot in the hot sun and I felt like crying. I ran back to the house and banged the door.

"Dad, she's screaming again!"

"Sure, sure," said Dad. "Come on." And he led me to my upstairs bedroom. "Here," he said. He made me lie down and put a cold rag on my head. "Just take it easy."

I began to cry. "Oh, Dad, we can't let her die. She's all buried, like that person in that story by Edgar Allan Poe, and think how awful it is to be screaming and no one paying any attention."

"I forbid you to leave the house," said Dad, worried. "You just lie there the rest of the afternoon." He went out and locked the door. I heard him and Mother talking in the front room. After a while I stopped crying. I got up and tiptoed to the window. My room was upstairs. It seemed high.

I took a sheet off the bed and tied it to the bedpost and let it out the window. Then I climbed out the window and shinnied down until I touched the ground. Then I ran to the garage, quiet, and I got a couple of shovels and I ran to the empty lot. It was hotter than ever. And I started to dig, and all the while I dug, the Screaming Woman screamed . . .

It was hard work. Shoving in the shovel and lifting the rocks and glass. And I knew I'd be doing it all afternoon and maybe I wouldn't finish in time. What could I do? Run tell other people? But they'd be like Mom and Dad, pay no attention. I just kept digging, all by myself.

About ten minutes later, Dippy Smith came along the path through the empty lot. He's my age and goes to my school.

"Hi, Margaret," he said.

"Hi, Dippy," I gasped.

"What you doing?" he asked.

"Digging."

"For what?"

"I got a Screaming Lady in the ground and I'm digging for her," I said.

"I don't hear no screaming," said Dippy.

"You sit down and wait a while and you'll hear her scream yet. Or better still, help me dig."

"I don't dig unless I hear a scream," he said.

We waited.

"Listen!" I cried. "Did you *hear* it?"

"Hey," said Dippy, with slow appreciation, his eyes gleaming. "That's okay. Do it again."

"Do what again?"

"The scream."

"We got to wait," I said, puzzled.

"Do it again," he insisted, shaking my arm. "Go on." He dug in his pocket for a brown aggie. "Here." He shoved it at me. "I'll give you this marble if you do it again."

A scream came out of the ground.

"Hot dog!" said Dippy. "Teach *me* to do it!" He danced around as if I was a miracle.

"I don't . . ." I started to say.

"Did you get the *Throw-Your-Voice* book for a dime from that Magic Company in Dallas, Texas?" cried Dippy. "You got one of those tin ventriloquist contraptions in your mouth?"

"Y-yes," I lied, for I wanted him to help. "If you'll help dig, I'll tell you about it later."

"Swell," he said. "Give me a shovel."

We both dug together, and from time to time the Woman screamed.

"Boy," said Dippy. "You'd think she was right under foot. You're wonderful, Maggie." Then he said, "What's her name?"

"Who?"

"The Screaming Woman. You must have a name for her."

"Oh, sure." I thought a moment. "Her name's Wilma Schweiger and she's a rich old woman, ninety-six years old, and she was buried by a man named Spike, who counterfeited ten-dollar bills."

"Yes, *sir*," said Dippy.

"And there's hidden treasure buried with her, and I, I'm a grave robber come to dig her out and get it," I gasped, digging excitedly.

Dippy made his eyes Oriental and mysterious. "Can I be a grave robber, too?" He had a better idea. "Let's pretend it's the Princess Ommanatra, an Egyptian queen, covered with diamonds!"

We kept digging and I thought, oh, we will rescue her, we *will*. If only we keep on!

"Hey, I just got an idea," said Dippy. And he ran off and got a piece of cardboard. He scribbled on it with crayon.

"Keep digging!" I said. "We can't stop!"

"I'm making a sign. See? SLUMBERLAND CEMETERY! We can bury some birds and beetles here, in matchboxes and stuff. I'll go find some butterflies."

"No, Dippy!"

"It's more fun that way. I'll get me a dead cat, too, maybe . . ."

"Dippy, use your shovel! Please!"

"Aw," said Dippy. "I'm tired. I think I'll go home and take a nap."

"You can't do that."

"Who says so?"

"Dippy, there's something I want to tell you."

"What?"

He gave the shovel a kick.

I whispered in his ear. "There's really a woman buried here."

"Why sure there is," he said. "You said it, Maggie."

"You don't believe me, either."

"Tell me how you throw your voice and I'll keep on digging."

"But I can't tell you, because I'm not doing it," I said. "Look, Dippy. I'll stand way over here and you listen there."

The Screaming Woman screamed again.

"Hey!" said Dippy. "There really *is* a woman here!"

"That's what I tried to say."

"Let's dig!" said Dippy.

We dug for twenty minutes.

"I wonder who she is?"

"I don't know."

"I wonder if it's Mrs. Nelson or Mrs. Turner or Mrs. Bradley. I wonder if she's pretty. Wonder what color her hair is? Wonder if she's thirty or ninety or sixty?"

"Dig!" I said.

The mound grew high.

"Wonder if she'll reward us for digging her up."

"Sure."

"A quarter, do you think?"

"More than that. I bet it's a dollar."

Dippy remembered as he dug. "I read a book once of magic. There was a Hindu with no clothes on who crept down in a grave and slept there sixty days, not eating anything, no malts, no chewing gum or candy, no air, for sixty days." His face fell. "Say, wouldn't it be awful if it was only a radio buried here and us working so hard?"

"A radio's nice, it'd be all ours."

Just then a shadow fell across us.

"Hey, you kids, what you think you're doing?"

We turned. It was Mr. Kelly, the man who owned the empty lot. "Oh, hello, Mr. Kelly," we said.

"Tell you what I want you to do," said Mr. Kelly. "I want you to take those shovels and take that soil and shovel it right back in that hole you been digging. That's what I want you to do."

My heart started beating fast again. I wanted to scream myself.

"But Mr. Kelly, there's a Screaming Woman and . . ."

"I'm not interested. I don't hear a thing."

"Listen!" I cried.

The scream.

Mr. Kelly listened and shook his head. "Don't hear nothing. Go on now, fill it up and get home with you before I give you my foot!"

We filled the hole all back in again. And all the while we filled it in, Mr. Kelly stood there, arms folded, and the woman screamed, but Mr. Kelly pretended not to hear it.

When we were finished, Mr. Kelly stomped off, saying, "Go on home now. And if I catch you here again . . ."

I turned to Dippy. "He's the one," I whispered.

"Huh?" said Dippy.

"He *murdered* Mrs. Kelly. He buried her here, after he strangled her, in a box, but she came to. Why, he stood right here and she screamed and he wouldn't pay any attention."

"Hey," said Dippy. "That's right. He stood right here and lied to us."

"There's only one thing to do," I said. "Call the police and have them come arrest Mr. Kelly."

We ran for the corner store telephone.

The police knocked on Mr. Kelly's door five minutes later. Dippy and I were hiding in the bushes, listening.

"Mr. Kelly?" said the police officer.

"Yes, sir, what can I do for you?"

"Is Mrs. Kelly at home?"

"Yes, sir."

"May we see her, sir?"

"Of course. Hey, Anna!"

Mrs. Kelly came to the door and looked out. "Yes, sir?"

"I beg your pardon," apologized the officer. "We had a report that you were buried out in an empty lot, Mrs. Kelly. It sounded like a child made the call, but we had to be certain. Sorry to have troubled you."

"It's those blasted kids," cried Mr. Kelly, angrily. "If I ever catch them, I'll rip 'em limb from limb!"

"Cheezit!" said Dippy, and we both ran.

"What'll we do now?" I said.

"I got to go home," said Dippy. "Boy, we're really in trouble. We'll get a licking for this."

"But what about the Screaming Woman?"

"To heck with her," said Dippy. "We don't dare go near that empty lot again. Old man Kelly'll be waitin' around with his razor strap and lambast heck out'n us. An' I just happened to remember, Maggie. Ain't old man Kelly sort of deaf, hard-of-hearing?"

"Oh, my gosh," I said. "No *wonder* he didn't hear the screams."

"So long," said Dippy. "We sure got in trouble over your darn old ventriloquist voice. I'll be seeing you."

I was left all alone in the world, no one to help me, no one to believe me at all. I just wanted to crawl down in that box with the Screaming Woman and die. The police were after me now, for lying to them, only I didn't know it was a lie, and my father was probably looking for me, too, or would be once he found my bed empty. There was only one last thing to do, and I did it.

I went from house to house, all down the street, near the empty lot. And I rang every bell and when the door opened I said: "I beg your pardon, Mrs. Griswold, but is anyone missing from your house?" or "Hello, Mrs. Pikes, you're looking fine today. Glad to see you *home*." And once I saw that the lady of the house was home I just chatted a while to be polite, and went on down the street.

The hours were rolling along. It was getting late. I kept thinking, oh, there's only so much air in that box with that woman under the earth, and if I don't hurry, she'll suffocate, and I got to rush! So I rang bells and knocked on doors, and it got later, and I was just about to give up and go home, when I knocked on the *last* door, which was the door of Mr. Charlie Nesbitt, who lives next to us. I kept knocking and knocking.

Instead of Mrs. Nesbitt, or Helen as my father calls her, coming to the door, why it was Mr. Nesbitt, Charlie, *himself*.

"Oh," he said. "It's you, Margaret."

"Yes," I said. "Good afternoon."

"What can I do for you, kid?" he said.

"Well, I thought I'd like to see your wife, Mrs. Nesbitt," I said.

"Oh," he said.

"May I?"

"Well, she's gone out to the store," he said.

"I'll wait," I said, and slipped in past him.

"Hey," he said.

I sat down in a chair. "My, it's a hot day," I said, trying to be calm, thinking about the empty lot and air going out of the box, and the screams getting weaker and weaker.

"Say, listen, kid," said Charlie, coming over to me, "I don't think you better wait."

"Oh, sure," I said. "Why not?"

"Well, my wife won't be back," he said.

"Oh?"

"Not today, that is. She's gone to the store, like I said, but, but, she's going on from there to visit her mother. Yeah. She's going to visit her mother, in Schenectady. She'll be back, two or three days, maybe a week."

"That's a shame," I said.

"Why?"

"I wanted to tell her something."

"What?"

"I just wanted to tell her there's a woman buried over in the empty lot, screaming under tons and tons of dirt."

Mr. Nesbitt dropped his cigarette.

"You dropped your cigarette, Mr. Nesbitt," I pointed out, with my shoe.

"Oh, did I? Sure. So I did," he mumbled. "Well, I'll tell Helen when she comes home, your story. She'll be glad to hear it."

"Thanks. It's a real woman."

"How do you know it is?"

"I heard her."

"How, how you know it isn't, well, a *mandrake* root."

"What's that?"

"You know. A mandrake. It's a kind of a plant, kid.

They scream. I know, I read it once. How you know it ain't a mandrake?"

"I never thought of that."

"You better start thinking," he said, lighting another cigarette. He tried to be casual. "Say, kid, you, eh, you *say* anything about this to anyone?"

"Sure, I told lots of people."

Mr. Nesbitt burned his hand on his match.

"Anybody doing anything about it?" he asked.

"No," I said. "They won't believe me."

He smiled. "Of course. Naturally. You're nothing but a kid. Why should they listen to you?"

"I'm going back now and dig her out with a spade," I said.

"Wait."

"I got to go," I said.

"Stick around," he insisted.

"Thanks, but no," I said, frantically.

He took my arm. "Know how to play cards, kid? Black jack?"

"Yes, sir."

He took out a deck of cards from a desk. "We'll have a game."

"I got to go dig."

"Plenty of time for that," he said, quiet. "Anyway, maybe my wife'll be home. Sure. That's it. You wait for her. Wait a while."

"You think she will be?"

"Sure, kid. Say, about that voice; is it very strong?"

"It gets weaker all the time."

Mr. Nesbitt sighed and smiled. "You and your kid games. Here now, let's play that game of black jack, it's more fun than Screaming Women."

"I got to go. It's late."

"Stick around, you got nothing to do."

I knew what he was trying to do. He was trying to keep me in his house until the screaming died down and was gone. He was trying to keep me from helping her. "My wife'll be home in ten minutes," he said. "Sure. Ten minutes. You wait. You sit right there."

We played cards. The clock ticked. The sun went

down the sky. It was getting late. The screaming got fainter and fainter in my mind. "I got to go," I said.

"Another game," said Mr. Nesbitt. "Wait another hour, kid. My wife'll come yet. Wait."

In another hour he looked at his watch. "Well, kid, I guess you can go now." And I know what his plan was. He'd sneak down in the middle of the night and dig up his wife, still alive, and take her somewhere else and bury her, good. "So long, kid. So long." He let me go, because he thought that by now the air must all be gone from the box.

The door shut in my face.

I went back near the empty lot and hid in some bushes. What could I do? Tell my folks? But they hadn't believed me. Call the police on Mr. Charlie Nesbitt? But he said his wife was away visiting. Nobody would believe me!

I watched Mr. Kelly's house. He wasn't in sight. I ran over to the place where the screaming had been and just stood there.

The screaming had stopped. It was so quiet I thought I would never hear a scream again. It was all over. I was too late I thought.

I bent down and put my ear against the ground.

And then I heard it, way down, way deep, and so faint I could hardly hear it.

The woman wasn't screaming any more. She was singing.

Something about, "I loved you fair, I loved you well."

It was sort of a sad song. Very faint. And sort of broken. All of those hours down under the ground in that box must have sort of made her crazy. All she needed was some air and food and she'd be all right. But she just kept singing, not wanting to scream any more, not caring, just singing.

I listened to the song.

And then I turned and walked straight across the lot and up the steps to my house and I opened the front door.

"Father," I said.

"So there you are!" he cried.

"Father," I said.

"You're going to get a licking," he said.

"She's not screaming any more."

"Don't talk about her!"

"She's singing now," I cried.

"You're not telling the truth!"

"Dad," I said. "She's out there and she'll be dead soon if you don't listen to me. She's out there, singing, and this is what she's singing." I hummed the tune. I sang a few of the words. "I loved you fair, I loved you well . . ."

Dad's face grew pale. He came and took my arm.

"What did you say?" he said.

I sang it again, "I loved you fair, I loved you well."

"Where did you *hear* that song?" he shouted.

"Out in the empty lot, just now."

"But that's *Helen's* song, the one she wrote, years ago, for *me!*" cried Father. "You *can't* know it. *Nobody* knew it, except Helen and me. I never sang it to anyone, not you or anyone."

"Sure," I said.

"Oh, my God!" cried Father and ran out the door to get a shovel. The last I saw of him he was in the empty lot, digging, and lots of other people with him, digging.

I felt so happy I wanted to cry.

I dialed a number on the phone and when Dippy answered I said, "Hi, Dippy. Everything's fine. Everything's worked out keen. The Screaming Woman isn't screaming any more."

"Swell," said Dippy.

"I'll meet you in the empty lot with a shovel in two minutes," I said.

"Last one there's a monkey! So long!" cried Dippy.

"So long, Dippy!" I said, and ran.

THE SMILE

In the town square the queue had formed at five in the morning while cocks were crowing far out in the rimed country and there were no fires. All about, among the ruined buildings, bits of mist had clung at first, but now with the new light of seven o'clock it was beginning to disperse. Down the road, in twos and threes, more people were gathering in for the day of marketing, the day of festival.

The small boy stood immediately behind two men who had been talking loudly in the clear air, and all of the sounds they made seemed twice as loud because of the cold. The small boy stomped his feet and blew on his red, chapped hands, and looked up at the soiled gunny sack clothing of the men and down the long line of men and women ahead.

"Here, boy, what're you doing out so early?" said the man behind him.

"Got my place in line, I have," said the boy.

"Whyn't you run off, give your place to someone who appreciates?"

"Leave the boy alone," said the man ahead, suddenly turning.

"I was joking." The man behind put his hand on the boy's head. The boy shook it away coldly. "I just thought it strange, a boy out of bed so early."

"This boy's an appreciator of arts, I'll have you know," said the boy's defender, a man named Grigsby. "What's your name, lad?"

"Tom."

173

"Tom here is going to spit clean and true, right, Tom?"

"I sure am!"

Laughter passed down the line.

A man was selling cracked cups of hot coffee up ahead. Tom looked and saw the little hot fire and the brew bubbling in a rusty pan. It wasn't really coffee. It was made from some berry that grew on the meadow-lands beyond town, and it sold a penny a cup to warm their stomachs; but not many were buying, not many had the wealth.

Tom stared ahead to the place where the line ended, beyond a bombed-out stone wall.

"They say she *smiles*," said the boy.

"Aye, she does," said Grigsby.

"They say she's made of oil and canvas."

"True. And that's what makes me think she's not the original one. The original, now, I've heard, was painted on wood a long time ago."

"They say she's four centuries old."

"Maybe more. No one knows what year this is, to be sure."

"It's 2061!"

"That's what they say, boy, yes. Liars. Could be 3000 or 5000, for all we know. Things were in a fearful mess there for a while. All we got now is bits and pieces."

They shuffled along the cold stones of the street.

"How much longer before we see her?" asked Tom uneasily.

"Just a few more minutes. They got her set up with four brass poles and velvet rope, all fancy, to keep folks back. Now mind, no rocks, Tom; they don't allow rocks thrown at her."

"Yes, sir."

The sun rose higher in the heavens, bringing heat which made the men shed their grimy coats and greasy hats.

"Why're we all here in line?" asked Tom at last. "Why're we all here to spit?"

Grigsby did not glance down at him, but judged the sun. "Well, Tom, there's lots of reasons." He reached absently for a pocket that was long gone, for a cigarette that wasn't there. Tom had seen the gesture a million times. "Tom, it has to do with hate. Hate for everything in the past. I ask you, Tom, how did we get in such a state, cities all junk, roads like jigsaws from bombs, and half the cornfields glowing with radioactivity at night? Ain't that a lousy stew, I ask you?"

"Yes, sir, I guess so."

"It's this way, Tom. You hate whatever it was that got you all knocked down and ruined. That's human nature. Unthinking, maybe, but human nature anyway."

"There's hardly nobody or nothing we don't hate," said Tom.

"Right! The whole blooming kaboodle of them people in the past who run the world. So here we are on a Thursday morning with our guts plastered to our spines, cold, live in caves and such, don't smoke, don't drink, don't nothing except have our festivals, Tom, our festivals."

And Tom thought of the festivals in the past few years. The year they tore up all the books in the square and burned them and everyone was drunk and laughing. And the festival of science a month ago when they dragged in the last motorcar and picked lots and each lucky man who won was allowed one smash of a sledgehammer at the car.

"Do I remember *that,* Tom? Do I *remember?* Why, I got to smash the front window, the window, you hear? My Lord, it made a lovely sound! *Crash!*"

Tom could hear the glass fall in glittering heaps.

"And Bill Henderson, he got to bash the engine. Oh, he did a smart job of it, with great efficiency. Wham!"

"But best of all," recalled Grigsby, "there was the time they smashed a factory that was still trying to turn out airplanes.

"Lord, did we feel good blowing it up!" said Grigsby. "And then we found that newspaper plant and the munitions depot and exploded them together. Do you understand, Tom?"

Tom puzzled over it. "I guess."

It was high noon. Now the odors of the ruined city

stank on the hot air and things crawled among the tumbled buildings.

"Won't it ever come back, mister?"

"What, civilization? Nobody wants it. Not me!"

"I could stand a bit of it," said the man behind another man. "There were a few spots of beauty in it."

"Don't worry your heads," shouted Grigsby. "There's no room for that, either."

"Ah," said the man behind the man. "Someone'll come along someday with imagination and patch it up. Mark my words. Someone with a heart."

"No," said Grigsby.

"I say yes. Someone with a soul for pretty things. Might give us back a kind of *limited* sort of civilization, the kind we could live in in peace."

"First thing you know there's war!"

"But maybe next time it'd be different."

At last they stood in the main square. A man on horseback was riding from the distance into the town. He had a piece of paper in his hand. In the center of the square was the roped-off area. Tom, Grigsby, and the others were collecting their spittle and moving forward—moving forward prepared and ready, eyes wide. Tom felt his heart beating very strongly and excitedly, and the earth was hot under his bare feet.

"Here we go, Tom, let fly!"

Four policemen stood at the corners of the roped area, four men with bits of yellow twine on their wrists to show their authority over other men. They were there to prevent rocks being hurled.

"This way," said Grigsby at the last moment, "everyone feels he's had his chance at her, you see, Tom? Go on, now!"

Tom stood before the painting and looked at it for a long time.

"Tom, spit!"

His mouth was dry.

"Get on, Tom! Move!"

"But," said Tom, slowly, "she's *beautiful!*"

"Here, I'll spit for you!" Grigsby spat and the missile flew in the sunlight. The woman in the portrait smiled serenely, secretly, at Tom, and he looked back at her, his heart beating, a kind of music in his ears.

"She's beautiful," he said.

"Now get on, before the police——"

"Attention!"

The line fell silent. One moment they were berating Tom for not moving forward, now they were turning to the man on horseback.

"What do they call it, sir?" asked Tom, quietly.

"The picture? *Mona Lisa,* Tom, I think. Yes, the *Mona Lisa.*"

"I have an announcement," said the man on horseback. "The authorities have decreed that as of high noon today the portrait in the square is to be given over into the hands of the populace there, so they may participate in the destruction of——"

Tom hadn't even time to scream before the crowd bore him, shouting and pummeling about, stampeding toward the portrait. There was a sharp ripping sound. The police ran to escape. The crowd was in full cry, their hands like so many hungry birds pecking away at the portrait. Tom felt himself thrust almost through the broken thing. Reaching out in blind imitation of the others, he snatched a scrap of oily canvas, yanked, felt the canvas give, then fell, was kicked, sent rolling to the outer rim of the mob. Bloody, his clothing torn, he watched old women chew pieces of canvas, men break the frame, kick the ragged cloth, and rip it into confetti.

Only Tom stood apart, silent in the moving square. He looked down at his hand. It clutched the piece of canvas close to his chest, hidden.

"Hey there, Tom!" cried Grigsby.

Without a word, sobbing, Tom ran. He ran out and down the bomb-pitted road, into a field, across a shallow stream, not looking back, his hand clenched tightly, tucked under his coat.

At sunset he reached the small village and passed on through. By nine o'clock he came to the ruined farm dwelling. Around back, in the half silo, in the part that still remained upright, tented over, he heard the sounds of sleeping, the family—his mother, father, and brother. He slipped quickly, silently, through the small door and lay down, panting.

"Tom?" called his mother in the dark.

"Yes."

"Where've you been?" snapped his father. "I'll beat you in the morning."

Someone kicked him. His brother, who had been left behind to work their little patch of ground.

"Go to sleep," cried his mother, faintly.

Another kick.

Tom lay getting his breath. All was quiet. His hand was pushed to his chest, tight, tight. He lay for half an hour this way, eyes closed.

Then he felt something, and it was a cold white light. The moon rose very high and the little square of light moved in the silo and crept slowly over Tom's body. Then, and only then, did his hand relax. Slowly, carefully, listening to those who slept about him, Tom drew his hand forth. He hesitated, sucked in his breath, and then, waiting, opened his hand and uncrumpled the tiny fragment of painted canvas.

All the world was asleep in the moonlight.

And there on his hand was the Smile.

He looked at it in the white illumination from the midnight sky. And he thought, over and over to himself, quietly, *the Smile, the lovely Smile.*

An hour later he could still see it, even after he had folded it carefully and hidden it. He shut his eyes and the Smile was there in the darkness. And it was still there, warm and gentle, when he went to sleep and the world was silent and the moon sailed up and then down the cold sky toward morning.

DARK THEY WERE, AND GOLDEN-EYED

The rocket metal cooled in the meadow winds. Its lid gave a bulging *pop*. From its clock interior stepped a man, a woman, and three children. The other passengers whispered away across the Martian meadow, leaving the man alone among his family.

The man felt his hair flutter and the tissues of his body draw tight as if he were standing at the center of a vacuum. His wife, before him, seemed almost to whirl away in smoke. The children, small seeds, might at any instant be sown to all the Martian climes.

The children looked up at him, as people look to the sun to tell what time of their life it is. His face was cold.

"What's wrong?" asked his wife.

"Let's get back on the rocket."

"Go back to Earth?"

"Yes! Listen!"

The wind blew as if to flake away their identities. At any moment the Martian air might draw his soul from him, as marrow comes from a white bone. He felt submerged in a chemical that could dissolve his intellect and burn away his past.

They looked at Martian hills that time had worn with a crushing pressure of years. They saw the old cities, lost in their meadows, lying like children's delicate bones among the blowing lakes of grass.

"Chin up, Harry," said his wife. "It's too late. We've come over sixty million miles."

The children with their yellow hair hollered at the

deep dome of Martian sky. There was no answer but the racing hiss of wind through the stiff grass.

He picked up the luggage in his cold hands. "Here we go," he said—a man standing on the edge of a sea, ready to wade in and be drowned.

They walked into town.

Their name was Bittering. Harry and his wife Cora; Dan, Laura, and David. They built a small white cottage and ate good breakfasts there, but the fear was never gone. It lay with Mr. Bittering and Mrs. Bittering, a third unbidden partner at every midnight talk, at every dawn awakening.

"I feel like a salt crystal," he said, "in a mountain stream, being washed away. We don't belong here. We're Earth people. This is Mars. It was meant for Martians. For heaven's sake, Cora, let's buy tickets for home!"

But she only shook her head. "One day the atom bomb will fix Earth. Then we'll be safe here."

"Safe and insane!"

Tick-tock, seven o'clock sang the voice-clock; *time to get up*. And they did.

Something made him check everything each morning—warm hearth, potted blood-geraniums—precisely as if he expected something to be amiss. The morning paper was toast-warm from the 6 A.M. Earth rocket. He broke its seal and tilted it at his breakfast place. He forced himself to be convivial.

"Colonial days all over again," he declared. "Why, in ten years there'll be a million Earthmen on Mars. Big cities, everything! They said we'd fail. Said the Martians would resent our invasion. But did we find any Martians? Not a living soul! Oh, we found their empty cities, but no one in them. Right?"

A river of wind submerged the house. When the windows ceased rattling Mr. Bittering swallowed and looked at the children.

"I don't know," said David. "Maybe there're Martians around we don't see. Sometimes nights I think I hear 'em. I hear the wind. The sand hits my window. I get scared. And I see those towns way up in the mountains where the Martians lived a long time ago. And I think I see things moving around those towns, Papa. And I wonder if those Martians *mind* us living here. I wonder if they won't do something to us for coming here."

"Nonsense!" Mr. Bittering looked out the windows. "We're clean, decent people." He looked at his children. "All dead cities have some kind of ghosts in them. Memories, I mean." He stared at the hills. "You see a staircase and you wonder what Martians looked like climbing it. You see Martian paintings and you wonder what the painter was like. You make a little ghost in your mind, a memory. It's quite natural. Imagination." He stopped. "You haven't been prowling up in those ruins, have you?"

"No, Papa." David looked at his shoes.

"See that you stay away from them. Pass the jam."

"Just the same," said little David, "I bet something happens."

Something happened that afternoon.

Laura stumbled through the settlement, crying. She dashed blindly onto the porch.

"Mother, Father—the war, Earth!" she sobbed. "A radio flash just came. Atom bombs hit New York! All the space rockets blown up. No more rockets to Mars, ever!"

"Oh, Harry!" The mother held onto her husband and daughter.

"Are you sure, Laura?" asked the father quietly.

Laura wept. "We're stranded on Mars, forever and ever!"

For a long time there was only the sound of the wind in the late afternoon.

Alone, thought Bittering. Only a thousand of us here. No way back. No way. No way. Sweat poured from his face and his hands and his body; he was drenched in the hotness of his fear. He wanted to strike Laura, cry, "No, you're lying! The rockets will come back!" Instead, he stroked Laura's head against him and said, "The rockets will get through someday."

"Father, what will we do?"

"Go about our business, of course. Raise crops and children. Wait. Keep things going until the war ends and the rockets come again."

The two boys stepped out onto the porch.

"Children," he said, sitting there, looking beyond them, "I've something to tell you."

"We know," they said.

In the following days, Bittering wandered often through the garden to stand alone in his fear. As long as the rockets had spun a silver web across space, he had been able to accept Mars. For he had always told himself: Tomorrow, if I want, I can buy a ticket and go back to Earth.

But now: The web gone, the rockets lying in jigsaw heaps of molten girder and unsnaked wire. Earth people left to the strangeness of Mars, the cinnamon dusts and wine airs, to be baked like gingerbread shapes in Martian summers, put into harvested storage by Martian winters. What would happen to him, the others? This was the moment Mars had waited for. Now it would eat them.

He got down on his knees in the flower bed, a spade in his nervous hands. Work, he thought, work and forget.

He glanced up from the garden to the Martian mountains. He thought of the proud old Martian names that had once been on those peaks. Earthmen, dropping from the sky, had gazed upon hills, rivers, Martian seats left nameless in spite of names. Once Martians had built cities, named cities; climbed mountains, named mountains; sailed seas, named seas. Mountains melted, seas drained, cities tumbled. In spite of this, the Earthmen had felt a silent guilt at putting new names to these ancient hills and valleys.

Nevertheless, man lives by symbol and label. The names were given.

Mr. Bittering felt very alone in his garden under the Martian sun, anachronism bent here, planting Earth flowers in a wild soil.

Think. Keep thinking. Different things. Keep your mind free of Earth, the atom war, the lost rockets.

He perspired. He glanced about. No one watching. He removed his tie. Pretty bold, he thought. First your coat off, now your tie. He hung it neatly on a peach tree he had imported as a sapling from Massachusetts.

He returned to his philosophy of names and mountains. The Earthmen had changed names. Now there were Hormel Valleys, Roosevelt Seas, Ford Hills, Vanderbilt Plateaus, Rockefeller Rivers, on Mars. It wasn't right. The American settlers had shown wisdom, using old Indian prairie names: Wisconsin, Minnesota, Idaho, Ohio, Utah, Milwaukee, Waukegan, Osseo. The old names, the old meanings.

Staring at the mountains wildly, he thought: Are you up there? All the dead ones, you Martians? Well, here we are, alone, cut off! Come down, move us out! We're helpless!

The wind blew a shower of peach blossoms.

He put out his sun-browned hand and gave a small cry. He touched the blossoms and picked them up. He turned them, he touched them again and again. Then he shouted for his wife.

"Cora!"

She appeared at a window. He ran to her.

"Cora, these blossoms!"

She handled them.

"Do you see? They're different. They've changed! They're not peach blossoms any more!"

"Look all right to me," she said.

"They're not. They're wrong! I can't tell how. An extra petal, a leaf, something, the color, the smell!"

The children ran out in time to see their father hurrying about the garden, pulling up radishes, onions, and carrots from their beds.

"Cora, come look!"

They handled the onions, the radishes, the carrots among them.

"Do they look like carrots?"

"Yes . . . no." She hesitated. "I don't know."

"They're changed."

"Perhaps."

"You know they have! Onions but not onions, carrots but not carrots. Taste: the same but different.

Smell: not like it used to be." He felt his heart pounding, and he was afraid. He dug his fingers into the earth. "Cora, what's happening? What is it? We've got to get away from this." He ran across the garden. Each tree felt his touch. "The roses. The roses. They're turning green!"

And they stood looking at the green roses.

And two days later Dan came running. "Come see the cow. I was milking her and I saw it. Come on!"

They stood in the shed and looked at their one cow.

It was growing a third horn.

And the lawn in front of their house very quietly and slowly was coloring itself like spring violets. Seed from Earth but growing up a soft purple.

"We must get away," said Bittering. "We'll eat this stuff and then we'll change—who knows to what? I can't let it happen. There's only one thing to do. Burn this food!"

"It's not poisoned."

"But it is. Subtly, very subtly. A little bit. A very little bit. We mustn't touch it."

He looked with dismay at their house. "Even the house. The wind's done something to it. The air's burned it. The fog at night. The boards, all warped out of shape. It's not an Earthman's house any more."

"Oh, your imagination!"

He put on his coat and tie. "I'm going into town. We've got to do something now. I'll be back."

"Wait, Harry!" his wife cried.

But he was gone.

In town, on the shadowy step of the grocery store, the men sat with their hands on their knees, conversing with great leisure and ease.

Mr. Bittering wanted to fire a pistol in the air.

What are you doing, you fools! he thought. Sitting here! You've heard the news—we're stranded on this planet. Well, move! Aren't you frightened? Aren't you afraid? What are you going to do?

"Hello, Harry," said everyone.

"Look," he said to them. "You did hear the news, the other day, didn't you?"

They nodded and laughed. "Sure. Sure, Harry."

"What are you going to do about it?"

"Do, Harry, do? What *can* we do?"

"Build a rocket, that's what!"

"A rocket, Harry? To go back to all that trouble? Oh, Harry!"

"But you *must* want to go back. Have you noticed the peach blossoms, the onions, the grass?"

"Why, yes, Harry, seems we did," said one of the men.

"Doesn't it scare you?"

"Can't recall that it did much, Harry."

"Idiots!"

"Now, Harry."

Bittering wanted to cry. "You've got to work with me. If we stay here, we'll all change. The air. Don't you smell it? Something in the air. A Martian virus, maybe; some seed, or a pollen. Listen to me!"

They stared at him.

"Sam," he said to one of them.

"Yes, Harry?"

"Will you help me build a rocket?"

"Harry, I got a whole load of metal and some blueprints. You want to work in my metal shop on a rocket, you're welcome. I'll sell you that metal for five hundred dollars. You should be able to construct a right pretty rocket, if you work alone, in about thirty years."

Everyone laughed.

"Don't laugh."

Sam looked at him with quiet good humor.

"Sam," Bittering said. "Your eyes——"

"What about them, Harry?"

"Didn't they used to be gray?"

"Well now, I don't remember."

"They were, weren't they?"

"Why do you ask, Harry?"

"Because now they're kind of yellow-colored."

"Is that so, Harry?" Sam said, casually.

"And you're taller and thinner——"

"You might be right, Harry."

"Sam, you shouldn't have yellow eyes."

"Harry, what color eyes have *you* got?" Sam said.

"My eyes? They're blue, of course."

"Here you are, Harry." Sam handed him a pocket mirror. "Take a look at yourself."

Mr. Bittering hesitated, and then raised the mirror to his face.

There were little, very dim flecks of new gold captured in the blue of his eyes.

"Now look what you've done," said Sam a moment later. "You've broken my mirror."

Harry Bittering moved into the metal shop and began to build the rocket. Men stood in the open door and talked and joked without raising their voices. Once in a while they gave him a hand on lifting something. But mostly they just idled and watched him with their yellowing eyes.

"It's suppertime, Harry," they said.

His wife appeared with his supper in a wicker basket.

"I won't touch it," he said. "I'll eat only food from our Deepfreeze. Food that came from Earth. Nothing from our garden."

His wife stood watching him. "You can't build a rocket."

"I worked in a shop once, when I was twenty. I know metal. Once I get it started, the others will help," he said, not looking at her, laying out the blueprints.

"Harry, Harry," she said, helplessly.

"We've got to get away, Cora. We've *got* to!"

The nights were full of wind that blew down the empty moonlit sea meadows past the little white chess cities lying for their twelve-thousandth year in the shallows. In the Earthmen's settlement, the Bittering house shook with a feeling of change.

Lying abed, Mr. Bittering felt his bones shifted, shaped, melted like gold. His wife, lying beside him, was dark from many sunny afternoons. Dark she was, and golden-eyed, burnt almost black by the sun, sleeping, and the children metallic in their beds, and the wind roaring forlorn and changing through the old peach trees, the violet grass, shaking out green rose petals.

The fear would not be stopped. It had his throat and heart. It dripped in a wetness of the arm and the temple and the trembling palm.

A green star rose in the east.

A strange word emerged from Mr. Bittering's lips.

"*Iorrt. Iorrt.*" He repeated it.

It was a Martian word. He knew no Martian.

In the middle of the night he arose and dialed a call through to Simpson, the archaeologist.

"Simpson, what does the word *Iorrt* mean?"

"Why that's the old Martian word for our planet Earth. Why?"

"No special reason."

The telephone slipped from his hand.

"Hello, hello, hello, hello," it kept saying while he sat gazing out at the green star. "Bittering? Harry, are you there?"

The days were full of metal sound. He laid the frame of the rocket with the reluctant help of three indifferent men. He grew very tired in an hour or so and had to sit down.

"The altitude," laughed a man.

"Are you *eating*, Harry?" asked another.

"I'm eating," he said, angrily.

"From your Deepfreeze?"

"Yes!"

"You're getting thinner, Harry."

"I'm not!"

"And taller."

"Liar!"

His wife took him aside a few days later. "Harry, I've used up all the food in the Deepfreeze. There's nothing left. I'll have to make sandwiches using food grown on Mars."

He sat down heavily.

"You must eat," she said. "You're weak."

"Yes," he said.

He took a sandwich, opened it, looked at it, and began to nibble at it.

"And take the rest of the day off," she said. "It's hot. The children want to swim in the canals and hike. Please come along."

"I can't waste time. This is a crisis!"

"Just for an hour," she urged. "A swim'll do you good."

He rose, sweating. "All right, all right. Leave me alone. I'll come."

"Good for you, Harry."

The sun was hot, the day quiet. There was only an immense staring burn upon the land. They moved along the canal, the father, the mother, the racing children in their swimsuits. They stopped and ate meat sandwiches. He saw their skin baking brown. And he saw the yellow eyes of his wife and his children, their eyes that were never yellow before. A few tremblings shook him, but were carried off in waves of pleasant heat as he lay in the sun. He was too tired to be afraid.

"Cora, how long have your eyes been yellow?"

She was bewildered. "Always, I guess."

"They didn't change from brown in the last three months?"

She bit her lips. "No. Why do you ask?"

"Never mind."

They sat there.

"The children's eyes," he said. "They're yellow, too."

"Sometimes growing children's eyes change color."

"Maybe *we're* children, too. At least to Mars. That's a thought." He laughed. "Think I'll swim."

They leaped into the canal water, and he let himself sink down and down to the bottom like a golden statue and lie there in green silence. All was water-quiet and deep, all was peace. He felt the steady, slow current drift him easily.

If I lie here long enough, he thought, the water will work and eat away my flesh until the bones show like coral. Just my skeleton left. And then the water can build on that skeleton—green things, deep water things, red things, yellow things. Change. Change. Slow, deep, silent change. And isn't that what it is up *there?*

He saw the sky submerged above him, the sun made Martian by atmosphere and time and space.

Up there, a big river, he thought, a Martian river, all of us lying deep in it, in our pebble houses, in our sunken boulder houses, like crayfish hidden, and the water washing away our old bodies and lengthening the bones and——

He let himself drift up through the soft light.

Dan sat on the edge of the canal, regarding his father seriously.

"Utha," he said.

"What?" asked his father.

The boy smiled. "You know. *Utha's* the Martian word for 'father.' "

"Where did you learn it?"

"I don't know. Around. *Utha!"*

"What do you want?"

The boy hesitated. "I—I want to change my name."

"Change it?"

"Yes."

His mother swam over. "What's wrong with Dan for a name?"

Dan fidgeted. "The other day you called Dan, Dan, Dan. I didn't even hear. I said to myself, That's not my name. I've a new name I want to use."

Mr. Bittering held to the side of the canal, his body cold and his heart pounding slowly. "What is this new name?"

"Linnl. Isn't that a good name? Can I use it? Can't I, please?"

Mr. Bittering put his hand to his head. He thought of the silly rocket, himself working alone, himself alone even among his family, so alone.

He heard his wife say, "Why not?"

He heard himself say, "Yes, you can use it."

"Yaaa!" screamed the boy. "I'm Linnl, Linnl!"

Racing down the meadowlands, he danced and shouted.

Mr. Bittering looked at his wife. "Why did we do that?"

"I don't know," she said. "It just seemed like a good idea."

They walked into the hills. They strolled on old mosaic paths, beside still pumping fountains. The paths were covered with a thin film of cool water all summer long. You kept your bare feet cool all the day, splashing as in a creek, wading.

They came to a small deserted Martian villa with a good view of the valley. It was on top of a hill. Blue marble halls, large murals, a swimming pool. It was refreshing in this hot summertime. The Martians hadn't believed in large cities.

"How nice," said Mrs. Bittering, "if we could move up here to this villa for the summer."

"Come on," he said. "We're going back to town. There's work to be done on the rocket."

But as he worked that night, the thought of the cool blue marble villa entered his mind. As the hours passed, the rocket seemed less important.

In the flow of days and weeks, the rocket receded and dwindled. The old fever was gone. It frightened him to think he had let it slip this way. But somehow the heat, the air, the working conditions—

He heard the men murmuring on the porch of his metal shop.

"Everyone's going. You heard?"

"All going. That's right."

Bittering came out. "Going where?" He saw a couple of trucks, loaded with children and furniture, drive down the dusty street.

"Up to the villas," said the man.

"Yeah, Harry. I'm going. So is Sam. Aren't you Sam?"

"That's right, Harry. What about you?"

"I've got work to do here."

"Work! You can finish that rocket in the autumn, when it's cooler."

He took a breath. "I got the frame all set up."

"In the autumn is better." Their voices were lazy in the heat.

"Got to work," he said.

"Autumn," they reasoned. And they sounded so sensible, so right.

"Autumn would be best," he thought. "Plenty of time, then."

No! cried part of himself, deep down, put away, locked tight, suffocating. No! No!

"In the autumn," he said.

"Come on, Harry," they all said.

"Yes," he said, feeling his flesh melt in the hot liquid air. "Yes, in the autumn. I'll begin work again then."

"I got a villa near the Tirra Canal," said someone.

"You mean the Roosevelt Canal, don't you?"

"Tirra. The old Martian name."

"But on the map—"

"Forget the map. It's Tirra now. Now I found a place in the Pillan Mountains—"

"You mean the Rockefeller Range," said Bittering.

"I mean the Pillan Mountains," said Sam.

"Yes," said Bittering, buried in the hot, swarming air. "The Pillan Mountains."

Everyone worked at loading the truck in the hot, still afternoon of the next day.

Laura, Dan, and David carried packages. Or, as they preferred to be known, Ttil, Linnl, and Werr carried packages.

The furniture was abandoned in the little white cottage.

"It looked just fine in Boston," said the mother. "And here in the cottage. But up at the villa? No. We'll get it when we come back in the autumn."

Bittering himself was quiet.

"I've some ideas on furniture for the villa," he said after a time. "Big, lazy furniture."

"What about your encyclopedia? You're taking it along, surely?"

Mr. Bittering glanced away. "I'll come and get it next week."

They turned to their daughter. "What about your New York dresses?"

The bewildered girl stared. "Why, I don't want them any more."

They shut off the gas, the water, they locked the doors and walked away. Father peered into the truck.

"Gosh, we're not taking much," he said. "Considering all we brought to Mars, this is only a handful!"

He started the truck.

Looking at the small white cottage for a long moment, he was filled with a desire to rush to it, touch it, say good-bye to it, for he felt as if he were going away on a long journey, leaving something to which he could never quite return, never understand again.

Just then Sam and his family drove by in another truck.

"Hi, Bittering! Here we go!"

The truck swung down the ancient highway out of town. There were sixty others traveling in the same direction. The town filled with a silent, heavy dust from their passage. The canal waters lay blue in the sun, and a quiet wind moved in the strange trees.

"Good-bye, town!" said Mr. Bittering.

"Good-bye, good-bye," said the family, waving to it.

They did not look back again.

Summer burned the canals dry. Summer moved like flame upon the meadows. In the empty Earth settlement, the painted houses flaked and peeled. Rubber tires upon which children had swung in back yards hung suspended like stopped clock pendulums in the blazing air.

At the metal shop, the rocket frame began to rust.

In the quiet autumn Mr. Bittering stood, very dark now, very golden-eyed, upon the slope above his villa, looking at the valley.

"It's time to go back," said Cora.

"Yes, but we're not going," he said quietly. "There's nothing there any more."

"Your books," she said. "Your fine clothes."

"Your *Illes* and your fine *ior uele rre*," she said.

"The town's empty. No one's going back," he said. "There's no reason to, none at all."

The daughter wove tapestries and the sons played songs on ancient flutes and pipes, their laughter echoing in the marble villa.

Mr. Bittering gazed at the Earth settlement far away

in the low valley. "Such odd, such ridiculous houses the Earth people built."

"They didn't know any better," his wife mused. "Such ugly people. I'm glad they've gone."

They both looked at each other, startled by all they had just finished saying. They laughed.

"Where did they go?" he wondered. He glanced at his wife. She was golden and slender as his daughter. She looked at him, and he seemed almost as young as their eldest son.

"I don't know," she said.

"We'll go back to town maybe next year, or the year after, or the year after that," he said, calmly. "Now— I'm warm. How about taking a swim?"

They turned their backs to the valley. Arm in arm they walked silently down a path of clear-running spring water.

Five years later a rocket fell out of the sky. It lay steaming in the valley. Men leaped out of it, shouting.

"We won the war on Earth! We're here to rescue you! Hey!"

But the American-built town of cottages, peach trees, and theaters was silent. They found a flimsy rocket frame rusting in an empty shop.

The rocket men searched the hills. The captain established headquarters in an abandoned bar. His lieutenant came back to report.

"The town's empty, but we found native life in the hills, sir. Dark people. Yellow eyes. Martians. Very friendly. We talked a bit, not much. They learn English fast. I'm sure our relations will be most friendly with them, sir."

"Dark, eh?" mused the captain. "How many?"

"Six, eight hundred, I'd say, living in those marble ruins in the hills, sir. Tall, healthy. Beautiful women."

"Did they tell you what became of the men and women who built this Earth settlement, Lieutenant?"

"They hadn't the foggiest notion of what happened to this town or its people."

"Strange. You think those Martians killed them?"

"They look surprisingly peaceful. Chances are a plague did this town in, sir."

"Perhaps. I suppose this is one of those mysteries we'll never solve. One of those mysteries you read about." ——

The captain looked at the room, the dusty windows, the blue mountains rising beyond, the canals moving in the light, and he heard the soft wind in the air. He shivered. Then, recovering, he tapped a large fresh map he had thumbtacked to the top of an empty table.

"Lots to be done, Lieutenant." His voice droned on and quietly on as the sun sank behind the blue hills. "New settlements. Mining sites, minerals to be looked for. Bacteriological specimens taken. The work, all the work. And the old records were lost. We'll have a job of remapping to do, renaming the mountains and rivers and such. Calls for a little imagination.

"What do you think of naming those mountains the Lincoln Mountains, this canal the Washington Canal, those hills—we can name those hills for you, Lieutenant. Diplomacy. And you, for a favor, might name a town for me. Polishing the apple. And why not make this the Einstein Valley, and farther over ... are you *listening*, Lieutenant?"

The lieutenant snapped his gaze from the blue color and the quiet mist of the hills far beyond the town.

"What? Oh, *yes*, sir!"

THE TROLLEY

The first light on the roof outside; very early morning. The leaves on all the trees tremble with a soft awakening to any breeze the dawn may offer. And then, far off, around a curve of silver track, comes the trolley, balanced on four small steel-blue wheels, and it is painted the color of tangerines. Epaulets of shimmery brass cover it, and pipings of gold; and its chrome bell bings if the ancient motorman taps it with a wrinkled shoe. The numerals on the trolley's front and sides are bright as lemons. Within, its seats prickle with cool green moss. Something like a buggy whip flings up from its roof to brush the spider thread high in the passing trees from which it takes its juice. From every window blows an incense, the all-pervasive blue and secret smell of summer storms and lightning.

Down the long, elm-shadowed streets the trolley moves, alone, the motorman's gray gloves touched gently, timelessly, to the controls.

At noon the motorman stopped his car in the middle of the block and leaned out. "Hey!"

And Douglas and Charlie and Tom and all the boys and girls on the block saw the gray glove waving, and dropped from trees and left skip ropes in white snakes on lawns, to run and sit in the green plush seats, and there was no charge. Mr. Tridden, the conductor, kept his glove over the mouth of the money box as he moved the trolley on down the shady block. "Hey," said Charlie. "Where are we going?"

"Last ride," said Mr. Tridden, eyes on the high electric wire ahead. "No more trolley. Bus starts tomorrow. Going to retire me with a pension, they are. So—a free ride for everyone! Watch out!"

He moved the brass handle, the trolley groaned and swung round an endless green curve, and all the time in the world held still, as if only the children and Mr. Tridden and his miraculous machine were riding an endless river, away.

"Last day?" asked Douglas, stunned. "They can't *do* that! They can't take off the trolley! Why," said Douglas, "no matter how you look at it, a bus ain't a trolley. Don't make the same kind of noise. Don't have tracks or wires, don't throw sparks, don't pour sand on the tracks, don't have the same colors, don't have a bell, don't let down a step like a trolley does!"

"Hey, that's right," said Charlie. "I always get a kick watching a trolley let down the step, like an accordion."

"Sure," said Douglas.

And then they were at the end of the line; the tracks, abandoned for thirty years, ran on into rolling country. In 1910 people took the trolley out to Chessman's Park with vast picnic hampers. The track still lay rusting among the hills.

"Here's where we turn around," said Charlie.

"Here's where you're wrong!" Mr. Tridden snapped the emergency generator switch. "Now!"

The trolley, with a bump and a sailing glide, swept past the city limits, turned off the street, and swooped downhill through intervals of odorous sunlight and vast acreages of shadow that smelled of toadstools. Here and there creek waters flushed the tracks and sun filtered through trees like green glass. They slid whispering on meadows washed with wild sunflowers, past abandoned way stations empty of all save transfer-punched confetti, to follow a forest stream into a summer country, while Douglas talked. "Why, just the *smell* of a trolley, *that's* different. I been on Chicago buses; they smell funny."

"Trolleys are too slow," said Mr. Tridden. "Going to put buses on. Buses for people and buses for school."

The trolley whined to a stop. From overhead Mr. Tridden reached down huge picnic hampers. Yelling, the children helped him carry the baskets out by a creek that emptied into a silent lake, where an ancient bandstand stood crumbling into termite dust.

They sat eating ham sandwiches and fresh strawberries and waxy oranges, and Mr. Tridden told them how it had been forty years ago: the band playing on that ornate stand at night, the men pumping air into their brass horns, the plump conductor flinging perspiration from his baton, the children and fireflies running in the deep grass, the ladies with long dresses and high pompadours treading the wooden xylophone walks with men in choking collars. There was the walk now, all softened into a fiber mush through the years. The lake was silent and blue and serene, and fish peacefully threaded the bright reeds, and the motorman murmured on and on, and the children felt it was some other year, with Mr. Tridden looking wonderfully young, his eyes lighted like small bulbs, blue and electric. It was a drifting, easy day, nobody rushing, and the forest all about, the sun held in one position, as Mr. Tridden's voice rose and fell, and a darning needle sewed along the air, stitching, restitching, designs both golden and invisible. A bee settled into a flower, humming and humming. The trolley stood like an enchanted calliope, simmering where the sun fell upon it. The trolley was on their hands, a brass smell, as they ate ripe cherries. The bright odor of the trolley blew from their clothes on the summer wind.

A loon flew over the sky, crying.

Somebody shivered.

Mr. Tridden worked on his gloves. "Well, time to go. Parents'll think I stole you all for good."

The trolley was silent and cool-dark, like the inside of an ice-cream drugstore. With a soft green rustling of velvet buff, the seats were turned by the quiet children so they sat with their backs to the silent lake, the deserted bandstand, and the wooden planks that made a kind of music if you walked down the shore on them into other lands.

Bing! went the soft bell under Mr. Tridden's foot, and they soared back over sun-abandoned, withered flower meadows, through woods, toward a town that

seemed to crush the sides of the trolley with bricks and
asphalt and wood when Mr. Tridden stopped to let the
children out.

Charlie and Douglas were the last to stand near the
opened tongue of the trolley, the folding step, breathing
electricity, watching Mr. Tridden's gloves on the brass
controls.

Douglas ran his fingers over the green creek moss,
looked at the silver, the brass, the wine color of the
ceiling.

"Well . . . So long again, Mr. Tridden."

"Good-bye, boys."

"See you around, Mr. Tridden."

"See you around."

There was a soft sigh of air; the door collapsed
gently shut, tucking up its corrugated tongue. The trolley sailed slowly down the late afternoon, brighter than
the sun, all tangerine, all flashing gold and lemon,
turned a far corner, wheeling, and vanished, gone
away.

"School buses." Charlie walked to the curb. "Won't
even give us a chance to be late for school. Come get
you at your front door. Never be late again in all our
lives. Think of that nightmare, Doug, just think it all
over."

But Douglas, standing on the lawn, was seeing how
it would be tomorrow, when the men would pour hot
tar over the silver tracks so you would never know a
trolley had ever run this way. He knew it would take as
many years as he could think of now to forget the
tracks, no matter how deeply buried. Some morning in
autumn, spring, or winter, he knew he'd wake, and if
he didn't go near the window, if he just lay deep and
snug and warm in his bed, he would hear it, faint and
faraway.

And around the bend of the morning street, up the
avenue, between the even rows of sycamore, elm, and
maple, in the quietness before the start of living, past
his house, he would hear the familiar sounds. Like the
ticking of a clock, the rumble of a dozen metal barrels
rolling, the hum of a single immense dragonfly at
dawn. Like a merry-go-round, like a small electrical

storm, the color of blue lightning, coming, here, and gone. The trolley's chime. The hiss like a soda-fountain spigot as it let down and took up its step, and the starting of the dream again, as on it sailed along its way, traveling a hidden and buried track to some hidden and buried destination. . . .

"Kick-the-can after supper?" asked Charlie.

"Sure," said Douglas. "Kick-the-can."

THE FLYING MACHINE

In the year A.D. 400, the Emperor Yuan held his throne by the Great Wall of China, and the land was green with rain, readying itself toward the harvest, at peace, the people in his dominion neither too happy nor too sad.

Early on the morning of the first day of the first week of the second month of the new year, the Emperor Yuan was sipping tea and fanning himself against a warm breeze when a servant ran across the scarlet and blue garden tiles, calling, "Oh, Emperor, Emperor, a miracle!"

"Yes," said the Emperor, "the air *is* sweet this morning."

"No, no, a miracle!" said the servant, bowing quickly.

"And this tea is good in my mouth, surely that is a miracle."

"No, no, Your Excellency."

"Let me guess then—the sun has risen and a new day is upon us. Or the sea is blue. *That* now is the finest of all miracles."

"Excellency, a man is flying!"

"What?" The Emperor stopped his fan.

"I saw him in the air, a man flying with wings. I heard a voice call out of the sky, and when I looked up there he was, a dragon in the heavens with a man in its mouth, a dragon of paper and bamboo, colored like the sun and the grass."

"It is early," said the Emperor, "and you have just wakened from a dream."

"It is early, but I have seen what I have seen! Come, and you will see it too."

"Sit down with me here," said the Emperor. "Drink some tea. It must be a strange thing, if it is true, to see a man fly. You must have time to think of it, even as I must have time to prepare myself for the sight."

They drank tea.

"Please," said the servant at last, "or he will be gone."

The Emperor rose thoughtfully. "Now you may show me what you have seen."

They walked into a garden, across a meadow of grass, over a small bridge, through a grove of trees, and up a tiny hill.

"There!" said the servant.

The Emperor looked into the sky.

And in the sky, laughing so high that you could hardly hear him laugh, was a man; and the man was clothed in bright papers and reeds to make wings and a beautiful yellow tail, and he was soaring all about like the largest bird in a universe of birds, like a new dragon in a land of ancient dragons.

The man called down to them from high in the cool winds of morning, "I fly, I fly!"

The servant waved to him. "Yes, yes!"

The Emperor Yuan did not move. Instead he looked at the Great Wall of China now taking shape out of the farthest mist in the green hills, that splendid snake of stones which writhed with majesty across the entire land. That wonderful wall which had protected them for a timeless time from enemy hordes and preserved peace for years without number. He saw the town, nestled to itself by a river and a road and a hill, beginning to waken.

"Tell me," he said to his servant, "has anyone else seen this flying man?"

"I am the only one, Excellency," said the servant, smiling at the sky, waving.

The Emperor watched the heavens another minute and then said, "Call him down to me."

"Ho, come down, come down! The Emperor wishes

to see you!" called the servant, hands cupped to his shouting mouth.

The Emperor glanced in all directions while the flying man soared down the morning wind. He saw a farmer, early in his fields, watching the sky, and he noted where the farmer stood.

The flying man alit with a rustle of paper and a creak of bamboo reeds. He came proudly to the Emperor, clumsy in his rig, at last bowing before the old man.

"What have you done?" demanded the Emperor.

"I have flown in the sky, Your Excellency," replied the man.

"What *have* you done?" said the Emperor again.

"I have just told you!" cried the flier.

"You have told me nothing at all." The Emperor reached out a thin hand to touch the pretty paper and the birdlike keel of the apparatus. It smelled cool, of the wind.

"Is it not beautiful, Excellency?"

"Yes, too beautiful."

"It is the only one in the world!" smiled the man. "And I am the inventor."

"The *only* one in the world?"

"I swear it!"

"Who else knows of this?"

"No one. Not even my wife, who would think me mad with the sun. She thought I was making a kite. I rose in the night and walked to the cliffs far away. And when the morning breezes blew and the sun rose, I gathered my courage, Excellency, and leaped from the cliff. I flew! But my wife does not know of it."

"Well for her, then," said the Emperor. "Come along."

They walked back to the great house. The sun was full in the sky now, and the smell of the grass was refreshing. The Emperor, the servant, and the flier paused within the huge garden.

The Emperor clapped his hands. "Ho, guards!"

The guards came running.

"Hold this man."

The guards seized the flier.

"Call the executioner," said the Emperor.

"What's this!" cried the flier, bewildered. "What have I done?" He began to weep, so that the beautiful paper apparatus rustled.

"Here is the man who has made a certain machine," said the Emperor, "and yet asks us what he has created. He does not know himself. It is only necessary that he create, without knowing why he has done so, or what this thing will do."

The executioner came running with a sharp silver ax. He stood with his naked, large-muscled arms ready, his face covered with a serene white mask.

"One moment," said the Emperor. He turned to a nearby table upon which sat a machine that he himself had created. The Emperor took a tiny golden key from his own neck. He fitted this key to the tiny, delicate machine and wound it up. Then he set the machine going.

The machine was a garden of metal and jewels. Set in motion, birds sang in tiny metal trees, wolves walked through miniature forests, and tiny people ran in and out of sun and shadow, fanning themselves with miniature fans, listening to the tiny emerald birds, and standing by impossibly small but tinkling fountains.

"Is *it* not beautiful?" said the Emperor. "If you asked me what I have done here, I could answer you well. I have made birds sing, I have made forests murmur, I have set people to walking in this woodland, enjoying the leaves and shadows and songs. That is what I have done."

"But, oh, Emperor!" pleaded the flier, on his knees, the tears pouring down his face. "I have done a similar thing! I have found beauty. I have flown on the morning wind. I have looked down on all the sleeping houses and gardens. I have smelled the sea and even *seen* it, beyond the hills, from my high place. And I have soared like a bird; oh, I cannot say how beautiful it is up there, in the sky, with the wind about me, the wind blowing me here like a feather, there like a fan, the way the sky smells in the morning! And how free one feels! *That* is beautiful, Emperor, that is beautiful too!"

"Yes," said the Emperor sadly, "I know it must be

true. For I felt my heart move with you in the air and I wondered: What is it like? How does it feel? How do the distant pools look from so high? And how my houses and servants? Like ants? And how the distant towns not yet awake?"

"Then spare me!"

"But there are times," said the Emperor, more sadly still, "when one must lose a little beauty if one is to keep what little beauty one already has. I do not fear you, yourself, but I fear another man."

"What man?"

"Some other man who, seeing you, will build a thing of bright papers and bamboo like this. But the other man will have an evil face and an evil heart, and the beauty will be gone. It is this man I fear."

"Why? Why?"

"Who is to say that someday just such a man in just such an apparatus of paper and reed, might not fly in the sky and drop huge stones upon the Great Wall of China?" said the Emperor.

No one moved or said a word.

"Off with his head," said the Emperor.

The executioner whirled his silver ax.

"Burn the kite and the inventor's body and bury their ashes together," said the Emperor.

The servants retreated to obey.

The Emperor turned to his hand-servant, who had seen the man flying. "Hold your tongue. It was all a dream, a most sorrowful and beautiful dream. And that farmer in the distant field who also saw, tell him it would pay him to consider it only a vision. If ever the word passes around, you and the farmer die within the hour."

"You are merciful, Emperor."

"No, not merciful," said the old man. Beyond the garden wall he saw the guards burning the beautiful machine of paper and reeds that smelled of the morning wind. He saw the dark smoke climb into the sky. "No, only very much bewildered and afraid." He saw the guards digging a tiny pit wherein to bury the ashes. "What is the life of one man against those of a million others? I must take solace from that thought."

He took the key from its chain about his neck and once more wound up the beautiful miniature garden. He stood looking out across the land at the Great Wall, the peaceful town, the green fields, the rivers and streams. He sighed. The tiny garden whirred its hidden and delicate machinery and set itself in motion; tiny people walked in forests, tiny foxes lóped through sun-speckled glades in beautiful shining pelts, and among the tiny trees flew little bits of high song and bright blue and yellow color, flying, flying, flying in that small sky.

"Oh," said the Emperor, closing his eyes, "look at the birds, look at the birds!"

ICARUS MONTGOLFIER WRIGHT

He lay on his bed and the wind blew through the window over his ears and over his half-opened mouth so it whispered to him in his dream. It was like the wind of time hollowing the Delphic caves to say what must be said of yesterday, today, tomorrow. Sometimes one voice gave a shout far off away, sometimes two, a dozen, an entire race of men cried out through his mouth, but their words were always the same:

"Look, look, we've done it!"

For suddenly he, they, one or many, were flung in the dream, and flew. The air spread in a soft warm sea where he swam, disbelieving.

"Look, look! It's done!"

But he didn't ask the world to watch, he was only shocking his senses wide to see, taste, smell, touch the air, the wind, the rising moon. He swam along in the sky. The heavy earth was gone.

But wait, he thought, wait now!

Tonight—what night is this?

The night before, of course. The night before the first flight of a rocket to the Moon. Beyond this room on the baked desert floor one hundred yards away the rocket waits for me.

Well, does it now? Is there *really* a rocket?

Hold on! he thought, and twisted, turned, sweating, eyes tight, to the wall, the fierce whisper in his teeth. Be certain-sure! You, now, who *are* you?

Me? he thought. *My* name?

Jedediah Prentiss, born 1938, college graduate 1959,

licensed rocket pilot, 1971. Jedediah Prentiss . . . Jedediah Prentiss. . . .

The wind whistled his name away! He grabbed for it, yelling.

Then, gone quiet, he waited for the wind to bring his name back. He waited a long while, and there was only silence, and then after a thousand heartbeats he felt motion.

The sky opened out like a soft blue flower. The Aegean Sea stirred soft white fans through a distant wine-colored surf.

In the wash of the waves on the shore, he heard his name.

Icarus.

And again in a breathing whisper.

Icarus.

Someone shook his arm and it was his father saying his name and shaking away the night. And he himself lay small, half-turned to the window and the shore below and the deep sky, feeling the first wind of morning ruffle the golden feathers bedded in amber wax lying by the side of his cot. Golden wings stirred half-alive in his father's arms, and the faint down on his own shoulders quilled trembling as he looked at these wings and beyond them to the cliff.

"Father, how's the wind?"

"Enough for me, but never enough for you. . . ."

"Father, don't worry. The wings seem clumsy now, but my bones in the feathers will make them strong, my blood in the wax will make it live!"

"My blood, my bones too, remember; each man lends his flesh to his children, asking that they tend it well. Promise you'll not go high, Icarus. *The* sun or *my* son, the heat of one, the fever of the other, could melt these wings. Take care!"

And they carried the splendid golden wings into the morning and heard them whisper in their arms, whisper his name or a name or some name that blew, spun, and settled like a feather on the soft air.

Montgolfier.

His hands touched fiery rope, bright linen, stitched

thread gone hot as summer. His hands fed wool and straw to a breathing flame.

Montgolfier.

And his eye soared up along the swell and sway, the oceanic tug and pull, the immensely wafted silver pear still filling with the shimmering tidal airs channeled up from the blaze. Silent as a god tilted slumbering above French countryside, this delicate linen envelope, this swelling sack of oven-baked air would soon pluck itself free. Draughting upward to blue worlds of silence, his mind and his brother's mind would sail with it, muted, serene among island clouds where uncivilized lightnings slept. Into that uncharted gulf and abyss where no bird-song or shout of man could follow, the balloon would hush itself. So cast adrift, he, Montgolfier, and all men, might hear the unmeasured breathing of God and the cathedral tread of eternity.

"Ah . . ." He moved, the crowd moved, shadowed by the warm balloon. "Everything's ready, everything's right. . . ."

Right. His lips twitched in his dream. Right. Hiss, whisper, flutter, rush. Right.

From his father's hands a toy jumped to the ceiling, whirled in its own wind, suspended, while he and his brother stared to see it flicker, rustle, whistle, heard it murmuring their names.

Wright.

Whispering: wind, sky, cloud, space, wing, fly . . .

"Wilbur, Orville? Look, how's *that?*"

Ah. In his sleep, his mouth sighed.

The toy helicopter hummed, bumped the ceiling, murmured eagle, raven, sparrow, robin, hawk; murmured eagle, raven, sparrow, robin, hawk. Whispered eagle, whispered raven, and at last, fluttering to their hands with a susurration, a wash of blowing weather from summers yet to come, with a last whir and exhalation, whispered hawk.

Dreaming, he smiled.

He saw the clouds rush down the Aegean sky.

He felt the balloon sway drunkenly, its great bulk ready for the clear running wind.

He felt the sand hiss up the Atlantic shelves from the

soft dunes that might save him if he, a fledgling bird, should fall. The framework struts hummed and chorded like a harp, and himself caught up in its music.

Beyond this room he felt the primed rocket glide on the desert field, its fire wings folded, its fire breath kept, held ready to speak for three billion men. In a moment he would wake and walk slowly out to that rocket.

And stand on the rim of the cliff.

Stand cool in the shadow of the warm balloon.

Stand whipped by tidal sands drummed over Kitty Hawk.

And sheathe his boy's wrists, arms, hands, fingers with golden wings in golden wax.

And touch for a final time the captured breath of man, the warm gasp of awe and wonder siphoned and sewn to lift their dreams.

And spark the gasoline engine.

And take his father's hand and wish him well with his own wings, flexed and ready, here on the precipice.

Then whirl and jump.

Then cut the cords to free the great balloon.

Then rev the motor, prop the plane on air.

And crack the switch, to fire the rocket fuse.

And together in a single leap, swim, rush, flail, jump, sail, and glide, upturned to sun, moon, stars, they would go above Atlantic, Mediterranean; over country, wilderness, city, town; in gaseous silence, riffling feather, rattle-drum frame, in volcanic eruption, in timid, sputtering roar; in start, jar, hesitation, then steady ascension, beautifully held, wondrously transported, they would laugh and cry each his own name to himself. Or shout the names of others unborn or others long dead and blown away by the wine wind or the salt wind or the silent hush of balloon wind or the wind of chemical fire. Each feeling the bright feathers stir and bud deep-buried and thrusting to burst from their riven shoulder blades! Each leaving behind the echo of their flying, a sound to encircle, recircle the earth in the winds and speak again in other years to the sons of the sons of their sons, asleep but hearing the restless midnight sky.

Up, yet farther up, higher, higher! A spring tide, a summer flood, an unending river of wings!

A bell rang softly.

No, he whispered, I'll wake in a moment. Wait . . .

The Aegean slid away below the window, gone; the Atlantic dunes, the French countryside, dissolved down to New Mexico desert. Is his room near his cot stirred no plumes in golden wax. Outside, no wind-sculpted pear, no trapdrum butterfly machine. Outside only a rocket, a combustible dream, waiting for the friction of his hand to set it off.

In the last moment of sleep someone asked his name.

Quietly, he gave the answer as he had heard it during the hours from midnight on.

"Icarus Montgolfier Wright."

He repeated it slowly so the questioner might remember the order and spelling down to the last incredible letter.

"Icarus Montgolfier Wright.

"Born: nine hundred years before Christ. Grammar school: Paris, 1783, High school, college: Kitty Hawk, 1903. Graduation from Earth to Moon: this day, God willing, August 1, 1971. Death and burial, with luck, on Mars, summer 1999 in the Year of Our Lord."

Then he let himself drift awake.

Moments later, crossing the desert Tarmac, he heard someone shouting again and again and again.

And if no one was there or if someone was there behind him, he could not tell. And whether it was one voice or many, young or old, near or very far away, rising or falling, whispering or shouting to him all three of his brave new names, he could not tell, either. He did not turn to see.

For the wind was slowly rising and he let it take hold and blow him all the rest of the way across the desert to the rocket which stood waiting there.

ABOUT THE AUTHOR

RAY DOUGLAS BRADBURY was born in Waukegan, Illinois, in 1920. He graduated from a Los Angeles high school in 1938. His formal education ended there, but he furthered it by himself—at night in the library and by day at his typewriter. He sold newspapers on Los Angeles street corners from 1938 to 1942—a modest beginning for a man whose name would one day be synonymous with the best in science fiction. Ray Bradbury sold his first science fiction short story in 1941, and his early reputation is based on stories published in the budding science fiction magazines of that time. His work was chosen for best American short story collections in 1946, 1948 and 1952. His awards include: The O. Henry Memorial Award, The Benjamin Franklin Award in 1954 and The Aviation-Space Writer's Association Award for best space article in an American magazine in 1967. Mr. Bradbury has written for television, radio, the theater and film, and he has been publishd in every major American magazine. Editions of his novels and shorter fiction span several continents and languages, and he has gained worldwide acceptance for his work. His titles include: *The Martian Chronicles, Dandelion Wine, I Sing the Body Electric!, The Golden Apples of the Sun, A Medicine for Melancholy, The Illustrated Man* and *Long After Midnight.*

RAY BRADBURY

America's most daring explorer of the imagination

☐	13504	S IS FOR SPACE	$1.95
☐	12588	SOMETHING WICKED THIS WAY COMES	$1.95
☐	11997	THE HALLOWEEN TREE	$1.75
☐	13247	THE ILLUSTRATED MAN	$2.25
☐	13155	DANDELION WINE	$1.95
☐	11931	R IS FOR ROCKET	$1.75
☐	10249	TIMELESS STORIES FOR TODAY AND TOMORROW	$1.50
☐	11942	I SING THE BODY ELECTRIC	$1.95
☐	2834	MACHINERIES OF JOY	$1.50
☐	11582	THE WONDERFUL ICE CREAM SUIT & OTHER PLAYS	$1.50
☐	13179	THE MARTIAN CHRONICLES	$2.25
☐	12164	GOLDEN APPLES OF THE SUN	$1.75
☐	13285	LONG AFTER MIDNIGHT	$2.25
☐	10390	A MEDICINE FOR MELANCHOLY	$1.75

Buy them at your local bookstore or use this handy coupon for ordering:

OUT OF THIS WORLD!

That's the only way to describe Bantam's great series of science fiction classics. These space-age thrillers are filled with terror, fancy and adventure and written by America's most renowned writers of science fiction. Welcome to outer space and have a good trip!